risk

ELANA DYKEWOMON

Ann Arbor
2009

Bywater Books, Inc.
PO Box 3671
Ann Arbor MI 48106-3671
www.bywaterbooks.com

Printed in the United States of America on acid-free
paper.

Bywater Books First Edition: July 2009

Cover designer: Bonnie Liss (Phoenix Graphics)

ISBN 978-1-932859-69-0

This novel is a work of fiction. All persons, places,
and events were created by the imagination of the
author.

Mixed Sources
Product group from well-managed
forests and other controlled sources
www.fsc.org Cert no. SW-COC-002283
© 1996 Forest Stewardship Council
FSC

For

Susan Levinkind
partner of my heart and home these twenty years
and
Gloria Anzaldúa
not a week goes by when I don't miss and bless you

Acknowledgments

So much appreciation to all the women who helped this book into being: to Casey Fisher, whose early astrological reading for Carol Schwartz illuminated her depth for me; to my intimate and best critic, Dolphin Waletzky; to Toni Lester, Lucy Jane Bledsoe, Tryna Hope, Michal Brody, and Susan Jill Kahn for their insightful readings and thoughtful responses (and fun!); and to my smart, engaged agent, Frances Goldin.

Many thanks to my wonderful publisher and editor, Kelly Smith and the phenomenal Carol Seajay, who shepherded this project into being.

For the great gifts of time and solitude: Soapstone, a Writing Retreat for Women; the Rhys Cottage space at Norcroft, where these characters were first imagined; and Tracy Moore and Lisa Edwards, in whose home the final revisions were made.

Special thanks to the following friends who have supported my life as a writer. It would take another book to describe all the gifts our interactions have given me: Abby Bogomolny, Amelia Maria de la Luz Montes, Andrea Krug, Barbara DiBernard, barbara findlay, Barbara Ruth, Barbara Wilt, Betty Sullivan, Cathy

Cade, Charles Flowers, Chrystos, Cindy Chan, Claire Wings, Clare Kinberg, Dan Nachman, Diane Sabin, Dorothy Allison, Esther Rothblum, Eva Schocken, Evelyn Averbuck, Fan Warren, Fran Day, Gail Lang, Gale Kissin, Gila Svirsky, Hadas Rivera-Weiss, Happy Hyder, Irena Klepfisz, Jamie Lee Evans, Jan Hoffman, Jennifer Brier, Pam Brier, Pam Mitchell, Jay Sky, Jewelle Gomez, Jess Wells, Joan Drury, Joan Nestle, Judith Katz, Judy Freespirit, Jo Ann Smith, Karen X. Tulchinsky, Katherine Acey, Katherine V. Forrest, Laura Rifkin, Lilian Mohin, Linda Zeiser, Margo Rivera-Weiss, Marilyn Kallman, Merry Gangemi, Patsy Engel, Rachel Nachman, Raelyn Gallina, Red She Bear, Rhea, Rose Weisberg, Ruth Gundle, Sandy Butler, Sara Felder, Sheila Gilhooly, Susan Goldberg, Susan Stinson, Terry Hill, Teya Schaffer, and Tova.

1

Carol had just turned seven when Harold Schwartz cast his lot with the Vietnam war in September of 1969. Many women, some of Carol's best friends, would object to starting a story with a father, with the father of an incipient lesbian. But it is where her memory starts, so she wants to be clear about men up front. She is a woman who values clarity, equations, the calculation of risk. Nothing was dramatic in her life before her father died, and afterward the drama was so thick she fled into fractions, decimals, the rough comforts of math.

She became a woman who valued both impulse and the calculation of risk. In that early life, her father was a pair of pants who taught her how to use a compass, who made fun of her when she couldn't learn to tie her shoes. Their relationship consisted of small humiliations, learning motor skills, and a few gifts: a red Schwinn bike, geography lessons, a box of rock crumbs with labels—feldspar, granite, quartz. Harold was an ordinary Jewish father, almost a 1950s' prefabrication, a counterbalance in the house, fitted to her mother, Molly, like the flywheel in a pocket watch, part of the machinery that drove expectation. Carol couldn't know how fragile their timekeeping was. When he put on his uniform the first time, they had lived in Rogers Park, on the north side of Chicago, for two years—their own apartment, after living with Harold's mom and dad since they got married.

"Dashing," he said, looking in the full-length mirror of her parents' bedroom.

"That was World War I. Nothing's dashing now." Her mother

ground a cigarette out in a beanbag ashtray, sitting on the edge of their double bed.

"What do you think, sweetheart?" he asked Carol.

"Oh leave her out of it, Harold."

"Doesn't your daddy look handsome?"

"Will you bring me back a present?" She was sitting on the floor beside the open suitcase, rolling marbles around on the green shag carpet.

"If you tell me I look dashing."

"Carol, don't pay any attention to him. He's going to war, and you don't get presents from the war."

Carol squeezed her eyes shut for a minute. She could make a bright light in the dark that way, and the light sucked up the noise. She wasn't allowed to say bad words, but "war" wasn't the same as swearing, since everybody talked about it. It was a mean word, though, and her mom and dad fought about it when they thought she was asleep. Grown-ups sounded hard when they used that word, hard as marbles, misshapen cat's-eyes with muddy centers. Sometimes marbles got chipped and rolled crooked. War was the kind of marble you'd try to palm off on a kid you didn't like.

"Hey, I'm a lieutenant. I'm sure the commissary will have gifts we can send our kids, Molly."

"Harold, I'm telling you, drop it."

Harold bent down and tugged on Carol's sleeve. "C'mon honey. Open your eyes. Don't you have a kiss for your dashing dad?"

"Dashing dad," she said, and kissed him on his clean cheek. He smelled pretty.

"That's my girl."

"Honestly," Molly said, and got another pair of socks out of the drawer, putting them in his suitcase. "You can't have too many socks in Vietnam."

"The air force takes care of its guys, Molly. They give us socks."

"Not thick ones like these."

"For chrissake, it's a tropical jungle. Take them out and close that thing. We've got to get a move on or we'll be late."

2

"No such thing as late for war," Molly said, inhaling her words with the next cigarette.

"What did you say?"

"Nothing."

And then Harold Schwartz left.

He was a pilot and sent Carol a picture of himself in uniform, autographed at the bottom like a movie star's photo, "For my brave girl. Love, Dad." His letter said he was sorry he couldn't come home for summer, to mind her mother, and be sure to get some extra swimming in for him. He did look handsome, with his deliberate snapshot grin. He had a curl that came down out of his cap. What did she know about the air force? She wished she could fly in an airplane too. All winter, she looked up at the sky, wondering what kept the planes from falling through clouds. Her teacher said it was because they went so fast. If she could go fast enough, could she zoom straight up? But she'd have to run faster than a bus, even, and she knew that was impossible.

"Does Dad fly a plane like that one?" she pointed high with her right hand, clasping Molly's fingers with her left. Molly made her hold on when they went downtown and she was glad, even though she protested that she wasn't a baby anymore.

"What? Oh, Carol. No. The planes your father flies are small. That's a passenger plane—it takes people from city to city very quickly. Almost like a time machine." The idea of a time machine distracted Carol, and she forgot to ask where her father's plane went. So many people were zooming around—how come she couldn't get to him?

When summer came, her front tooth was loose. Her mother sent her away to Brownie camp for a week in July, with her friend Alice from school. She told the other kids that it was great to wear the Brownie uniform, it made them like their dads in the war. She showed them the photo her dad had sent.

3

Alice, who had long, red pigtails, said, "My dad won't go to the war. He says we have no business over there."

"A lot you know. Your dad's a coward."

"He is not. Your dad's a pawn." Alice pursed her lips and pulled on her hair.

"What's a pawn?"

"It's what my dad said."

"So what. I'm not going to be your swimming partner anymore," Carol mumbled, trying not to cry. It was hard enough being away from home, and now this. Alice had been so nice just this morning, showing her how to do the frog kick. She liked the way Alice's braids stuck out of her swimming cap.

"Fine. I don't care."

Carol found a new swimming partner, who yakked all the time about her doll collection at home, and how she was learning to sew clothes for them—"itsy bitsy booties!" That sounded boring.

"Want to cannonball off the dock?" Carol asked.

"We're not allowed," her partner whined.

"So what?" Alice would have done it with her. Now she had to do it alone. No one was watching them—her counselor, Alice, most of the girls were splashing around in the shallows; some were standing at the shore, shoving their hair into bathing caps, and the older campers were waving and laughing on the raft anchored at the end of the roped-off swimming area. Canoes were tied up alongside the dock, which ended in pretty deep water, beyond where anyone was supposed to swim. But she was a good swimmer, everybody said so. They didn't say it like a compliment—more as if it was a miracle a chubby kid like her could be good at any sport.

Carol bit her lip and took a deep breath. She kicked off her sandals, dropped her towel, and started to run.

"Hey!" her new partner called.

Zooming must be like this. *Is* this! The hot wooden boards creaked as she slapped down on them, and her feet prickled, throbbed as she gained speed. Something wide opened in her chest. The edge of the dock was coming up fast—she saw it just

4

in time to jump, suck a breath, and grab her legs. Then the long wild second that stretches and bends time sent her careening through that local slice of sky—boom! Landing almost flat, shoulders, back, calves stung as the water spanked her baby flesh.

She must have yelped. A counselor was yanking her arm, growling, "Young lady! You should know better than that!"—dragging her back to shore. But a bunch of the girls were cheering. Even Alice, she noticed. Her new partner was telling her bunk captain, "I toooold her not to do it." She had to stay on her cot all afternoon and "think about it." She thought: worth it, worth it, double worth it with hot fudge. And at dinner, although Alice still avoided her, they did exchange a quick smile.

When Alice's mom picked them up at the end of the week, she noticed the tension that persisted. "You girls are awfully quiet. Didn't you have a good time?"

"Yeah, sure."

"Yes ma'am, Mrs. Abrams."

But when Mrs. Abrams bought them soft freeze ice cream cones, they giggled at each other as the melting goo trickled down their sleeves at the same moment.

"Hey, we can still be friends, can't we? I'm sorry I called your dad a bad name." Alice pushed her braid away from her cone.

"I'm sorry too. Want to taste my chocolate?"

"Sure. That was cool, what you did at the lake. I wish I could have done it with you," Alice said.

"Thanks. Maybe next time," she grinned.

Alice's mom smiled at them in the rear view mirror. "Here we are, dear—but I don't see your mother's car," she said when they got to Carol's house. "Can you get in alright? You're okay carrying that duffle bag?"

"I'm fine, Mrs. Abrams. There's a key under the door. And Mom usually parks around the corner, anyway."

"Well, all right, Carol. Be good. Say hi to your mom for me." She watched the child struggle the bag up the walk and find the key before driving off.

◆ ◆ ◆

5

"Ma?" Carol let her duffle bag fall on the floor, and a little puff of dust swirled up. It gave her the shivers. She kept calling, but Molly didn't answer. The sound carried through the apartment like a stone dropped into a well. She knocked her knuckles against the wallpaper—a pattern of bumblebees and flowers that she didn't like, especially at night when it sometimes seemed like the bees could fly off the paper and sting her. She heard a noise in the back yard.

It wasn't much of a yard—a slab of concrete with a few chairs, and rows of flowers along the sides that they shared with their up-stairs neighbors. Her mother was starting a fire in the trash can with what looked like an American flag. It *was* an American flag. Carol had heard that only nasty people and hippies burned flags, but it was her mother, standing there in the humid afternoon, trying to get the flag to ignite, burning her fingers in a stray summer wind off Lake Michigan.

"Mom, what are you doing?"

"Your mother has become a war protester," she said, in a voice that sounded like it was on TV, formal and not quite real. Carol thought it was strange to protest the war with no one else around—she'd seen the protests on TV, and she had fought with Alice about it for the last three days, but she didn't know what they were fighting about.

"Why?"

"Your father—" she looked up behind her head and Carol turned, expecting to see him. "Your father is dead, and they gave me this fucking flag."

"Who?"

"Some soldiers came an hour ago." Molly turned back to the can and prodded the ashy cloth with a stick. "You think a flag is better than a man, even a nebbishy man like your father? You got another think coming."

Carol liked that expression, another think coming. She liked to imagine the air thick with thinks, flying in every direction. Big thinks and little thinks that could be caught like Frisbees, and thrown back. What could she think now?

"Mom?"

"Oh, honey, I'm so sorry." Molly came over and squeezed Carol so hard she started to cough. It was the last time she saw Molly cry.

Carol lay on her belly, crayons fanned out along the right side of the picture she was drawing. Molly, coming in from the kitchen, squinted at it—flames and stick people throwing their arms up in the air, the gray wing of an airplane that Carol was bearing down on, over and over.

"I haven't had time to go shopping," Molly said, "hot dogs and lima beans okay for dinner, kiddo?"

"Uhuh." She didn't look up.

Molly perched on the sofa arm and lit a cigarette. She was partial to Kools, for the menthol, but kept a package of Benson & Hedges in her office drawer, which she thought might help impress her in-law's real estate clients. Silly, wanting to support them with status symbols. She should throw them out. It sickened her, to see Harold's parents every day, but they were flexible about childcare—the least they could do for their own damn granddaughter. She took a deep drag and let the smoke stream out of her nose.

"Your father could have had ten deferments, you know."

"What's a deferment?" Carol looked up for a moment before switching to the orange crayon and drawing in a new row of flames.

"It's when the Army decides you can stay home because you have a good reason—like you have flat feet or you're in school or you have a family."

Her hand paused in the air. "Did Daddy have flat feet?"

"No, honey," Molly smiled. "He had beautiful arches, actually."

"Didn't he tell them about us?"

"Of course he did—that's how they knew to bring me that flag. But he said he didn't want to use us as an excuse when so many others were being forced to go."

"Oh." Carol sat up and looked at the bottom of her feet. Then she flopped back on her stomach and stared at the drawing. "But Mom, aren't we as important as the war?"

Molly ground her cigarette out and kneeled down next to Carol. She ran her fingers through her daughter's fine hair. Carol didn't look up. "It's complicated, kiddo. I think he got caught up in wanting to prove that Jews could be fighters."

Carol cocked her head to the side. "Huh? Why? That's silly. Benjy Green is Jewish, and he's the biggest fighter in my school."

"He is, is he? And do you fight him?"

"Moooommm."

"Okay, I was only asking."

"So why would Dad have to prove he could?"

Molly closed her eyes for a second, considering. "Oh, a couple wars back—you must have heard your grandparents talking about this—a lot of people said bad things about the Jews and wanted to get rid of them."

"Get rid of us?"

"Not us, honey. That happened in Europe, before you were born."

"I'm never going to Europe, then."

Molly laughed and picked up a crayon. "We'll talk about that when you're seventeen. Can I color too?"

"Well—over there—you can draw a river."

"Okay." They drew in silence until Molly sighed, "Your father was a schlemiel."

"Yeah," she bit her lip. "Yeah, my dad was a schlemiel."

"Schlemiel" was nearly all her mother ever said afterward if Carol asked about her father. She went through a period of thinking schlemiel was his first name. Lieutenant Schlemiel Schwartz, killed while bombing a Vietnamese village on the Mekong Delta, not even enough left of him to send home in a box.

Oh Dad, she said to the dark. Come home, open the door, say it was a mistake, just because you're missing in action doesn't mean you're gone—maybe you gave your dog tags to another soldier, you fell into the ocean like Icarus in mythology, but then you were swallowed as if you were Jonah into the belly of the whale, who threw you up on a beach in Canada, and you had to hitchhike all the way back to us on West Leland Ave. Right? You promised you'd bring me a present—I don't care if it's a carving you made on the ribs of the whale while you were in its belly, or necklaces of fishbone and ocean stones. You promised.

She was eight, nine, ten, eleven and thought if she stopped believing he was alive even for a second, that he would drown then, in that instant. As long as she believed he was coming back, he might, he would. Every time Molly made them move, she stomped around the house. "But how will Dad find us?"

"Carol, your father, the schlemiel, died. They sent me his dog tags. Do I have to show them to you again?"

"But what about the body?"

"It was burned up. Planes burn when they crash. I know you want your father, honey. I miss my own father too. I know what it's like."

She didn't see how that could possibly be true. Molly's father had died a couple years before Harold went to Vietnam, but they made her stay home with a babysitter because they said she was too young for funerals. Everyone knows what happens at a funeral, though. She knew when she was six, and she knew now. A body in a box goes into the ground. A real body, into a cemetery you can visit. She kicked at the baseboard.

"Cut that out, Carol. You got over the tooth fairy, you'll get over this."

"But Mom, maybe it wasn't really him if the body was burned. How will he find us if we keep moving around?"

Molly gave in, trying to comfort the best she could. "We're in the phone book," she said.

2

Five years out of UC Berkeley, Carol found July the slowest time for her tutoring business. No one wanted to study and no parent wanted to suffer their child's humid academic anguish—the middle class ones especially, the ones who could afford to pay. They cleaved to the romance that summers were what made a childhood. Who was Carol to convince them otherwise? Besides, she had discovered the summer race horse circuit at the county fairs, which combined almost everything she loved: figuring the odds, taking a chance, strolling through rabbit, pig, and llama 4-H barns while eating funnel cakes and sausage sandwiches. Fried onion grease dripping onto the racing form—that was her current vision of paradise, though she was fastidious in keeping her hands clean. Turned out advanced calculus gave Carol the concentration of a halfway decent handicapper, clearing at least fifty bucks most afternoons she went.

Yearning for the fairground barn where quilts hung and asparagus lined up perfectly, spear to spear, she sighed, listening to Molly on the phone. Carol had told her mother that she kept busy volunteering at the Women's Building in San Francisco, picturing Molly's bookshelf bulging with new titles at the end of the '70s—*Sisterhood is Powerful, Monster, The Erotic As Power*, Emma Goldman's life. Most of the time she enjoyed their weekend calls, but today Molly was on her case. "I put you through UC Berkeley so you can be a goddamn math tutor?"

"Mom, you might remember I put myself through." Carol was sitting by the window of her second floor walk up, which had a great view of 40th St. in Oakland. Not much happened out her window besides traffic, the occasional ambulance going to or from the hospital eight blocks away. She was studying that afternoon's racing program for the Alameda County Fair. She hoped no one could see her sweating there in her lace bra with the little pink bows.

"Well, you put me through the wringer."

"What's that supposed to mean, Mom?"

"Just an expression—you're a good child, I've always said. But listen, kiddo, I don't care that you got religion—"

"I do not have religion."

"Yeah? That lesbian thing, that's religion."

"What does sex have to do with religion, mom?" Heaven's Heartbeat, an 8-1 longshot in the third race, probably because of that woman jockey riding. Maybe. She circled it.

"Aha! I can see college was wasted on you, but I thought you learned something from my old feminist books. Didn't you have to take anthropology or something?" Molly stopped for a fit of coughing.

"Mom—weren't you giving up smoking?" Carol put her pencil down.

"Don't distract me. Where was I? Whirling dervishes, virgin oracles, Abraham sending Hagar out into the desert because Sarah got jealous after she conceived at—what was that, ninety? That's all sexual politics."

"I guess." Some cat gave the kind of desperate wail it might make if it was being run over. Carol looked out the window, covering her breasts with her arm, but couldn't see anything unusual. She used an old dish towel to dab at the dampness in her pits and threw it against the wall. "I am following you now, though. Your thesis is that all religion is based on sexual power dynamics."

"Thesis my ass. This is my whole point. You spent five years in college so you can throw around words like 'thesis,' but you don't make any more money an hour than I do as a godforsaken real estate secretary—probably less. Now why is that?"

"Because there's a glut of college grads with B.S.s in the Bay Area?"

"Because your ambition got waylaid in the bedroom."

"Mom, don't go there." Carol ran her finger down the list of names for the fifth race. The names had to resonate first, but she always backed them up with stats. Green Moon, Vera's Dandy, Midwest Mama—oh, absolutely, even if it was a favorite.

"I'm not criticizing your lifestyle, sweetie. But what about graduate school? You have so much talent. You remember that spectroscope?"

The image of her 10th grade science-project spectroscope slammed into Carol's head. She stared at the wall, her eyes unfocused. That was the year Molly started going to a consciousness-raising group. She explained about feminism, about becoming aware. Molly said it was all in order to wake up, and Carol had formed the image of a hundred mothers—maybe all the mothers of her high school—looking down at piles of folded laundry and screaming in unison.

But how did they get that capacity to scream, to realize they were repeating the same meaningless motions every week? What was consciousness itself? For real answers about the mind, not complaints about laundry or even women's wages (which were, she granted, relevant), you needed science. So she conceived a science project to find out where human consciousness resided by tracing the pictures of human and animal brains on tissue paper. Layering them, she would be able to pinpoint the spot, the fold, the structure that differentiated her species from the others, that created conscience. Conscience—or morality—that thing that makes us know something is right or wrong, that makes us self-aware—Carol had been determined to find its source. All the great rivers of the world had been mapped, but not the mind. Carol doodled a picture of the medal she was going to get from the Society of Explorers of the Wild Conscience. Is there a difference between self-awareness and having a conscience? Maybe that too would show up in some secret drawer of the brain.

Molly had found her hunched over stacks of tracing paper, and when she pieced together what her daughter was up to, sighed, "If you were a couple years older, I'd buy you a drink. What you want to find out, you can't see in drawings. Trust me. What makes us different from animals—if we really are different—and you know there's some debate about that, don't you?" Carol nodded assent "—may not be in the brain at all. It might be some mixture of chemicals. Something that no scientist will ever be able to prove, even with cross sections and electron microscopes, which you ain't got here, cookie. What else are you interested in?"

Carol looked down at her collection of papers and blew her nose. Molly waited. Finally Carol decided to agree that what she was looking for was impossible to find, at least with the tools at her disposal. "Spectroscopes," she said.

"What are those?"

"A kind of telescope that measures what a star is made of by capturing a picture of the—the spectrum it emits."

"Nothing easy like a robot? A telephone? A volcano?"

"Mom, those are for kids."

Molly laughed. "Tell it to Alexander Graham Bell. OK. Spectroscope it is. You better get busy at the library tomorrow. You don't have to build a real working model of one, do you?"

While Carol was relieved that her mother had rescued her from the maze of brain diagrams, she got a B- on the spectroscope, which mortified her, although she could rationalize that it was on account of starting so late. Science projects are graded on results, not intentions. Even at the fringe of the universe, stars send out signals about what they're made of, delicate strands of light parting the dark sky of time, capable of being parsed, passed through series of prisms and studied. Easier to catalog the emissions of stars than to find the place in your own body where your spirit lives, where the paw prints of your ancestors are tucked.

"Carol? Are you still there?" Molly sounded worried.

"Yeah, mom, I was remembering the spectroscope." The image

13

of the Crab Nebulae, which had formed in front of Carol's face, dissolved. "But the heyday of great women astronomers is over."

"Hey, who do you think you're talking to? There never was a heyday for women in the sciences. So what? When did you ever let that stop you?"

"Mom, I don't feel stopped, just because I'm not going in the direction you want me to. Let up, OK?"

"Just promise me you'll consider going to graduate school."

"I promise."

Maybe her mother was right—she should do something big, molecular science, for instance—win a Nobel Prize. Definitely the Nobel or nothing. She shook her head until the idea rattled and dropped out of sight. It wasn't that she didn't aspire, but that she couldn't hold on to the idea of slow and steady wins the race. Her undergrad study buddies, now laboring to unearth original PhD ideas, bored her stiff, sucking up to their graduate mentors, attaching their lives to string theory. How many strings can we manage to get tangled in? She was waiting for the severing flash of inspiration, the idea, the hunch, that would kick her into the mouth of a life that would lick her clean.

The white enameled kitchen table she'd scored at the Ashby flea market a couple years ago had stacks of papers—racing forms, puzzle books, local news, *Science Digest*. Carol pushed the racing form aside—too damn hot out in Pleasanton today, anyway— then idly thumbed through a copy of the *Express*, the East Bay's weekly alternative paper. A notice that the Berkeley Rep was looking for ushers for *The Normal Heart*, a play about the AIDS epidemic, winked at her.

At Cal, she'd had one gay friend. The third week of school, a guy in a black cape walked by the bench where she was studying calculus derivatives. He was tall, dark, Jewish, as handsome a man as Carol had ever seen.

"Want to come look at my etchings?" she called to him. He stopped, stared at her, and laughed. Phillip and she became show tune friends, lying around eating potato chips, lamenting about their various unsuccessful liaisons, and indulging in the lyrics of *Guys and Dolls* and *Funny Girl*—albums their mothers had vacuumed to. She hadn't seen Phillip in what? Three years? Toward the end of their regular visits, she'd become bored with his sighing about his inability to feel love, to feel loved. "I don't know about gay men," he'd say, with a flourish. "All we seem to want are the senses, not the sensibilities."

If he, a liberal arts phi beta kappa dancer, couldn't sound out the depth of gay men, who could? "Perhaps we're different species after all, men and women," she suggested, more tentatively than she felt.

"Oh, perhaps!" He slapped the back of his palm against his forehead, and succeeded in proving her point, although he did make her laugh. The last she heard of him, he'd run off to Seattle with a former member of the Alvin Ailey Dance Theater. But he crossed her mind occasionally, and she worried for him. Worry hung around the gay community, a starving mutt growing sleek and fierce on the takeout gay men were too sick to eat. She avoided it as best she could, and not just because she didn't see herself as the nursing type. Some women appeared delighted to devote their energy to the epidemic, as if they had been bench-warmers finally called into the game; and some just had very sick friends whose illness compelled them to act. She respected that. But some of the older women she went to meetings with were still mad at the guys for having shut them out in the early days of gay liberation, making them run errands, brew coffee, and stuff envelopes. They complained that now, when the party was over, the guys came back to women to take care of them.

Carol wasn't angry. She just didn't see the point of spending so much time with men—wasn't the whole idea of being lesbians, and gay men for that matter, that you wanted to be with your own gender? That you craved their smells, shapes, forms of laughter, the particular bravado, the tenderness that echoed your own? Except for Philip, who had seemed like family, a spoiled younger

15

cousin, she'd never felt compelled to socialize with gay men. But this play might help her find a pulse that she realized she'd lost track of—maybe even some compassion, though she was jealous of her compassion, knowing that it was in limited supply.

Her astrologically inclined friends had warned her that big changes were coming with her 28th birthday this summer, when Saturn returned to the position it was in, more or less, when she was born. When she scoffed, Tourmaline said, "you think you're too big to be touched by the stars?"

"Too small for them to notice me," Carol replied.

"But I know you believe in small actions making change, the ripples of a stone in a pond, the butterfly effect."

"The butterfly effect is overrated." Carol patted Tourmaline's hand.

"Don't condescend to me. You'll see," Tourmaline said.

Maybe change was coming, maybe you could kick change in the butt and help it along. Carol decided, what the hell, she'd check out *The Normal Heart*, and went for the ushers' "orientation." She liked theaters—the inside dark of them when the audience wasn't there, when a world was nailed in place in six days and even the stage hands sounded like drama queens. Bad pun, she thought, glad the other usher wannabes couldn't hear her thoughts.

The WASPy woman in charge of volunteers was showing them the way the seats were numbered, while trying to keep them away from the stage, where another pale woman—the director maybe—was muttering and sighing and flinging her hands around. A white man on the stage yelled over to a brown butch in overalls to get a move on, and the butch went into slow motion, walking as if she waded in jello, while carrying a two by four. Someone Carol hadn't noticed before, sitting in the front row, laughed.

"Don't get distracted," the usher coordinator said, "and that's good advice for the night of the play. Students, especially, will try to distract you so they can move up front. We don't really want you to play cop out here, but try to be firm, and if there's a problem, go to Peter by the concession stand. Any questions?"

Carol got out her chapstick and coated her lips, shaking her head no, listening for that laugh again. It was like the first time she heard a rain stick—rough, pebbly, unexpected, a burst of sound that beats against the boundaries of what you think a laugh should be, and then trickles around your ears, warm, reminding you of something you lost that you can't put a finger on. The butch in overalls hoisted the two by four onto a platform and moved to the stage's apron, leaning over to talk to the laugher.

"... *my* damn set design ..." was all Carol could make out. Then the butch turned to the man who'd shouted at her and started pointing at things. A faint chuckle rose from the laugher's seat. The coordinator was finishing up her tour, telling them how lucky they were to see the process behind the magic that's the Rep. Carol asked where the bathroom was. Annoyed, the coordinator pointed out a door and said, "Down that hallway. Don't get lost in there."

That was, of course, her intent. Making sure no one was watching, Carol scouted out the stage doors, and found some very interesting curtains to inspect. She heard the coordinator go into the women's room, call out, "Still in here?", and then mumble, "must have left." The footsteps retreated. Carol knew better than to enter the theater through the stage—that would have been awkward, a dizzy blond act out of a Marx Brothers' movie. After waiting another ten minutes, listening to the stage hammering and shuffling, she went back into the orchestra section through a side door. The laugher's hair was visible—almost a crew cut, dark brown in the softened light. She made her way toward the front quietly. Suppose it was a guy, maybe even Larry Kramer, supervising every detail of his play's production. What would she say? "Gee, Mr. Kramer, I'd just like to get your autograph?" Not that she'd know Larry Kramer from Ronald Reagan, but still, it would be uncomfortable.

From the side, the profile was definitely a woman's. She was a white butch, probably a couple years older than Carol, wearing a muscle-T that showed she worked out. She had a stack of papers on her lap she was leafing through—her buddy on the stage was occupied now, looking at bands of paint on plywood—so she didn't hear Carol coming up. Maybe she was the stage manager, or the accountant, making sure they didn't go over their quota of nails.

"They should sell tickets to hear you laugh," Carol whispered.

Startled, the woman swiveled. Nice eyes, Carol thought, sea-washed bottle green.

"What?"

She sat down, one seat separating them, the one full of papers. "I'd buy a ticket to hear you laugh," Carol said. "Are you in the show?"

The woman narrowed her eyes, inspecting Carol curiously. "Not me. Nash—the assistant stage designer over there—" she gestured to the butch in overalls, a thin Latina "—is my buddy. Where'd you come from?"

Carol had an impulse to say something hokey, like—from your dreams—but thought better of it. "I'm an usher volunteer—I skipped out on orientation because I heard you laugh."

The woman laughed again, low and gratifying. Sometimes the second taste is better than the first. "Z.D.," she said, holding out her hand to shake. That's what butches do first, shake. Even butches who've been friends for ten years, when they see each other, they extend a hand. Femmes hug. But it was too early for hugging, so Carol took her hand and gave it a strong squeeze.

"Carol Schwartz."

Z.D. looked up at Nash on the stage, down at her papers, then back at Carol's lap, taking in her thin lavender skirt. She was thinking about it. Carol saw the thoughts move back and forth as Z.D. flexed her jaw muscles. She rubbed that little space people have under their noses—crossword puzzlers probably know what it's called, but Carol had forgotten. "Well, Carol Schwartz, would you like to get some—" she looked at her watch,

18

a basic black-banded chronometer type—"lunch? It's lunchtime in Berkeley, I think."

"That sounds fine," Carol flashed her a wide-eyed, close-mouthed smile.

"You know, I'm not in the habit of picking up women in the Rep," Z.D. said, straightening her papers into a neat stack.

"I hate to correct you so soon, Z.D., but I believe I'm the one picking."

She pursed her lips and grinned. "Hey, Nash, come on over here a minute."

Nash obliged—the other people on the stage gave them all a momentary glance, and went back to their chores. "Carol, this is my best friend Nash. Nash, Carol Schwartz, one of your new usher groupies. We're gonna go grab some lunch, OK?"

Nash made a quick survey of the situation, her right hand going into her pocket, fingering her change. "Sure," she said, "I'm here the rest of the day—probably until late tonight, by the look of things. Catch you later. I'll page you if there's any action." She winked, but Carol couldn't tell whether it was at her or Z.D.

"What kind of action does she mean?"

"Nothing important. So what do you want—burritos? hamburgers? Indian? I think there's an Indian place a couple blocks from here. You're not a vegetarian, are you?" Her voice took on a quick, wary edge.

"Not since I was in college, don't worry. Indian sounds good— I'd like something intricate," Carol said.

"Intricate," Z.D. repeated, as if she'd never heard the word before. "Intricate. This is going to be interesting."

"Yes, it is," Carol agreed.

3

First the rainstick laugh, then the smell of her, copper and dope, a fir-tree green, not pine, but the scent of greenness coming up through a snow bank, a promise. Z.D. was the kind of butch who checked her look quick and shy in the mirror, not knowing that it was the checking itself that brought out tenderness in women who might catch her in the act. She had a blue vein that pulsed in her left eyelid, and Carol thought that was sexy—attractive, a vulnerable spot, a place she'd like to kiss. They were scooping up their order of saag paneer with nan, which was one of Carol's all-time favorite breads. A confluence of sensualities was washing through her; she hoped through both of them.

"I like that vein," she said.

Z.D. looked into the serving dish, frowning. "The vein of spinach?"

"Well, yes, but that's not what I meant. I mean, on your eyelid."

Her hand went up to her forehead self-consciously. "I always thought that looked kind of odd, you know, too intense."

"I like intense."

"Do you always come on this strong to strangers, Carol Schwartz?"

"Not often, and I'll back off. It's just that I am finding myself unusually compelled. I don't go around picking up women, by the way. I tend to be the studious type."

"Yeah, sure. I bet you're the kind of woman everyone talks to, who gets strangers to spill their life stories in airplanes."

Good guess, Carol thought, but didn't let on. "Want to tell me yours?"

Z.D. cleared her throat, drank almost a full glass of water. "Okay, I walked into that one. It's not that interesting."

"Maybe not to Dan Rather, but believe me, I'm interested." Carol ran her tongue over her teeth, hoping that none of the spinach was stuck.

Z.D. wasn't looking at her, though. "Well," she said, sounding like someone at a job interview, "I come from Portland, I'm the second of five kids—the only girl—and I manage a discount paper outlet in downtown Oakland."

"That's impressive."

"Only because you've never been there. It's boring unless you really like paper—but I've been working for this company since I was in high school, so it's a living. Since I'm the manager, I have a lot of flexibility and I like that."

"Who wouldn't?"

"You'd be surprised. Lots of people want their schedules to fit them like—I don't know, like girdles." Z.D. snorted with pleasure at the image, relaxing visibly.

"You ever wear a girdle?" The idea of butches being tortured by their clothes was a mixed image for Carol—she had sympathy, of course, but also—what was that? A fantasy, she realized, of making a butch squirm, and then soothing that bruised ego.

"For a year when I was in Catholic school, it was supposed to be mandatory. I think the nuns just wanted an excuse to pat us down."

Catholic. Carol had been friends with some Catholic women, but never lovers. Ex-Catholic, Z.D. would probably protest, which is what Catholics say when they mean they don't agree with the doctrines they were brought up with. Who does? Not many lesbians. Carol liked what non-religious Jews said, secular. You never heard Catholics say they were secular Catholics, just ex-. As if you could change your childhood like a pair of earrings. But she didn't say any of that to Z.D. "Catholic school, huh?"

"Don't get me started."

"Actually, it's my intention to get you started."

21

Z.D. cleared her throat again. "So tell me about you."

"Chicago Jew, raised by a single mom—" she decided to leave out the part about Harold and Vietnam for the moment, although she was aware of swallowing hard, and a shift in Z.D.'s cheek muscles that meant she must have noticed "—came out in high school—well, it takes a while to come out, doesn't it? But I had my first lover in high school, a basketball player who broke my heart."

"First lovers always do." Z.D. stared into her plate, picking a strand of flesh off the bone of her Tandoori chicken.

"Well, she got a scholarship to University of Colorado." Carol paused and Z.D.'s smile locked onto her again.

"You didn't know she was going there?"

"Not a clue. I thought we were applying to all the same colleges so we could stay together. She never told me about Colorado. So I came to Cal, finally graduated, and was shocked to find out there weren't any job openings for lesbian mathematicians." Carol became aware that her head was bobbling from side to side, in a gesture that reminded her unpleasantly of her bubbe, her father's mother. She straightened in her chair. "Now I tutor middle and high school kids—it's an okay living. I work with LABIA sometimes, but I'm not much of an organization freak."

"What's LABIA?"

"Lesbian Amazon Brigade in Action. Cute, huh? Middle-class dykes raise money and working-class dykes figure out who to give it to—we have dances and garage sales."

"Oh, I went to one of those dances. I remember now. It was all right." A brief fog came and went on her face. "Are you a raiser or a giver?"

"Good question. I raise, but I think technically the daughter of a single-mom secretary is working class."

"Depends."

"Yup, I agree. Depends." Carol looked at Z.D. Tell her now? Oh, hell, why not. She had to endure Z.D.'s sympathy sometime, and it would be easier now, when she was a stranger, then later, when it might be read as manipulation. Cordelia, two lovers ago,

22

often made that accusation. Might have been right, too, three times out of seventeen. "My dad was killed in Vietnam—"

"Oh. That's hard."

"Yeah, but I'm kind of used to it by now. I was eight. Let's save that for another time." Carol shoved the sensation that she was lying behind a neuron curtain somewhere in the lower right hemisphere of her brain.

They looked down at their food and picked at it for a while. Death is a sure-fire conversation stopper. Z.D. stroked her upper lip again. "Well, besides death, class is what no one likes to talk about."

"No kidding. It's a lot easier to talk about sex, and actually, I find lesbians don't do such a good job of that either."

"That's because it's easier to do than talk about."

"Sometimes talking can be a lot of the doing."

"Like now?" Z.D. was watching Carol chew the last of the green bean curry.

Being watched made Carol nervous, but she tried not to let on. Unexpectedly, Z.D. reached across the table and stroked the side of her cheek, moving down her jawline with her knuckles. The fuzz on Carol's face picked up static electricity and gave her a shiver. "Like now." Carol swallowed hard.

"If you, uh, aren't busy this afternoon, we could go for a ride and, well, keep talking," Z.D. said.

"It's slow in tutoring over the summer, but it depends on what kind of ride you've got."

"Yeah, maybe working class. Middle class girls never ask that. I got a '84 Mustang ragtop—20th anniversary special edition."

"Oh, you like your car. Sounds nice."

"Nice is just the beginning of it. I've only ever had Mustangs. You could say I'm kind of a fanatic. Well, fanatic's too big a word for it—but I am into it. You?"

"Now I'm embarrassed to say I drive a ten-year old Corolla."

"That's OK. It's a safe, reliable car."

"You were going to say 'girl's car,' weren't you?"

23

Z.D. put her hands up. "Guilty. But you gotta give me points for knowing better than to say it."

"If you give me points for not saying that American cars are pieces of crap."

"Not my 'Stang. I take good care of it."

"I bet you do. Let's take a look."

Z.D. put the top down and they settled back in the red bucket seats. "Any preference for direction?"

"Not inland. It's too hot. You sure you don't have anyone waiting at home for you?"

"Nope—I broke up with my last girlfriend, Gloria, in March. If this is a date, it's my first one since then. You?"

"I'll say 'date' if you will. And no, no one's waiting for me." Carol didn't want to give out too much information all at once—that can spoil the pungency, she thought, tasting the curry spice behind her teeth. Besides, she was impressed by the Mustang—she'd never ridden in a convertible before. Z.D. popped a cassette of Anne Murray's hits in. Country, she smiled, just a good ol' girl looking smooth behind the wheel. Z.D. maneuvered past the Safeway lots and refineries of Richmond, heading north over the San Rafael bridge. Before Carol could get the toll out of her purse, Z.D. pulled a couple Susan B. Anthony dollars from a tray and passed them over.

"I thought they stopped making those."

"They did, but I've got a stash."

"Are you a fan of Susan B.?" It's hard talking in a convertible at highway speed, and especially when you're going over a long bridge.

"Don't know that much about her," Z.D. shouted, "but I like dollar coins. We'll be off the freeway in five minutes—look over there."

Too easy to take this Bay for granted, Carol realized. Everyone forgets how wild, how sensational, how lucky we are to have escaped wherever we came from and landed here, where creation flashes its naked, hungry teeth at the sea, where the ocean and the land dare each other to be brave and leap, piling up together in a tangle of boulders and foam. Now she was cannonballing, a kid taking a leap off the dock, not knowing where the landing was—and not caring. No dogs or cats at home, no friend waiting for a call, no old lovers making dates. She was free today, and lucky.

Z.D. got off at the downtown San Rafael exit and Carol looked at her puzzled when they stopped at a light.

"It's the way we get to Point Reyes—you said you wanted some place cool, didn't you?"

"I've never been there."

"I thought you said you went to Cal."

"I did, but most of my weekend expeditions were to Reno."

"Oh, gambler, huh?"

"Kind of, I guess. I don't have that much to gamble with, and I've never had a big lucky streak, but I come out ahead usually—thirty, fifty bucks. The track treats me a little better, though I prefer casinos, I have to admit."

"You are a gambler." Z.D. gunned the Mustang through a yellow light, winding through what seemed to be a very long suburb. "So whadya like so much about gambling?" Z.D. was grinning, holding the wheel low, steering against her lap. Her left hand thumped casually along to Anne Murray's sentimental singing on "You Needed Me."

"The money."

Z.D. laughed again, her rumbling rainstick laugh, which this time made Carol curl her toes, glad that Z.D. couldn't see her feet at that angle.

"No," Carol said, "I didn't mean it like that. Or only like that. I like to watch what goes on with the money—how people attach themselves to different postures, how everyone has a kind of money signature."

"Like a stance?"

"Exactly. You know the way butches stand?"

"Oh, we all stand a certain way?"

25

"Of course not. But you stand—like you belong where you are, even when you're not sure you do."

"Who told you that?" Z.D. turned to consider Carol as they passed the small shops of Fairfield.

"I like to watch."

"Butches?"

"Butches, sure."

"And how people act with their money in casinos?" It had never occurred to Z.D. to stand back and observe people handling money in such a dispassionate way.

"Yes—it's better than going to the movies. You can read the plot in a twitch of someone's muscles."

"That's a pretty way of saying you like to be close to the action."

"Guilty," Carol laughed. "But I also like the math part—the attention it takes to figure your bets. I drove across country when I came to Cal, and when I stopped in Reno that last night, got fascinated with the odds on the table games." They passed a golf course, full of the same guys who like to place big line wagers at the casino tables.

"What do you play?" Z.D. asked.

"Mostly craps now, sometimes blackjack, sometimes poker machines when I get tired."

"Huh," she said, "I've never played craps. It always seemed complicated, though I'm sure I could figure it out if someone showed me the ropes."

"You like to gamble?"

"Only on love, ma'am." Z.D. made a little salute with her right hand, steadying the wheel with her left as they entered a redwood grove. Suddenly they were the only car on the road.

"Hey, this is pretty."

"Yeah. I love driving out here when I can get away."

Z.D. slowed down, and Carol looked up. Redwood branches interlaced above them, and her eyes shook with an after-image pattern of red. She closed them and smelled ferns, mountain runoff in the creek, dirt. "I can see why," she said. She relaxed into

26

riding next to Z.D., heading toward the coast, crunching through the woods, wind in her ears, blowing the words out of them.

They came to a stop sign where the road ended. Z.D. took a right turn, and another by a forest service sign for Pt. Reyes National Park. "It's actually still a ways from here to the ocean. You OK? We can stop in Inverness and get some cokes or something."

The little grocery had a pit toilet behind, close to the water. Carol was not a fan of pit toilets—well, probably no one is, she thought—but she had to go, grateful to be wearing a skirt so she didn't have to worry about pants trailing on floor muck. On the way back, she saw a big blue bird—like a jay, but not with the same sweep of a jay's head that makes it so recognizable. Z.D. surprised her by pulling a bird book out of the trunk.

"That's a scrub jay," she patted the book. "I thought so, but I wanted to make sure. See the blue necklace going down the front? Not nearly as common as the Stellar jay we mostly see."

"So you're a birder?" Carol's image of birders was of middle-aged men in tweed and ladies with ankle length skirts tripping over tree roots to complete their Audubon lists, probably right out of a "Saturday Night Live" skit, or some PBS English drama. Funny how TV infects your head.

"Nah," Z.D. gestured, probably to get rid of that same image. "I like to identify things, that's all. I don't keep a list or anything like that. But the jays are cool—did you know they're the same family as the ravens?"

"If you're not a birder, you're a secret scholar."

"Don't tell. I got a rep to maintain."

"And what rep is that, exactly?"

"Stick around and find out."

"You're corny, you know that?"

Z.D. shrugged, got quiet, threw the bird book in the back seat. They wound along a bay shore full of motels that needed coats of paint and an out-of-place Russian structure with onion domes leaning out over the water, around a bend, and then down a long, green stretch of road. Carol wondered where the ocean was, but didn't want to ask for a map. Z.D. stopped by a sign for McClure's Beach. No one was behind them. "You know, I always go out to the lighthouse. But the lighthouse is closed today. Wanna take this fork? I like to try roads I've never been on before."

"Since they're all new to me, be my guest." Almost immediately they were on a ridge with a panoramic view of the Pacific on their left. A long gray hand of fog was fingering the coast. Carol inhaled. "Spectacular—if you don't have acrophobia."

"High places, right? You scared?"

"Nah. I'm just a Midwest girl, and it takes us a long time to get used to the West Coast's sharp edges."

"OK, if you say so—but I'll go slower if you like."

"Oh no—I like speed—and I like not being used to the sharp edge."

Before Z.D. could think of the snappy reply she was looking for, they came to another sign on the right, for Heart's Desire beach. Z.D. looked at Carol. "Who could resist?"

"Not me," Carol smiled at her as Z.D. turned.

No one was in the guardhouse, and they didn't bother to put three bucks in the little envelope like they were supposed to. Carol figured the percentage of people who do that at around fifteen— the law-abiding folks who plan on staying all afternoon and want to support the park service. When they passed the big wooden sign at the entrance to the beach with "Heart's Desire" burned into the wood, Carol said, "Now I wish we had a camera. I'd take a picture of you by that sign."

"Heart's Desire," Z.D. read, with a skeptical tone. "How would you know?"

"Call it a hunch."

"Gambling already, huh?"

Only a handful of cars were in the parking lot—an old Ford van, a couple Toyotas, a Civic. The park service is good at names, actually, Carol thought. Even from the parking lot, they could see a perfect crescent of beach facing the bay. A blue heron skittered over the surface, landing close to shore. Probably because the top was down, she could hear a small waterfall, water dropping over stone, somewhere close. She surveyed the apparently all-American family having a picnic and took a deep breath, letting the pine air coat her lungs with a tingle.

"Want to take a walk?" Z.D. asked.

Carol was not much of a hiker—though she used to love walking around the Loop, looking in the store windows, going to museums, and had walked up and down Virginia Street in Reno for hours. She had a fragmentary memory of those scout camps Molly used to send her to. What a trial, although the swimming and crafts were okay. But Z.D. seemed so eager, Carol didn't want to disappoint her. "These sandals aren't made for any serious hiking—"

"Don't worry—if it gets too rough, we'll turn back. Let's just investigate."

"Lead the way, investigator." Z.D. was about an inch taller than Carol, which would make her five seven or eight. Nice sized woman—muscular, tan, enough belly fat to make a small roll over her belted black jeans. Carol found herself longing to hook her fingers in those belt loops and pull Z.D. close.

A breeze was coming up over the bay, although the fog they'd seen from the ridge hadn't gotten there yet. Fine long June afternoon, a couple days past solstice. Cycles were important to Carol. Even though she wasn't a nature girl, she got pleasure from exactitude, enjoying the mental effort of slicing up the moment when one season turns into the next. Many things were changing this afternoon, but emotion was much harder to keep track of. Easier to fix the precise second that the last heavy-lidded mascara blue turns into the luxurious black fur of night than to know the one gesture your lover made, the one response you offered, that pulled you forward, until tasting each other seemed inevitable.

Like most paths through the woods, this one was narrow, so Carol followed Z.D. as closely as she could without bumping into her. As they walked, Z.D. rattled off the names of ferns and flowers—not in a show-offy way, more like a tour guide, taking pleasure whenever Carol bent to examine something more closely, or said she liked a particular smell. They had been walking about fifteen minutes when Z.D. stopped so abruptly Carol rear-ended her.

"Sorry!" she said, confused about what just happened.

Z.D. pivoted, put her hands on Carol's shoulders, and without saying anything, kissed her. Her lips still had the tang of curry. She parted Carol's cautiously, but when she found no resistance, her tongue moved into her mouth, asking a hundred questions as she probed, tasting the answers. Carol pushed her breasts against Z.D.'s chest and found herself encircled in warm arms. Z.D.'s nipples were hard—Carol knew better than to call attention to that on the first date, but she rocked into her arousal, trying to flatten her fatness into Z.D.'s muscles. How long do first kisses last? Years and years, with the lattice-work shadows falling on their skin, their hair, her eyelashes against Carol's cheeks, the left-over spices of their lunch lingering, merging with the chemistry of their hungers falling out of the secure place where they maintained their distances, falling as seeds fall, taking root, blooming in a stop-motion photograph that expands time into something wet, fertile, new, new for them.

Z.D. pulled her head away and rested her palms on Carol's upper arms, then ran her left hand into her hair, pulling it lightly, surprising Carol, as she watched her face. Carol kept her eyes open, focused on Z.D.'s, and smiled. "Were you apologizing for something?" Z.D. asked.

"Not now," Carol said, leaning to kiss her again. Then they heard a crunch of leaves, someone whistling, coming toward them. They shook themselves into their separate bodies as if they were teenagers who'd heard their moms coming up the stairs. The whistler—a gray-haired woman with a walking stick—was grinning as she passed them, probably having had her own voyeuristic moment before she started making noise.

"Nice afternoon," she half-whistled, half-spoke.

"Nice," they chorused.

"Let's turn back," Carol said, feeling flushed, and suddenly tired of being on her feet.

Back in the car, Z.D. took Carol's hand, rubbed it between hers as if she were polishing a stone. Carol's hands were slightly bigger, but Z.D. had wide, long fingers, the fingernails bitten and rough.

"I can see you were telling the truth about being single." Carol ran her finger over the sharp edge of the index nail.

"Yeah, I try to tell the truth." She looked a little ruefully at her hands.

"I'll give you time to work on your nails, then. Let's see where the road ends." Carol squeezed Z.D.'s wrist.

"Is that a request or a metaphor?"

"Right now, a request," Carol found herself giggling. "You'll have to excuse me—I don't usually giggle."

"I don't mind a little giggle once in awhile," Z.D. said, reaching out to trace the line of Carol's chin with the back of her hand.

Carol closed her eyes, expecting that hand to continue on, to cup her breast, and was surprised to hear Z.D. start the engine. When she opened them, she saw a man with two wet dogs getting into a VW bus, and another car coming into the parking lot. Shy, she thought, or cautious. Or maybe Z.D. is savoring this beginning. She looked over at Z.D.'s profile and felt breath fill her belly. We're old enough to know a beginning when it comes to us, she realized.

Back on the ridge, they passed dairy farms, labeled Historic Farm I, then H, then J, which Carol found spectacularly unimaginative, given the scenery. Did the cows think themselves blessed for wandering free in these fog-drenched pastures with enormous views, or did they wish for the warm monotony of the inland valleys? The fog was pulsing toward them now, blowing in wisps. A red-winged blackbird skittered to a stop on a fence post. Knowing what it was made her understand better why Z.D. kept a bird book in her car. Carol put her arm around Z.D.'s shoulder to keep her warm, and she leaned back into the seat.

"I've got jackets in the trunk if you need one," Z.D. said.

31

"I'm enjoying being cold, but thanks. You're well-prepared."

"Girl scout."

"Really?"

"No, I never wanted to join them, although Ma tried to convince me it was a good idea. Never been much of a joiner." Z.D. shook her head.

"I was."

"A scout or a joiner?"

"Was a scout, still a joiner—more of a hanger-on, I guess."

"Oh yeah. LABIA. What else?"

"Girls Inc.—I tutor first-grade girls on Wednesday afternoons during the school year. Kind of a busman's holiday."

"What's a busman's holiday?"

"Oh, when somebody who drives buses for a living drives a bus on their vacation, I think."

"I get it, teach."

They went over a cattle grate, and looking away from Z.D., Carol saw a long fence strung down a steep ravine. "Tule Elk Reserve." She read the sign out loud.

"Hey, cool," Z.D. said. "I didn't know this was here. Think we'll see some?"

Before Carol could answer, they spied a herd over the hill, a couple hundred feet away—twenty, maybe, large brown lumps. The fog was spreading across the road now, and it was hard to make them out. The word "gloaming" came to Carol's mind. Was this dim light what gloaming was? As they negotiated a hairpin turn, the fog parted. Then, startling them—two elk, antler-heads aimed at each other, were butting it out not ten feet from the car. Z.D. pulled over, incredulous. They were in the middle of a nature documentary, the two of them alone with the young elks storming, giving off the sparks of their youth—now they could make out six, seven pairs of them, in various stages of antler lock, ranged close to the road.

Struck with awe—bodies straining forward, throats tight, breath held. As what they saw opened them, they shed their fear of the huge animals colliding and became aware of each other's amazement. They were separately allowing the elk's power to stretch their hearts, the fibers of their spirits, into the world. Elk stench, elk youth, challenge and assent. Wisps of fog curled along the hillside, rode the elks' backs. Call me out, change me, charge me with your intent. Z.D.'s eyes were as wide as they could go. Carol reached for her hand, and this time it wasn't a stranger's hand but the hand of her companion on a journey. They were transformed on that Pacific ridge. Having shown up, they felt a singular bravery for letting the world enter them, letting themselves be shaken naked into wonder.

Later, when their friends asked them how they hooked up, they'd each say, "We fell in love watching the elk rut, as close to us as that doorway."

4

I wasn't the first one in my family to go to college. My ma's older brother Stan went, and my cousin Mary on my dad's side. My dad, Dad Dallas—who rides around in an old Ford pickup with Handy Andy stenciled on the sides—said Mary was a snob. "If you want to know stuff the nuns won't teach you—" here he paused to wink at the boys, like I wouldn't notice "— go to the library. If you're smart enough for college, Zenobia, you're smart enough not to waste your time and money on it." Ma would narrow her eyes, but wouldn't say anything. I hoped she'd stick up for me when the time came.

We went to Catholic schools, where they try to get kids like me to consider the possibilities. I mean, some nuns can't stand baby dykes, but there's always one—usually more than one—who counsels us. Sister Bernadette counseled me. She'd put her dry hand on mine and make a soft clicking noise against her teeth. "Zenobia, the world is something to see." You gotta wonder about a nun like that—a woman who loved the planet—maybe even lusted for it—the hundred kinds of green that interlace the tropics, morning light in Kathmandu as you prepare to trek in the Himalayas. She taught history and geography, and whether or not she'd actually been to any of the places she singled out, her descriptions were so enthusiastic I could feel the difference between morning light in a river city like Portland and the Italian Alps.

How is it women get this weird calling? I mean, one day you're drinking a beer in Singapore and God raps you on the head, saying:

Forget the world, marry Me? I liked Sister Bernadette okay, but she made me afraid that you could want the wrong thing. You could have your heart set on becoming a rocket scientist, but it wouldn't be what you were meant for, and you'd spend your whole life doing the wrong work. I didn't think she was meant to be a nun—but what do I know about religion? The kind of religion that grabs your guts and squeezes out everything else you ever wanted to do. I never much liked the idea of praying—it seemed self-indulgent and cowardly at the same time. But if I prayed for anything, it was to not get the call.

Sister's room was full of maps. I had to admit, Portland was a speck up close to the edge of the yawning Pacific. Our address in the universe was less than a dot. Maps put things into perspective and I liked to study them, trace the back roads of Oregon Dad poked around on. Sometimes, when Dad was flush and into his family man trip, we'd drive in the pickup out to the coast—all us kids in back. Four brothers and me. I was second oldest, and lucky that Billy, who beat me into the world by fourteen months, was OK. By "OK," I mean not a complete bastard—a regular boy's boy, like he'd read the script for life in a true adventure comic book and was sticking to it: sports, spitting, and looking out for his sibs when Ma made him. Try sleeping next to the bathroom where each of your brothers practices spitting as if that, perfected, would get him through the minefield of adolescence.

Jake, the one after me, was mean. If mean were a color, he'd be spotted ugly industrial shades of green under his clothes, a rash of mean under his armpits, around his nuts, making him squirm all day, looking for something, someone to take it out on.

We had a hamster—well, really it was my hamster, though the boys always jockeyed for the chance to feed her—when Jake was about nine. I named her Biscuit, because she liked to eat shredded wheat. Every week, I changed the cardboard on the bottom of Biscuit's cage—mostly cereal boxes, because I thought Biscuit would like the colors. Ma found Biscuit out in the yard, blown up. That's all she would say about it, "blown up." She buried Biscuit herself, before I could see, and she refused to let us get any other pets. Ma didn't put her foot down about much, but when she did, she was hard as the boulders in Mt. Tabor Park.

Until I was about fourteen, I was bigger than Jake, and I'd wrestled enough with Dad and Billy to be able to hold my own. I'd even sneak down in the basement and lift weights with them, though I had to promise not to tell Ma.

Jake had a growth spurt when I wasn't paying attention, and he caught up to me one day when I was walking home after school. "Bird's dying over there," he said, like it didn't mean much to him.

"Where?"

"I saw a cat drag it into that lot, and I scared the cat off." He pointed to an overgrown thicket that'd had a "for sale" sign in front of it for about a year. "C'mon, I'll show you."

Should have known better. Should have known he'd never scare off a killer cat. He'd watch it munch on a bird's head, and you could imagine he was savoring the crunch of live bones in his own mouth.

I was in front of him, edging past some brambles, and he pushed me down. He got his legs around my neck and started to squeeze. I grabbed hold of his ankles, trying to topple him. "Bitch," he yelled, "stupid cunt." He sounded like he'd said that plenty of times before. He was twelve. Fucking twelve. I was having trouble breathing, and he was beating on my head. Suddenly I was so pissed that a rush of strength flew into my arms and I managed to pull his left leg over. Then I slammed him in the shin sideways with my fist and he fell, his leg punching a hole in my ribs. "You fuckin' bitch," he yelped into the dirt, but then I was sitting on top of him, grabbing his hair, yanking his head up.

"You asshole, Jake. I'm no snitch, but I'm gonna tell Mom and Dad. You can't beat up on people whenever you fucking feel like it."

"I'm not scared of Mom and Dad."

"Then be scared of me." I shoved his face back into the ground and had my elbow dug in his shoulder. His feet were kicking uselessly and he was trying to throw stones with his free hand, but they weren't going anywhere. "Can't breathe? Huh? C'mon, say uncle." He made a muffled cry into the earth. I pulled his head up.

"Fucking cunt," he growled, spitting out dirt.

I slammed him back down. I lay full on top of him, keeping a grip on his hair and punching him with my free hand. "Was it going to be like this, Jake? You were going to get on top of me and show me who was the boss? You ever lay a hand on me again, or any other girl, I swear I'll kill you. I'll get every nun in the damn school to tie you up and whip you until you look like Saint Sebastian." Surprise—that made him stop squirming.

"Not afraid of Mom and Dad, but scared of nuns? Man, you are a piece of work." I stopped punching him and jerked his head back. "We're done here, right?"

"Yeah," he mumbled.

Keeping my hand on his head, I rolled off him and kneeled. "I'm going to let you up now, and you're going to run out of here. I'm not going to tell Ma and Dad, but if I ever hear about you going off on anyone—anyone—smaller, weaker than you, I am going to go to the nuns. That's a promise. You hear me, Jake?"

"Yeah, I fucking hear you." He spit dirt at his feet.

"Then get the fuck out of here." I let go, scared about what he'd do. But he got up and started running. As I was brushing myself off, he turned and threw a rock at my head, but I ducked in time. I felt like a garbage truck had backed over me. I knew I should have killed him when I had the chance—but after that, we both kept a wary distance.

So when Dad took us on his happy family outings, I always sat next to Billy or Amos, who was our family ghost, absent-minded, always reading comics or watching TV. But hell, I would have even sat next to Jake, maybe, for the chance to ride in the bed of that pickup. Looking at the world go away—each tree bending along the asphalt—was another moment separating me and our stinking house. I wished Dad would have kept driving—north, I thought, up through Washington to Canada, through Canada to

Alaska—as far as we could get, as far as the Northern Lights. But we always made that easy right or left, never farther than Lincoln City, which is south, or Astoria, which is north, towns set up to get the inland folks to spend their holiday dimes on salt water taffy. They used to be logging and fishing towns, and I guess some people still make their living that way because you can see the logs clogging up the sides of rivers and salmon jerky is all over the place, but in my lifetime I expect to see the salmon and the forests gone; close to gone, anyway.

Sometimes Dad would drive us over the bridge across the mouth of the Columbia, which, I have to admit, is a spectacular thing. "Better than any damn Disneyland," Dad said, reliably. But he was right. If I hadn't been sitting with all those boys, I would have thrown my cap in the air and yelled hooray! every time we went under the green ironwork. The Columbia spread her broad back, vast, reflecting the green of shear cliffs that open up a hidden country of imagination, and let us glide on the belt that spanned her waist. The coast is pretty, in every direction. Pretty is a girl's word. It isn't pretty, really. It's tough—it's the remnants of a great upheaval pounded by surf into forms that cut your mind to ribbons. There. Better. What I learned in school was that how you say things counts more than what you mean. I tried writing down words for things on scraps of paper, but I always threw them away because I didn't want the boys, or Ma, even, emptying out our pockets for the laundry, to find them.

The kids in my high school who went to college mostly went to community colleges or Portland State, or if they were really ambitious or desperate to get away from home, to the U. of O. in Eugene. Big whoop. Sister Bernadette said I was smart enough to get a scholarship anywhere I wanted. Good in science and physics—I hit the exact moment colleges were looking for girls like me. I got great scores on the SAT, though I don't know how—I mean, I studied for them, but the night before, I got stoned out of my mind on some very superior weed, and when I saw the test form, the little boxes where you fill up circles under the letters of your name struck me as hilarious. I had a theory that you needed to relax before you took tests because when the moment comes, being uptight is not going to get you through. So I guess my theory was right.

The Sister and I would spend afternoons working on my why-you-should-let-me-be-your-exceptional-working-class-student essay. She had sussed out my road lust, so she made me write about pressing up against the world's boundaries, which I guess was honest although I wasn't thrilled about revealing so much. Must have worked, because I got accepted at the University of Wisconsin and, miraculously, at Stanford. Both of them willing to foot the whole damn bill. I kinda wanted to go to Wisconsin because it was so far, and it snowed there. That was also why I didn't want to go. My mom said, "Zeeny, I can't stand to have you more than a day away. Please." It's a very long day between Portland and the Bay, but Mom didn't travel much beyond our visits to the coast. I guess she thought I could fly if she really needed me. I don't like to fly. I'm not afraid of it or anything—I'd just rather drive anyplace you can get to by car.

So I went to Stanford, but damn Stanford—even if it was their dime. Especially because it was. Talk about a fish out of water—I didn't make it through the first semester, and I didn't care when the counselor told me how disappointed he was, how my leaving was going to make it harder for other working-class kids. At least, I didn't show him that I cared. Salmon die when they leap upstream to spawn—I've seen them, turning into bright red, big-jawed monsters, heaving in the shallows. What if some of them opted out? Queer salmon, who looked at the incline and said, I'll take my chances in the ocean, thanks. Those colleges have some setup—they take a handful of poor kids, minority kids, to prove they shouldn't really take them. Yeah, a couple tough it out—or maybe they'd spent their childhoods longing for cashmere sweaters and practicing saying, "Well, actually, I went to Stanford," with a mouthful of bored superiority. Not me.

It took a couple years, but I landed at San Francisco State. By

39

then, all I wanted was a degree, so I could say I had one if I ever ran into any of those Stanford snots. But I ended up liking State—it's where I met Nash, who was in theater, learning the technical parts. I was living in Oakland, because it was cheaper than the City, and after classes Nash and I would cruise around the Peninsula, go down past Pescadero, visit the seals. Nash always got excited by seals, running down the path through the sand succulents and flopping down on the crumbling ledge, cooing at them—"hey mami, hey papi, looking good!"—until I pulled her away. Apparently, they don't have seals in the Tropics, where she comes from. Nash is kind of a restless type—jiggles the change in her pockets, makes twenty adjustments to her sets even though they seem perfect to me the moment they're up. But she could watch the seals for hours, binoculars wedged against her eyes in the middle of a winter storm. She'd shake her head in disbelief. "Imagine, these great beasts live next to us, and the only stage they have are clumps of rock. No Lope de Vega, no Hansberry. Only grunts and moans. But maybe great drama goes on out there we are simply too—what's the right word for it?—too limited to understand. What do you think, my friend?"

"Parallel universes, Nash. We can't know what we can't know." I'd say something like that, trying to be cool. Even though we'd grown up visiting the seals at the coast, I admired them almost as much as she did.

At first, I thought Nash liked me for the Mustang and my naturalist tours, because why would a serious Puerto Rican kid, the daughter of doctors, want to hang out with a white stoner like me, even if we did have that nun connection? After a while, though, I realized how hard it is to find a good butch buddy. A dyke you can feel totally relaxed with, who lets you get away with your postures. You know what I mean? Femmes always want to get in, beyond, through to some unguarded part of your psyche they think got wounded in childhood. A butch respects how you front, lets you be. And a buddy is always ready for the ride.

I got my first car the summer I was seventeen. The year before,

Dad got me a job cleaning up and doing inventory in this paper warehouse, because he'd done some wiring for the owner. Dusty work. "Hey, you wanna wear jeans? This is the kind of work people in jeans do. You wanna waitress instead?" He knew I'd rather eat sawdust in a sideshow. I started spitting up paper debris like hairballs, but that was easier to take than having some Jake-like loser call me "girlie," as if an order of fries made him a king.

Dad would drop me off in the mornings and I'd take the bus home in the afternoon. With the bus fares going up and having to chip in for groceries, since "you've gotta learn what it's like in the world," blah blah, I realized my $3-an-hour job wasn't going to support any kind of stylish wheels. My brother Billy and I had been smoking dope for a year or so, and that summer was when I started dealing. It's easy to start. You could buy a bag, a good sized bag, for a hundred bucks back then, and then I'd roll it—I was good at rolling straight, thin joints. I could get 40 or 50 if I was careful, and I'd sell them to kids from school or the neighborhood for 5 bucks a pop—if I liked them, I'd go down to 5 joints for 20. A lot more profit in that than at the warehouse, but the warehouse was a good cover for my folks.

I had my heart set on a Mustang convertible. All summer, I rolled joints in the basement. The warehouse job had the extra benefit of giving me an excuse to cough so much. I kept the money under a loose brick behind the water heater. By the time school started, I had $475 saved. Not hardly enough yet.

The guy who ran the warehouse—a big Polish guy—put in a good word for me on account of I was so diligent and uncomplaining, and in the fall I got an after-school job in a discount paper store that drew its stock from the warehouse. It was the same kind of damn work—keeping track of inventory, cleaning up, running errands for the full-time guys—but the store was a little cleaner and had the bonus of keeping me legitimately away from home. You never would have imagined that there were so many kinds of paper. I mean, we had all kinds of paper goods—plates, toilet paper, paper hats even—but there were three aisles of reams of paper and stacks of paper with little booklets of samples hanging off the sides. People liked to swipe the sample books, so one of my jobs was keeping an eye on them.

May that year I turned 17, I finally had enough saved. I'd been circling ads in the classifieds for months, and May 2nd, when I drew the circle around the Mustang for sale over on Yamhill, I knew in my gut it was the one for me. $750, firm. That would leave me enough for insurance and a couple tanks of gas.

My folks must have thought I was a genius at saving money—which I was, kinda—when I showed up with the '67 'Stang, burgundy with black bucket seats and dual exhaust, four on the floor, completely paid for. Even Jake gave it an approving whistle.

"How you gonna put gas in that thing? Do you know what gas costs now?" Dad asked; he was always going on about how gas was twelve cents when he started driving.

"I filled it up already, Dad. Sixty-two cents a gallon. You want to take it for a spin?"

Dad grinned at me, and I tossed him the keys. "Okay, since you sprung for the gas, we're going for ice cream, on me," he beamed. "Get your mom and brothers."

Jed was still small enough to fit on my mom's lap, and me, Billy, Amos, and Jake perched together on the tiny back seat—our butts pressed up to the trunk wall so we looked more like a gang than a family. That was before anyone cared about seat belts.

That car! It sure did eat gas, but the dope covered that. I spent Sundays, when Mom made Amos and Jed go to church with her, buffing the hell out of it. I loved pressing my hands into its indentations, and dragging the chamois along its curves. From the front, it looked a little like a fish with its mouth stuck open if you squinted a certain way, but I didn't mind.

Out to the Columbia Gorge with the top down, that's where I'd go whenever I had a whole afternoon—and it wasn't raining. It does rain a lot in Portland, like one of those ugly bargains God likes to make. "Hey there," God rumbles, "You can live next to the most beautiful set of waterfalls in the world, but it'll rain nine days out of ten, so you'll forget about going to see them. And here's something else, special for you. I'll give you a great pitching arm, but I'll make you a girl. Ha ha." The god of fire and brimstone settled for bad jokes in the 20th century. Maybe everyone got too mad at him after the concentration camps and the atom bomb, so he had to tone down his act. "Here, Zenobia, I'll give you the car keys, since you want it so much," and you know God had to be bored if he was bothering with me. Bored, and had a trick up his sleeve. But hell, I was 17 and I didn't really care what God was up to.

Someone else made green, made mist, made the rock that splits apart under the water's fist. Not god, not the god who gave up Jesus to the cross, bam bam, in go the nails—the nuns' god. I wasn't falling for that anymore. Okay, maybe somewhere there was a god of vengeance, a god of smiting. He could go smite Jake, but he couldn't ride in my Mustang. I wouldn't let him in. I like the world, that's my secret. I don't tell anyone about it, how much I like it. Man, just look at it! Canon Beach with its wild rocks shattering on the sand like so many seriously broken hearts—the fossils of some prehistoric romantic drama, earthquake and lava. It's great. And the Columbia Gorge—with its puny WPA road. I read about the WPA and the New Deal in American history, and it gave me a funny feeling to be riding on something that was part of a textbook. But I guess it wasn't all that different from any road crew—except now they let girls hold the flags, big deal. I mean, the road crews were always made up of young guys so desperate for work they'd do any hard thing. Guys who flunked history. Anyway, back then, when desperation was the only food they had and the road crews of young guys had sucked it dry, they built this delicate little road that clings to the cliffs so you can get as close to the falls as possible.

Any day I could, which wasn't all that many, between school, work, dealing, and the rain, zip I'd go, past Troutdale, into the core of rushing water. Sometimes even when it was raining, but then I'd have to have the top up. I'd walk for hours. Hike is what the tourists say, but what is that? Putting on a pair of leather britches and using a hundred-dollar walking stick? I used my hands to get up into muddy places on the rocks. Behind the falls you can see from the road, lurk a hundred falls more, hidden along the trails.

Sometimes I'd stand at the bottom of a falls—one of the big ones, like Multnomah—and was certain I could see an Indian looking down at me. It always gave me the willies when it happened. Down past the Dalles, there's a park with petroglyphs, but you have to get permission to see them, which is more planning than I ever could pull off. Indians started all these trails the rangers like to pretend they created, stalking deer and bear, eating salmon and thinking, What a great place. All the park service signs are full of stuff about geologic time, but the time it took us to steal the view was a minute. Why isn't everybody more ashamed? That's what I want to know. Maybe it's not so obvious. I didn't take the land away from anyone, I was born here, and probably that's what everyone says, if they even think about it.

Mostly people seem to pretend that we all stumbled onto the Pacific Northwest and since it was empty of people, people we recognized, we could pave whatever we wanted. WPA. At least back in the what, thirties?, they were more subtle. Now people whiz by on 84 and check off the Gorge on their sightseeing list because they can see some of the bigger cascades from the highway—even though they look like puny silver ribbons dangling along the cliffs.

That's the kind of stuff I thought about when I walked around the trails. I'd pack a couple bologna sandwiches and cokes, some guidebooks about geology and wildflowers I pinched from the library, and spend the day. From Wahkeena falls, there's a great trail to Fairy Falls that I liked to take because of the name. The names for nature—falls and flowers, strung together—made a kind of music to me when I wrote them down. Wahkeena's a tier fall, the water going over one terrace after another. I was happy alone back there, with the mist of rivers like feathers ruffling against my skin, and no brothers getting in my face. When I got tired, I'd sit by a falls, eat my lunch, and try to identify whatever plant I was sitting next to—Howell's Daisy, Long-Beard Hawkweed, Douglasia. It was my senior year, and I thought it would be cool to be some kind of botanist, maybe a geologist, tramp around the world for your work, discover a rare rock formation or a fern no one had noticed before, and get it named after you. Probably a lot of things are called Zenobia already, even if I haven't come across them yet.

5

"Yes," Carol said. "I want you. I still want you. I want the muscles of your arms and the hair on your legs and your morning breath and the way I make you blush. I want your love of nature, your persistence, your tender strength."

"And all this time I thought it was my car. So you want me enough to move in together?"

"I thought you'd never ask."

Z.D. pumped her fists in the air.

6

Nash never went to a party, never went anywhere except to work, without first ironing her outfit, making sure the crease down the front of her pants was dagger sharp. Sometimes even for stage crew, she'd iron her overalls. Years of uniforms had her in a groove—the clean lines of her parents' lab coats, her father's professional suit and tie, her mother's office wear coming back from the cleaners absolved of the baby shit she regularly put up with in her pediatric practice. Nash didn't have anything near the disposable income her parents did, and besides, she had decided that dry cleaning fluid was bad. "Toxic environments," Mamí would agree. That didn't keep Mamí from sending the clothes out, although now she bragged about her "green" dry cleaner, whatever that meant. But Nash preferred the control, convenience, cheapness of pressing her own clothes.

Nash was partial to whatever she could do with her hands. She liked to nail things together—she built her own bookcases, small stools, chairs. The afternoon she saw her first play, *West Side Story*, she fixed on her future career as stage carpenter, transformed by the fantasy world props create. Even at ten, though, she realized that the gang violence of New York City didn't exactly translate to the auditorium of her cousins' Episcopal high school in Santurce, despite Leonard Bernstein's belief that he understood Puerto Ricans. Not that there weren't gang fights over girls down in La Perla slum, according to her brothers, but it was different. Maybe Puerto Rico was "*in* America," as Bernstein's song went, but it was not America. Even a kid could make that distinction. Not long after, her parents, who had a different admiration for the U.S. than she did, decided that keeping their children out of harm's way would best be achieved if they accepted positions at the University of California at San Francisco Medical Center, and off they went, waving goodbye to their aunts and uncles and cousins.

From the airplane windows, Nash watched Puerto Rico turn into a series of jagged green-gold shores. Jade-black water turned to aquamarine at the cream edge of land where sand separated the water's colors from the fifty leafy tints that ran down from the mountains, shouting greetings. Then her childhood was a speck of land in the vast mono-color on which only their plane and a few stray clouds cast shadows; then it was gone. A shiver of color was all Nash remembered when she woke from her dreams.

Her parents figured her desire to see every show that came to San Francisco was evidence of a precocious literary tendency. Her parents were busy. Her teachers were oblivious. Nash was in a long-term rebellion against the language of "service"—both from her parents and from St. Ignatius College Prep. Her father was a big deal cardiac anesthesiology specialist, which she thought particularly ironic since he walked around the world without any visible emotion. Her mother at least seemed to care—she had causes, like reducing lead paint and, later, spearheading research on pediatric AIDS. But everything was presented as a grand moral opportunity, or a cautionary tale ("You don't know how lucky you are, mija, to be healthy. Promise me you'll stay that way," her mother fussed. "Promise you'll take, you know, precautions. If you must."). It made Nash fantasize about becoming a paid assassin, until she decided even that was too grandiose.

The world is a series of small sets we hammer together, is what she came to: rice paper partitions and the illusions created by taking a step through a doorframe. Her teachers were fond of saying that we create reality through language. No, she wanted to argue, we create reality by artifact—what we gather around us, what we get attached to. By our stuff. We give too much credit to words, when everyone knows we judge books by their covers, strangers by their clothes, schools by their facilities. We are less and less interested in etymology, precise description, as we become—or re-become—a visual and tactile species, moved by what we see, lusting for what we can touch. As soon as she was able to control it, Nash lived in a white room with a single bookcase, a double bed with a white bedspread, the cover of the Beatles white album tacked on the wall, white paper cut-outs and flowers, and nothing else. She said she was meditating on what it meant to be a woman of color in America.

"Sometimes a 'Rican's gotta show up for the white girls' party, though," she said out loud, admiring her look in the mirror. You weren't really supposed to tuck in a Guyabera shirt—at least, the guys back in San Juan didn't—but she thought it looked better, cleaner. Too sloppy if you let it hang out of the back of your jacket. Of course, in San Juan, only lawyers and bankers wore jackets. Not even butches going out on the town. California in February is a whole different scene.

It had taken Z.D. and Carol more than a year-and-a-half to move in together—Nash was surprised first that they hadn't merged their pots and pans during the initial three months, and then that they had stayed together long enough to pick out furniture that had to be delivered. Nash had three different affairs while those two had been working out their differences. Este, if you stop to think about that, you're definitely going to be late for their housewarming, she thought, grabbing her car keys from the rack by the door. Nash took pleasure in organization and punctuality.

And in finding the right presents.

"My grandmother had one almost exactly like this—how did you find it?" Carol marveled at the green glass swan with the miniature spoon, hollowed out in the back. Nash was the first one to arrive, which was fine with Carol. "A saltcellar. No one has these anymore. No one even knows about them."

"Some of the theater people I know use them for cocaine—these saltcellars have a whole new incarnation."

"Really?" Carol turned the saltcellar over in her hand.

"Don't let her tell you her imaginary theater people stories. The truth is she likes to go antiquing but doesn't think it fits her image." Z.D. came up and looked at the swan over Carol's shoulder.

"But you can never be sure exactly what the truth is, right? Anyway, my friend, I also got something for you." Nash handed Z.D. a large, store-wrapped box.

"Heavy. Big." Z.D. hefted it in her hand, showing off the muscle in her arms.

"Bigger than a—" Nash prompted.

"Bigger than a—than a breadbox?"

"You'll thank me someday."

"I thank you right now," Z.D. said, tearing off the wrapping and admiring it—an old wooden breadbox with a slatted roll top. "It's beautiful."

"And your grandmother had one, right?"

"Actually, I think she might have. Not as nice as this, though. Thanks, man."

"What made you come up with these, Nash?" Carol was sitting down, still staring at the swan and the little spoon.

"You know I've dated my share of Jewish girls. It's customary to bring bread and salt to new homes, is it not? And here—" she fished in the shopping bag the presents had come out of "—are the bread and salt." Nash handed over a whole-wheat Acme loaf and a small container of Mediterranean sea salt.

"Well done, Nash. Very nice." Carol clapped, and Nash took a bow. The doorbell rang.

"I'll put this stuff in the kitchen—you get the door, okay, darling?" Z.D. said.

"Okay, honey."

Oh darling! Oh honey! Nash thought but only smiled, noticing the lacy fringe of a red bustier surrounding Carol's excellent cleavage.

"Hey, Carol, how you doing? This place is great!" Tourmaline and Ginny came in, folding up their umbrellas in the hallway. Before they could close the door, Miranda, Roz, and Myra showed up.

"Nice apartment. How'd you find it?" Miranda asked.

50

"Z.D. apparently has connections. One of her paper suppliers turned her on to it." Carol was showing off the living room with a flourish.

Nash turned and considered Carol. Well, maybe it was one of the paper suppliers and not one of their dope connections. Or maybe Carol was naïve, or, maybe not. She'd have to ask Z.D. how much she'd told Carol about their side business again—the last time she asked, Z.D. hummed and then said, "Don't worry. Carol's cool." Cool and cognizant are not necessarily the same things. She didn't want to accidentally drop some hint that would blow Z.D.'s cover. Or her own.

"And you look pretty well-connected yourself, honey. I love that nail polish—very plum-y." Myra raised one eyebrow, expertly.

"If it were up to me, I'd call it 'Inner Lips.'" Carol waved her hand in the air while everyone giggled.

"If lesbians named colors, we'd have a sexual revolution in the spectrum, sweetie," Myra said.

Nash realized Myra and Carol were doing a femme flirt, admiring each other's style. All props, she thought, that's how we humans do it. What we say to each other is frosting, insubstantial. It's the decoration that's the cake. Nice decoration on Myra, though, and also something solid emanating from underneath. Worth investigating, maybe.

"But they call it 'Royal Bride'—honest to god. Straight people have no imagination," Carol laughed.

"It could be some gay man with a sense of irony," Nash said. She scooped up Myra's coat with a barely perceptible half-bow flourish. Myra smiled.

"Could be, Nash," Carol allowed, smoothing the line of her velour pants. Nail polish was an indulgence you couldn't hide anymore than you could hide your hips. At least she could lay claim to fat politics, the theories of which read to her like good science, radical science that poked holes in conventional wisdom. But makeup—artificial, billion-dollar industry as nasty as the diet empire—and colluding with it to keep women attached to form

51

over content—she could find no excuse for using makeup beyond wanting to.

Carol's grandfather used to tell a joke about the Russian revolution—after the revolution, one man will want to keep a garden, just for his family; the next will agree as long as he can keep his cow; the next uses that to justify keeping family heirlooms, silver, paintings; the official listening nods, and decides to keep his mistress. Was that a joke? Her grandfather laughed when he told it. Z.D. said she thought too much—why worry about makeup? We should take every opportunity for pleasure that we can, so long as—Z.D. laughed when she said this, although Carol believed she meant it—it was cruelty-free. Turned out Z.D. had a secret nail polish fetish, and brought her home extravagant purple, magenta, silver blue shades, many of which Carol would only use on her toes in winter.

"At least our sense of irony is intact," Myra said, taking another look at Nash just as she turned away.

"Irony can be one of life's small consolations," Nash was saying as she swiveled toward Miranda, a former flame. "Can I take your coat too, Miranda?"

"Hey, Natividad—what's up?" Miranda slid out of her jacket, while Carol swayed in her heels, going to check on the living room, beckoning them to follow.

"Nash," Nash said.

"Oh, c'mon, an old novia has to have a few privileges."

"Yeah, but in private."

"In private, what?" Tanya, Miranda's latest girlfriend, who had been parking the car, squinted at what she overheard.

"It's nothing, Tanya. Old business," Nash said.

"Looks like old flirting to me," Tanya took hold of Miranda's arm, lightly, anxious but willing to relax, since it was a party celebrating a happy couple, after all.

Nash was content to leave it there, because tonight she had her eye on someone other than Miranda. She smiled before she left them, explaining she needed to help out in the kitchen.

◆ ◆ ◆

52

"Did you notice that your friend Nash left with Myra over an hour ago?" Carol asked, throwing remnants of over twenty glasses of wine and beer down the drain. It was after 1 a.m.

"Nash is a player," Z.D. said, wiping up the counters.

"You sound envious." Carol came up behind her, and wiggled against her rear.

"How can I be envious when I have this at home?" She twisted around and grabbed Carol's behind. "You've been showing your ass off to the girls all night. Time you showed it off just for me."

"Z.D., you're going to embarrass me."

"How about I see how much I can embarrass you. You know we've never done it on the living room rug."

"Unless you think hoovering is sexy, the living room will have to wait for another time. The only place in the house not covered with debris is our bed."

"See, using those old fashioned mid-Western words can really get someone hot. I could hoover you right up." Z.D. felt the muscles in her thighs twinge.

Then she and then she: pressed, swayed, buckled. Kneaded flesh up against the kitchen cabinets, Carol's shoulders a mottled pink, Z.D. slightly tan, freckled, blushing underneath, a bead of sweat rolling down her neck. Z.D. lifted her knee high into Carol's crotch and Carol, deliberate, breathing thickly, strained into Z.D., straining against the give of the velour pants, tight across the wide arc of her belly. "Dammit, Z.D., in the bedroom."

"You don't want it here, hard? What were your friends talking about tonight, that being in your Saturn return is all about dramatic change? Let me change you."

"You already were my Saturn return, Z.D. and all you do is change me." Kaleidoscopic, catastrophic, metamorphic, she didn't care, didn't want to care, wanted her boundaries to disappear, wanted even her skin to slough off, to be left twinging, ragged in the elements.

"And that's what you want, isn't it?"

"So much. But you can change me lying down."

While Carol stripped to the red lace underwear that matched her bustier, Z.D. arranged lube, silk scarves, a long wide flap of soft leather—a cast-off scrap she'd picked up from one of the craft fair vendors—on the night stand. She folded her jeans, t-shirt, and vest neatly over a chair, leaving on a white undershirt, jockey briefs. She lit candles, turned off the lights, humming. Sometimes you just go at it, primordial elks on the coastal hills, and sometimes you get all human, arranging the equipment of romance. Carol settled in amid their six pillows.

"Comfortable? Because you know once I get started, I'm not going to let up."

"I'm counting on you, Zenobia."

"Counting on me to what?" Z.D. was beside her, her breath a current, an entire atmosphere, as she pressed Carol's wrists back above her head. She felt her muscles stiffen, containing her strength.

"Counting on you to insist." Carol shuddered, holding still.

"Open your eyes, baby. Look at me. Insist on what?"

"Insist on taking me, gathering me up, splitting me apart—"

"Tying you up?"

"Tying me up. Please, tie me up."

"That's my girl. You know what you like." Z.D. took the scarves—she'd seen the padded faux-leather cuffs for sale at Good Vibrations, maybe she'd get some for a present—but Carol's scarves would carry Z.D.'s scent, carry her body—and later, when Carol wore one to a meeting, she'd remember and her belly would tremble in the midst of serious business. If they were out together, in the movies, say, Z.D. could tug on the scarf and make Carol wet, creating intimacy islands while her body stirred. Now she was quick, looping scarves around Carol's fists, knotting them to the iron bed posts—the bed frame Carol had chosen. Good choice. Z.D.'s hunger made her want to lunge, to swallow Carol whole. Slow down, she told herself, you'll get what you want, you have what you want. The woman you want, wants you. The silk shivered along her fingers.

54

"Don't—"

"I'm in charge now, you can't tell me what to do. You understand?" Saying it sounded over the top. But over the top was the name of this game. Z.D. tried not to grin.

Carol spread her arms until the silk bit into her skin.

Z.D. took the piece of suede and rubbed it against the fat of Carol's upper arms, then undid the bustier and pushed it open. She flicked the leather against Carol's shoulder. "Understand?"

"I understand. I'll do whatever you say."

"You know you will. You can't stop me, can you?"

"I appear, uh, to be tied up." Carol's ribcage undulated with the laugh she held in.

"No jokes." Z.D. swatted her belly, suppressing her own laugh. This line was so delicate. Here she was determined to never let anger even flicker in her stomach or her mind. What she wanted was texture, sensation. A purity stronger than prayer. Ritual in which control and desire rewired them, changed all the residual shames—polluted water into wine. Z.D. circled Carol's nipples with the leather, and Carol groaned. Carol's left breast was slightly larger than her right, so Z.D. bent to the right one, while she rubbed the leather against the left, sucking, tugging, giving the smaller breast encouragement, although she wouldn't have been able to say why. Carol pulled at the restraints, longing to rub Z.D.'s head, to touch her lover.

"Go on, the more you struggle, the tighter those knots are going to get. You have to give in to me. Say it."

"I give in to you. I give in. Please, Z.D.—get inside me." Her body buckled and creased with urgency.

"When I'm ready, greedy girl. Aren't you my greedy girl?"

"Yes." Carol's voice sounded tattered, strips of a flag that had been torn apart in gale force wind. "Yes, you make me lust and greed." A dark heat, the red of coals, infiltrated her tissues, body shame and body pride competing currents of sensation, lapping into flame.

Z.D. lay on top of her, her hands grabbing Carol's upper arms, rubbing her stomach along Carol's belly. Her undershirt bunched up and she pulled it off quickly in the semi-dark, throwing it on the floor, letting herself relax, naked, arcing, until she felt her skin soften, fuse into Carol's smooth, oiled body.

"I'm so hungry for you—" Carol's internal imagery changed, then, and Z.D. became a waterfall, inevitable, necessary energy bearing down into bedrock. Waterfalls have to have their way. Carol wanted to let Z.D. pour through her, craved to be the one who could contain that rush, the secret weeping nerve of her. Then she was swimming again, not separated by air, by anything—becoming the water in which she moved. The muscles in her shoulders and thighs ached to stroke, power bunching in the bundles of cells. Sex is all about power, she thought, no matter what anyone says. Z.D. pulled the snaps on Carol's silky lace undies open. And power is pure energy. Everything here is energy—vigorous intersections of will, the need to molt, to shed your skin, your sea hard shell, to turn yourself inside out, to turn the other inside out, to feel her tendons in your mouth, her hands reshaping your skeleton.

"Oh, baby." Z.D. felt the full strength of her torso digging into Carol's legs as she licked, swallowing the distilled juice of party tequila and crab dip, nuzzling her cheeks among Carol's soft soft thighs. She felt how Carol wanted to fill her, to offer herself, pushing her labia, the long brown wrinkled winking leaves, up against Z.D.'s cheeks. Hair and globes, mouth in the fur, now fingers, fist, twisting, and Carol rocking, her hands grabbing air, grabbing the scarves, an undulation, coming into being, new, now, come on, do it, you're so close, your lips engorge, clitoris jumps— jumps and arcs, down in the bone screaming, Carol screaming yes, oh, Zenobia, oh oh oh—

Then Carol caught her breath, stilled, went somewhere with her eyes closed, Z.D. watching, her neck curved up from between Carol's thighs, trying to read the flickering muscles in her face. For a moment we are one, one motion, one shout, one strength— and then, what? Carol's hands hung limp above her head, and Z.D. realized she best untie her before her arms went numb. She kissed her way up Carol's torso, grabbing mouthfuls of sweet fat between her teeth, which caused Carol to moan and shiver, but not open her eyes.

Before unloosening the scarves, Z.D. wiped her hands on the side of the bed, thinking she'd change the sheets tomorrow. She rubbed each hand as she freed it, and now Carol was watching her, hooded and dreamy. "Where'd you go?"

"I'm right here with you." Carol lay in the crook of Z.D.'s arm, idly stroking her shoulder.

"Yeah? How?"

Carol's breast heaved with the in and out of her breath. "Close, Z.D., half my cells have migrated to your face, your hands, can't you feel me?"

Z.D. held her fingers up, sniffed. "Well, I can smell you—don't worry, it's one of my favorite smells in the universe."

"I'm glad." Carol was slow, hoping her lover would relax. Then she remembered what she'd seen behind her eyes. "You know those waterfalls you told me about—where are they?"

"In the Columbia Gorge?"

"Mmm. That's what I saw—that's what you are, what you do to me."

"Really?" Z.D. filled with happiness, a pride that she could so please the woman she desired, that the woman she desired could feel, could sense, into Z.D.'s spirit. Could see her for who she was. She suffered an exquisite ache of expansion—of being so porous that all the sensations of living matter swept through her cells.

"Yes, really. You come through, thousands of tons of water, changing me, making me find a way to let you through. You waterfall me."

"Mmhmm."

Carol squinted, seeing an image of mist, monochrome, like an old tintype, brown and white, jangle on the border of memory. Brown mist, a man in a brown trench coat. "You know, I think my father took us to Niagara Falls when I was a kid."

"You just remembered that?" Z.D. turned lazily, relaxing now, letting the high drift off while looking into Carol's eyes, umber eyes, she thought, like a color in the Zellerbach premium paper line.

"Maybe. I'm not sure—I would have been between five and seven. It could have been something I saw on TV once—I'd like to think it was my father, that he'd take me and Molly on a trip like that."

"Yeah, I bet." Dad Dallas wouldn't have won any prizes in a father sweepstakes, but he had taken them to see the sights close by. Still, Z.D. didn't think she'd miss him much when he was gone. Carol poked around in her memory for her dad way too often—Z.D. didn't like him showing up in their bedroom, but she figured it would be insensitive to make a big deal about it. He'd go back to ghost land in a minute.

"Not many waterfalls around Chicago. After it was Molly and me, we rarely took trips out of state. But she did drag me to every two-bit museum in a fifty-mile radius. I have to confess I rather enjoyed those outings. Being with Mom, anyway." She grew quiet, smoothing Z.D.'s hair. After a while, she whispered, "Will you take me there?"

"To the Gorge?"

"Yeah. To your waterfall country."

"Someday. If you're good."

"Haven't I been good?"

"Oh," Z.D. said, "very."

7

But Z.D. said spring was the best season for a beginner to see the Gorge, spring for the melt-off or early winter when the first hard rains come. In spring, they were both busy—Carol had more tutoring clients than ever; Z.D.'s store was in the midst of expansion. In summer, they wanted to stay in town for the film festivals. They felt it was a mark of maturity, of taking their place as a couple in their community, to pony up for passes. Z.D. was particularly pleased with Castro passes from the Frameline Gay and Lesbian festival, and felt clever for getting the store to take out a small ad in the program, which underwrote most of the cost of their tickets. Yeah, yeah, it was really called LGBT—too much of a mouthful. She was grateful that the language had reclaimed "queer" and they could get on with going to the movies.

Carol wanted to know how many bad shorts about butches showing off they could possibly see, but had agreed to get their money's worth out of the Frameline pass if Z.D. promised to go to more of the shows at the Jewish Film Festival this year— besides, the Jewish films were closer, running in Berkeley after being at the Castro. Z.D. didn't mind going into the City, even though it took an extra half hour to park, because she loved the Castro Theater, inside and out—to her, it was the apex of big city life, something you couldn't find in Portland, or even Seattle. It was like being in the heart of a jukebox—flashing colors on the outside, busy with important fun. But inside, in the cool dark where the old 45s lay in stacks, waiting to be chosen, lurked the true center of the beat, the place a culture, a time, finds its rhythm.

At weekend shows, inside the Castro's ornate cavern, an organ came up from under the stage ("the proscenium," Nash whispered), a man played show tunes, ending with "San Francisco," and the audience sang along. In the Castro, you weren't just with people, you were a people. For the big nighttime shows, Z.D. shined her shoes and wore her best ties.

"Maybe we can go to that Italian one Wednesday night with Nash and Myra," Carol said, as they marked up their Jewish Film Festival catalogs. Nash's romance with Carol's friend Myra had lasted six months, not a record, certainly, but its longevity appeared to surprise Nash as much as it had her friends. Now that they were in the surfacing-from-bed, time-to-circulate phase, Z.D. agreed to give them a call.

No excuses for skipping the films this year, Carol insisted, and she was right, really. Last year Z.D.'d gotten away with saying she was busy—training someone new, big orders. The Jewish films made her nervous. It was inevitable that she'd make some comment— an "I never thought Jews were good with money"—or even an inadvertent grunt at a joke only Jews were supposed to get—and Carol would arch an eyebrow, letting her body go cold. Man, they had that Medusa myth all wrong. It wasn't that looking at Medusa would turn you into a rock—incurring Medusa's wrath turned *her* into stone, and that's the one thing no one can stand. The untouchable, unmovable other.

Even if Nash agreed to double date, Nash would likely whisper, "Este, buddy, where's the 'Rican festival?" Would Nash be joking or not? Half and half. Maybe there were more Puerto Ricans in the States than Jews, maybe back East, but probably not in San Francisco. "Aren't there Jewish Puerto Ricans?" Z.D. had asked.

"Not really." Nash stopped to consider. "No, I don't think so. Cuban Jews, I met some of them—but the Jews in Puerto Rico were all business people from the States, or else old refugees from the war." Nash was trying to sound like she knew what she was talking about, and maybe she did, but Z.D. was as confused as before. Weren't Jews always from someplace else?

60

Jews and Puerto Ricans seemed to Z.D. to be caught in some sticky business about race she couldn't get, a flypaper. She realized it had been a long time since she'd seen flypaper anywhere. No one wants to look at bugs wriggling to get free, except people like Jake, maybe. So we zap 'em, or suck them up with vacuums, or poison the world. Anything but deal with them one by one. Jews—she sucked on her lip. People aren't bugs, but we don't treat them much better. Carol's breasts, Carol's mouth, Carol throwing her head back in the car, letting wind unwind her hair—that Carol was her home. Nash was her partner in crime, funny, ironic, good. But when they were Jew and Latina instead of Carol and Nash, they became categories, engraved in stone, and the gulf between them felt impassable. She'd go quiet when that shift overtook them, not wanting to let on.

Maybe they felt as pricklish, as isolated, on their sides of the divide. And sometimes Z.D. caught herself thinking, Hey, look at me, I'm so cool that I have a Jewish lover, a Puerto Rican best friend. Then she'd be ashamed, hoping they'd never feel her thinking that. Objectifying. But was it objectifying to acknowledge their differences? See, she thought, the Jewish Film Festival gets me in trouble before I even go to any damn movies. Don't the Black women say Black is key—look how race in America infects every-thing? Z.D. was pretty sure they were not talking about Jews. But something about it applied to Jews. Fucking race does infect everything, and there's no penicillin for it.

Before she met Carol, she'd gone to the Jewish films a couple times with friends. At Stanford, hell, even at State, folks said Portland was a provincial town, and whatever they meant, she had decided that going to film festivals was a good way to get over it. International, Native American, Jewish—Queer she liked best, naturally, but even then she made an effort to see the films from Germany and India. Once, she'd checked out one of the gay guys' films from—what was it? Norway?—but it was all about cock. Some of her friends were into strap-ons, and more power to them, but she'd seen enough cocks in her house to last a lifetime. What

61

was the big fucking deal? She could be nice to guys if she had to be, but she sure as hell didn't want to mimic their kind of sexuality. You can only think about race for so long, she thought, before you get distracted.

"What did Nash say, honey?" Carol asked.

"Wednesday night is fine. Want to go to that Thai restaurant near the theater first?"

"I don't think it's as good as it used to be. How about the Italian one down the street?"

"When did you become another yuppie food snob?" Z.D. licked Carol's ear lobe.

"When you heightened my sense of taste," Carol whispered back, and then they were tangled in each other's mouths again.

Z.D. liked the feature-length movies from France or South America at the Jewish films—the one they'd chosen for their double date featured Sophia Loren, which she experienced as a brilliant bit of luck. What bothered her, she realized, was that even when the movies weren't about the Holocaust, they were. The Holocaust was a note, a background sound, like when you hear crickets or cicadas at night and you think there's words to it, if only you can make them out. People make noises like that, almost unhearable noises. Maybe she was part dog, Z.D. thought. Dog enough to hear the sad language the Jews never speak out loud when the movies are set in modern Europe.

But if they were about Israel, what a mess that was. How could it be that a people who had been so nearly wiped out, obliterated, would turn around and treat the Palestinians like shit? Carol told her the Oslo accords were going to change that, but she didn't think Carol believed it; Z.D. certainly didn't. To Z.D. it smacked of a cosmic joke, putting the State of Israel in the middle of Arab countries. It was so far from her life that she'd probably never think about it if it wasn't for Carol, who found Z.D.'s detachment irritating.

Mostly they didn't talk about it. What would they say? And even if they could talk about it, how was that going to change anything? Okay, suppose a Jewish and white Catholic dyke come to common definitions. Even if the answer were revealed to them in a sudden flash of epiphany, a burning bush, hah hah, nobody would pay any attention. They could agree all they liked. Carol said that Jews weren't any better than anyone else on the planet, and to expect them to be is another form of anti-Semitism, like thinking all Jews are smart.

"I get that," Z.D. nodded, although damn if she'd ever met one who wasn't. She figured Jews had developmentally disabled kids like everyone else, but that wasn't what she meant by smart/not smart. She'd been in high school with hundreds of not smart kids. Hell, her brothers weren't all that bright, unless you counted meanness as being its own form of genius. Yeah, sure, Jake the genius.

Once she said to Carol, "You know that thing about Jews being smart?"

"Uh-huh."

Z.D. heard the cautiousness in Carol's throat. "The thing is, Jews are smart. I mean, your friend Sandy is a writer, and Hannah and Myra are therapists, and Naomi does some lawyer thing with the city, and—"

"Yup. We run the world." Carol put down the math puzzle she was working on and gave her that squinty look that meant: watch out.

"I didn't say you were *that* fucking smart."

"Oh. So we're *not* smart enough to run the world?"

"C'mon Carol. I know there are plenty of Jewish guys somewhere working in factories or being salesmen or doing some kind of middle-middle job like I've got, and maybe there are straight Jewish women who like bubblegum music and don't care about politics, but I've never met a Jewish woman who didn't have it going on upstairs."

"Yeah, we're smart enough to run the world and smart enough not to try."

"Smart enough to run me." Z.D. decided it was time to get

out of this dead end. The only way to do it was to jump sideways.

"I'll run right through you."

"I'd like to see you try."

Right about there, as she'd hoped, they stopped talking.

But Carol did have a point—if the Jewish dykes were so damn smart, how come they weren't running the world? Of course you didn't have to be smart to have power. Probably helped not to be too smart if you wanted to be in charge. At some concert Z.D. had gone to, at Mama Bears, probably, Alix Dobkin said the patriarchy was in its death throes, and like any writhing beast, lashed out. Right. Lashed out for two thousand years. Were the Jewish dykes smart enough to get out of the way? Were any of them?

This was why she liked to go to the "Fun in Girls Shorts" programs at the queer festival—the sex films, the comedies. What were they going to solve? Treat each other decently, with respect. Share resources, privilege, when you can. Go out on the streets when it counts, or sometimes even when it doesn't count, because you gotta show up for each other, even if that doesn't change the way things work, or changes it so slowly the glaciers could melt and re-form before the assholes running things would give that power up. She'd like to be able to sigh and say, "oy," but she figured that was cultural appropriation. Been told, actually.

Talking about it wasn't a sport that Z.D. liked, even with Carol and Nash when she felt relatively comfortable, like they were working it out instead of judging each other. So many discussions—and she'd done it too, around class—were trials. She could cop to that feeling: wanting to put someone on trial. Someone close. Someone she could get to. Here's the evidence, I can prove that on the night of September 3rd your heart was not in the right place. On the morning of February 16th, you had a racist thought about a guy who cut you off in traffic. In July, you could have sprung for beer for the softball team, but all you did was put in your lousy three bucks. Plus, you told that woman you would lend her the money for rent, and then you blew it off, had to be reminded twice, and her landlord threatened her with eviction while you went to a bed and breakfast for the weekend. Had a nice time, didn't you? Well, now I sentence you to a hundred hours of community service. If only we had a community for you to give service to.

8

Z.D. refused to go to meetings, said she'd jump on a barricade, picket, march, commandeer the paper store's truck to haul tag sale donations on her day off (something she'd actually been asked to do), anything but sit through a meeting.

"What do you think happens in meetings? Orgies?" Nash was looking up, trying to identify constellations from where they were parked on Skyline Boulevard, waiting for their connection. A lattice of tree branches rubbed out sections of the view to the west.

"Orgies of self-flagellation. Look, you got me into those woman's center meetings when we were at State, and that was enough." Z.D. was lying over the hood of her car, with a backpack next to her, from which she'd taken binoculars to look at the stars. Nash and Z.D.—just a couple of amateur astronomers.

"It was that bad that it's soured you for fifteen years?"

"Nash, give it up. I don't have the temperament for it. Hey, look—a shooting star."

Nash looked in the direction Z.D. was pointing, but missed it. "Did you make a wish?"

"Yeah, that you would stop bugging me about LABIA. It's enough that you and Carol desert me in the middle of basketball season to argue about class with strangers."

"Hey, my friend, someone has to make up for what the menfolk have done to the world. If we cannot stop war, at least we can help each other out."

Z.D. narrowed her eyes at Nash, but smiled. A beat-up VW van with a "My other car is a broom" bumper sticker pulled onto the

dirt shoulder where they were parked. "You think that's them?"
Nash looked the van over as if she were a cop—not so much as a
broken taillight, nothing to distinguish it from any other hippy
feminist van, nothing you'd get stopped for if you didn't run any
lights, and you were white.

Up around Honeydew in Humboldt County, scores of entre-
preneurs made a good living, growing weed. Every season, the
Feds would find somebody's secret garden on state land and zap
it; one of the women told them that the growers got together to
plant a decoy patch, which was usually the one that got found.
Z.D.'s contact kept bees, for real, providing for a nice sideline in
organic hemp honey and legitimate posting of "Caution—Bees!"
signs. She sold the honey in general stores along Route 101 and
the Avenue of the Giants, and everyone called her Aunt Bee. They
should call California the Big Easy, not New Orleans, Nash
thought, a memory of French Quarter wrought-iron work taking
her back to the ornate balconies of Old San Juan, when they'd go
visit her cousins on Navidads if her parents could spare a week
from their busy doctor schedules. Her parents liked to posture
that their work was so important it would upstage Christmas. She
rubbed her forehead hard to clear her mind. Even in the Oakland
hills on an August night, it was important to stay alert.

Aunt Bee had a couple young dykes who cleaned and distributed
for her—good money in season. Z.D. was buying four kilos. When
the VW pulled in, she put the binoculars down and hopped off
the Mustang's hood.

"Hey, got any water? My dog's thirsty and I knocked over the
jug," a woman said.

"Sure," Z.D. answered. "I've got a couple bottles in my pack."
She approached the van, taking out a large plastic Vulvic water
bottle. The woman swung her door open and let a small golden
retriever out the back. Nash, watching sideways while appearing
to take in the view, noticed how smoothly they switched identical
packs while Z.D. bent down to pet the dog. "Nice dog."

"It's good to have company on the road." The woman dropped

67

her voice, "Mind hanging around a couple minutes while we count?"

"Dogs are good company. I saw a shooting star a couple minutes ago—I'm going to hang around for a while, see if I can spot anymore."

"Oh yeah, it's August—that would be the Perseids, right?"

"Perseids. Yeah, probably."

When Z.D. got back to the car, she swung the backpack in beside Nash, who chuckled. "Este, what do you know about Perseids?"

"Perseids—they're, uh, a bunch of comets, or, wait, I know, a band of space debris that circles the sun and shows up in August."

"Meteors," Nash said, fingering the contents of the backpack without even glancing at it, looking at Z.D. instead, who had the binoculars up against the sky, scanning the horizon surreptitiously. So much drama, Nash thought, and no one is paying any attention to us at all. She had a pinch of dope between her fingers, which she crumbled into the bag she pulled it from, then held her fingers to her nose. "Very nice bouquet. I'd say Garberville, 1996, fresh harvest."

The woman by the van called her dog. "Thanks for the water," she called as she pulled back on the road.

"You're welcome," Z.D. responded. She got up, brushed off her jeans. "Meteors. I knew that. Besides, meteors are space debris."

"You couldn't ask for a better stage." Nash said as Z.D. threw the pack in the trunk and headed to town, "meteor shower and all. Sometimes I think I should start writing my own plays."

"Probably make more money being a set designer, though." Z.D. was barely paying attention. She felt powerful, dangerous, raw. Anything could happen and she'd be ready for it.

"Money isn't everything, my friend. At least, after you have some."

"Tell it to your LABIA friends. You'll never convince them—and you sure won't convince me."

"You still think you're Mack the Knife—'the bulging pocket

68

makes the easy life.' Maybe we should think about growing up."

"C'mon Nash—we just had a perfect score. What's eating you tonight?"

"I don't know. Was thinking I should be doing something more productive with my life, give into my parents' nagging."

"Hell, you're as productive as anybody. You do beautiful work on stage—everyone says so. You go to those damn meetings faithfully—aren't you organizing the next dance?" Z.D. felt the rear of her 'Stang fishtail slightly in the curve, coming down the hill. She knew the Japanese sports cars handled better, but what the hell—they'd never be Mustangs.

"Yeah—me, your girlfriend, a couple others. But dances and dope—I don't know." Nash shook her head. "Hey—watch your speed there."

Z.D. slowed down, giving her a sheepish grin. "Dances and dope—what's wrong with that? We're doing community service, completely. Did you know that more people die from aspirin overdose than pot? I don't think anybody's ever died from smoking dope, not that's been documented anyway."

"So this is all a humanitarian enterprise to you?"

Z.D. beamed. "Yup, humanitarian. Besides," she slowed down to avoid hitting a squirrel, "I have that mentoring gig going at the store—I'm a model citizen."

"Yeah, you look very good on paper," Nash smiled at her own pun, "but Z.D., I'm going to be forty next year. Seems like I should do something else. Change."

"Aw, you're having a mid-life crisis. That's cute."

"Knock it off!" Nash punched her lightly in the arm. The lights of Oakland flashed in the grid below them, and they could still make out the outline of the coastal hills punctuated by smaller, more rural illuminations above the dark bay as they descended Redwood Road.

Marijuana smuggling one night, lesbian philanthropy the next, an outlaw's work is never done, Nash thought, parking in front of

Kaneesha's apartment building on 52nd Street. Good thing she was between productions. And besides, Myra was going to be there tonight. It had been at least a year since they officially broke up, and at first Nash had dropped out of LABIA—in deference to Myra's long standing in the group, she'd said, although really because most of the women were more Myra's friends than hers, and she didn't like to be scrutinized. A couple weeks ago, Myra called. "There's no reason we can't work together. That we have different visions of fidelity doesn't mean we don't have to negate our mutual commitment to community."

What a way to make up! "Different visions of fidelity." Why couldn't she say, I miss you even if you are a two-timing piece of work? And yet, Nash found that seriousness, that round-about attempt at reconciliation, extremely appealing. Myra—maybe it could work. Hey, hermana, you are way ahead of yourself here. All she did was try to get you to come back to the meetings, and probably because the group wants more women of color. That's me, the parity kid.

Kaneesha answered the bell with a spray of gladiolas in one hand. "You're the first one here. Come on in—I was about to put these in a vase."

"Stereotype busters are us," Nash said. Carol came up from the stairwell behind her.

"Hi, Nash. What stereotype is that?"

Nash nodded at her, feeling a vague discomfort for knowing how much Z.D. hid the dope business from her girlfriend—reason number seventy-three for not making long-term commitments. "You know, women of color time, like dyke time."

"Not us serious types," Carol flirted with her.

"What can I get you serious women to drink?" Kaneesha asked. When they answered "water," she pointed to a pitcher on the dining room table. "Hey, Nash, do you mind if I ask you why you picked that name?" She called over her shoulder, arranging the flowers.

"I didn't pick it. It's my real name. Kind of."

"Kind of?" Carol tilted her head, teasing.

"OK, smarty, then you tell her what it stands for."

"Okay, let's see if I can remember. Natividad, right? And something with an A—Aida?"

"Not even my parents would name a girl Aida." Nash turned to Kaneesha with an apologetic shrug. "Natividad Alíta Sanchez Herrera. My family calls me Alíta, but my friends call me Nash."

"Huh—it's a nice name, Natividad especially. Nash erases your heritage, you know." The doorbell rang again, and Kaneesha got up to answer.

"Ay, Kaneesha, if only it were that simple. Just do me a favor and call me Nash."

"Everyone gets to choose the name that suits them," she said reassuringly, but her gaze was perplexed.

The small apartment quickly filled with lesbians then, and Carol and Kaneesha reverted to the small talk that precedes the political discussion of women who mostly know each other through their cause. Carol, Miranda, Tourmaline, and Myra squeezed onto the couch; Nash, Kaneesha, Tina circled them in a variety of chairs, Janine and Sandra, who'd been late, sat on the floor. Ginny found a stool in the kitchen and perched next to the couch; her girlfriend, Tourmaline, rubbed her shoulder briefly, lest anyone accuse them of couple-ism. Miranda took notes. Nash gave Myra a half-questioning/half-damn-I'm-glad-to-see-you-again grin, and Myra grinned back, saying something about how well Nash looked before Kaneesha made them get started. The six middle-class girls were reporting on their fall fundraisers—the dance and weekend tag sale.

Kaneesha grimaced. "You've got the easy part. Now that we've got a rep, we're beginning to have dykes who need more money than we have to give. And you don't have to sort out some funky story about not having the rent. Do you think I like telling dykes we don't have enough money and trying to shake out information about their resources and friends?"

"It feels good to be able to make a difference in someone's life, though. There sure were times when fifty bucks meant I didn't get evicted," Janine volunteered.

"For real. But I'm saying we have to have a better way to check out folks' stories than we do now," Kaneesha said.

"Maybe we should have a form," Miranda ventured, looking up from her pad.

"You gonna fill out some form for a bunch of dykes?" Sandra asked.

"Hell, yes, if I'm hungry. Better for dykes than for the welfare office."

"We're not the welfare office."

"That's the point, isn't it? We're trying to share the money in our community."

"Yeah, but sometimes I feel like women who aren't even dykes find out about this and rip us off."

"It's better to be ripped off once or twice than to shut down to the people who need us," Myra said. Myra was firm and clear. Nash admired that.

"That's why I think anybody who applies should know somebody we know."

"Like a referral system? Doesn't that sound kind of classist?"

"What's classist about it? We're trying to build community. It doesn't mean you have to be friends with middle-class women—it just means you have to know someone, anyone. For god's sake, you know by the time we get to the woman who knows to call Nash over there because her ex-lover's mechanic heard about the fund from the woman she goes running with on Sundays who stopped by the garage sale last year, we'll have spread the word to hundreds of dykes. Sounds like good old tell-a-dyke to me."

"Yeah, but what about the dyke who just moved here and doesn't know anyone? Or whose car broke down and she's living in it while she's panhandling on Telegraph to get the money to fix it?"

"Or who was in an abusive relationship and got isolated from everyone?"

"So how would she find out about us?"

"She'd see the flier and come to the dance. You gonna tell her, 'Sorry, you don't know the right people for us to help you'?"

"Then she can know me."

"Okay, but then what if she's scamming and brings the money back to her boyfriend? Or what if she shoots it up?"

"That goes back to my original point. We can't start being suspicious of every woman who calls, trying to figure out if she's a liar. It's the opposite of what we want to be doing. And I don't want to filter what lesbians tell me with some kind of cop mentality."

"Amen to that."

"I appreciate that figuring out who gets the money has gotten much harder the last couple years, but shouldn't we be talking about having more money to give first?"

"That's the middle-class group's responsibility, not all of ours."

"Yeah, talk amongst yourselves for that. I've got enough work now."

"But I thought we all wanted to talk about what we were going to say at the dance and what to put on the fliers."

"Yeah, sure."

"I agree. Let's get down to that and maybe we can break into two groups after we decide what goes on the flier—it's only five weeks away."

"Oh yeah, about that. Wasn't someone supposed to check on the Jewish New Year date?"

"It's okay," Carol said. "The dance comes in-between Rosh Hashanah and Yom Kippur, which starts Sunday night. Not a problem."

Nash had added a few points, but had been mostly quiet. She was having trouble picking up her passion for this. If it's dollars that change the world, then their pile of dyke dollars was pitiful next to even, say, the money raised from church bake sales in a year. But maybe it wasn't just dollars that made change. She'd argued—hadn't she?—that these very conversations about money, about redistribution, about power, changed them all. But were they changed? Even if they were, what difference did the changes

73

a handful of dykes made create in the vastness of the world? She squeezed her eyes together and in the speckled after-image saw Puerto Rico disappearing, a dot of green on the horizon.

After nearly another hour, Ginny agreed to do the photocopying at her job if Tourmaline got her the flier by the next Wednesday, and they went into separate rooms to complain about each other. And to organize. Ironic, Nash thought, that I have to go in with the middle-class girls and Myra's with the others.

9

Whenever she wasn't distracted by waking to the smell of Z.D.'s flapjacks (a term Carol found endearing), which signaled a lazy, amorous Sunday morning, Carol headed north on 80 for the weekly fat women's swim at Albany High. She sometimes swam closer to home at Oakland's Temescal municipal pool, but it was outdoors, cold in winter, and although her body was a pleasure to Z.D. and a plum under her own fingers, Carol didn't see that reflected back in the faces of the regular swimmers. They rarely appeared content with their own bodies, and tried not to even look at Carol's. Thin and average-sized women glanced at her quickly and turned away, compressing their lips into tight lines as they went through their shoulder warm-ups and stretches.

Carol struck up conversations with the few other unconventionally shaped women in the locker room—old women, women who'd had mastectomies, or whose doctors prescribed swimming for one ailment or another. She hoped her happiness and ease served as a rebuke to those who judged her, although she figured they mostly took it as a form of pitiable courage.

But, oh, Sunday mornings with the other fat women in the locker room! Even though the locker room often smelled like stale farts, she never hurried, hanging her blouse carefully on the third hook on the far wall. She had a pink and orange gym bag she'd picked out at the Berkeley Flea Market, which she kept filled with the necessities—swimmer's shampoo, powder, body lotion, hand cream, mini hair dryer. One of the fat swim's founders made bathing suits to order, and, although it took her a year or two,

Carol got up the courage to order a two-piece—bright magenta with fuchsia polka dots. She had a plain blue one-piece for public pools, and a few others in assorted colors for vacations, but here she was comfortable, silly, enjoying the spill of flesh across her waistband, the admiration of butches in the shower, the soft wobble of her upper arms as she spiked a volleyball in the shallow end.

And underwater, counting laps, Carol reveled in the distraction of shapes. What equations can there be for the volumes of fat bodies? She smiled, remembering a chapter on calculating asymmetrical forms. Every belly, hip, thigh, calf, shoulder, its own sweet irregular series of swell and shadow. Are equations the equivalent of girdles, by which we seek to conform the world to set principles, and feel, therefore, in control? Every woman in that pool had at some point slipped the reins. Likely they were adept at counting, even the ones who'd flunked algebra in some distant course. Counting is the required vocabulary of fat women—80 calories in a banana, 300 in a scoop of vanilla ice cream, 40 calories in a smile, only 20 in a frown, why not smile, you have such a pretty face, one more hour of grief to take before I can slip away into the water.

She peered through the blue tint of her goggles at a massive belly, three times the size of her own, gliding to her right. Manatee gardens, easy home, all these bodies out of control, and yet, so tame. Carol felt the freedom to expand into her body, and then beyond her body, in the moving light, into the physics of waves. I am only an electron here, a small nucleus of energy, flashing in the cool blue refractions. I am thirty-four and strong. She felt the smooth motion of her shoulder breaking the surface, the muscle glistening with fat and water, a power, a happiness of power.

The women hung by the pool sides in friendship groups, exchanging gossip or film reviews of *Fargo* and *Shine* or mourning the passing of Ella Fitzgerald. Some of them planned demonstrations against the Rwandan genocide, organized the dyke march, critiqued the last fat feminist caucus gathering and many gave each other tips on the best places to get skirts or leotards or shoes.

In the shower, they scoped out the variety of bodies, trying surreptitiously to compare size. That one's thighs are much bigger than mine, but my butt is bigger than hers. Some of them were ambivalent about fatness, some took it as a simple given, some reveled in it. A few younger women had tattoos (snakes, dragons, chains) that gained a new dimension when soaped. Sometimes they sang—arias, show tunes, pop music—the notes pulsing through the soft pouches on their throats, the best among them as rousing as any diva. Carol adored the fat swim. And it was a perfect place to leave fliers.

DYKES OF ALL TYPES!

COME TO THE DANCE

SUPPORT LABIA

Your **L**esbian **A**mazon **B**rigade **I**n **A**ction
Raising Consciousness and Cash!

Share whatever you can with
lesbians who need help—
no donations too small or too big.
8 pm-1 am, Saturday, September 21, 1996
The Brick Hut, Berkeley

In consideration of our sisters,
No drugs, alcohol or scents, please

"Mmm-mmm, fun," Z.D. smacked her lips, crumpled the flier and flipped it into the trash. "Score a point for the kid."

"It's a good thing I have another hundred of those," Carol said, kissing Z.D. on the neck, deciding not to fall for the needling.

"How did I know that? I suppose you're going to drag me to this."

"You are my favorite dancing partner, you know." Carol moved behind Z.D. and pressed her belly into the small of her back. Putting her hands on her shoulders, Carol slowly ground herself into Z.D.'s body, leaning in to lick her neck.

Z.D. spun around, returning the embrace. "Since you're asking me so nicely, I'll go. But I want you to put on that underwear I got you—that red stuff. And I want to be the only one who knows you've got it on."

"See, dykes can have fun sober," Carol whispered in her ear.

"Yeah, but if you get me started like this I'm sure to give off a scent—and I know you will."

"Those scents we allow. Encourage, even."

Carol conceded that women would come with flasks in their hip pockets, or having polished off a joint in the car, or would go to the bathroom with their friends who had just scored something excellent—probably from Z.D., about whose sideline she was more aware than she let on. The point was the advertisement. They could flirt, dance, gossip, shine without drugs. Not that she wanted to judge anyone's hungers. It's hard enough to survive the twentieth century. But lesbian culture could use a makeover, an evening at the anti-corporate shadow and blush counter, she thought.

"You know, we have a couple free hours this beautiful Sunday afternoon. No games on that I'm interested in," Z.D. said. "Whadya think?"

"It's not the most romantic proposal I ever got. But I think it's about time I flipped you over."

"Uhuh," Z.D. cleared her throat. "We'll see about that."

"Oh, stop being so tough. You know you like it when you let me."

Z.D. cleared her throat, shrugged her shoulders. "We'll see. I'm gonna wash up. Light a candle, okay?"

Lying naked on their bed while Z.D. got out the lube and

cleaned up in the bathroom, Carol imagined herself testifying to a city council, or whoever would listen: we are the dykes about love. We are the serious dykes, the ones who have the heart to change how the heart works after it learns its muscular pattern as a shield. We are the ones who want to change the world, but have learned we can't force that on you. We can hold dances to raise money for dykes to go to the dentist, get new glasses, buy a retread, make the rent. And maybe you'll be inspired. To love. It can't be wielded as punishment or reward. Love has to be love. It can't be a stick, even a stick of butter, nor an inducement, a promise (oh, if only love could be a promise!), an investment. And you have to not care if the energy that comes to meet you isn't the same love returning, not be bound to outcomes, payback, romantic illusions. When love comes out of a person, out of a woman, it has to be—so full of self, so full of pleasure, so amused, so in balance, that nothing matters but to listen and respond with an open mind. Gotcha—you thought I was going to say, open heart.

But it's a hell of a lot harder to open your mind than your heart. A heart's got little doors all over it, and each one has the word "hope" stamped in different color foil stapled on to its flocking. And hope—we hope—for everything. We hope to be touched and comforted and given what we want and to die at home being stroked and to never feel pain or fear or even discomfort. Z.D. hopes to have the best damn car on the road, and Nash hopes to be called to Broadway and I hope to be the winner, to have a long roll at the crap table, to come out ahead, hell, I even still hope that my father is alive, an amnesiac mechanic in Hanoi, and that is what the heart is about.

But the mind can let go of that, in its best moments, and hear how the dark comes in through the window screens along with the gristly car noises that want to mimic undertow but can't quite. At its best, the mind itself loves. It says yes. Yes, I will pour my imagination into creating lesbian culture. Yes, I will dance with you, expecting and wanting nothing. Yes, I will admire the way your hips move and long for you biting my arm as I push against your body as soon as you finish up in the bathroom. Yes, I will listen to everything you have to say and admire you without desire. Damn, Carol laughed, as Z.D. appeared in the doorway in her undershirt, the mind can be an asshole. All we have is desire.

Carol looked out at the dance floor and giggled, and Z.D. wanted to know why. "C'mon, honey," she said, looking at Carol who was so familiar, whose smell lingered all day in the hair along Z.D.'s arms. "Tell me what's funny."

"Oh god, Z.D., I wish I had words for it." Carol had an overwhelming apparition of how folks like their distractions. The meaning of life is given to each of us on wafers when we're five, and we swallow. Oh, now I've conflated Catholic with Jewish ritual, but what the hell. That femme in the center of the room will like her party dresses; that one needs a father figure's approval; the butch by the wall over there will always define herself against, in opposition; the young woman leaning into her will let pain bind her to another so she doesn't have to feel alone—pleasure is unreliable but when you ache, the ache is clear. And I, I have swallowed the change-the-world and wanna-bet? wafers, along with god knows what else. Somehow that seemed funny, with dykes disco-ing in the spangled dark to Gloria Gaynor's "I Will Survive."

Z.D. stood still for a minute regarding her, and then walked with the beat. "You can laugh at something you don't know how to tell me? Is it a picture or something?"

"No, it's words, but they're all bunched together like flowers some kid picked, weeds and tulips rubbing up against each other—"

"That's you and me, a weed and a tulip."

"Are you calling me a weed?"

"You know, Carol, that you are always my tulip." Z.D. bowed slightly, and gave Carol's neck a quick, sharp bite.

"Ow! Z.D., people are watching us."

"So what? It's a damn dyke dance after all."

"Hey, Z.D.!" Nash called her from across the room.

"Oh, man. What now?"

"Go on over, honey. I know where we can finish this."

"I bet you do."

"I always bet with the house when I can, and you're home to me."

"God you can be annoying," Z.D. said, squeezing Carol's hand.

One of the ways Carol knew Z.D. was in the midst of some drug deal was that it increased her sexual appetite—three times in a week was a lot, now. Danger pops us into attention, makes our cells alert. Not all that unlike gambling, she realized. Mixed blessings.

"Hey, Z.D." A small, fat woman standing next to Nash called, by way of greeting.

"I'm coming."

Nash figured conducting business wasn't the same as using. She told the dykes who approached her to remember it was a dope-free dance, smoke at home—or at least wait until you get in the car. They trusted her. Nash and Z.D. pretty much followed the same guidelines that LABIA did—you had to know someone who knew someone they knew. And even then they were careful.

Z.D. had a lot to lose now, but she was loath to give up dealing. It wasn't the money anymore, although she liked the extra cash, the ability to spring for the check at restaurants or drop an extra twenty bucks in the hat at events like these. Conflicted, unwilling to let go of an image. She'd modernized the store, put in a completely new inventory tracking system that she'd designed with a little help from Carol. A big raise followed that, and then some of the downtown merchants started coming to her for advice. They sought her out not only because of her computer smarts—although talking to Z.D. was considerably cheaper for the business folk than calling up Oracle. She was good with the local kids, training them, spotting the scam artists and occasionally turning them around. She and a couple others set up an after-school mentoring program for the high school. Hands on. She liked the kids, even the boys, liked seeing how everyone wanted a chance to prove themselves. Didn't want to throw that away. But didn't want to give up being an outlaw, either.

Ginny came up to Carol. "Can you take a turn selling drinks? Someone told me a cop car is circling the block and I want to check it out."

"Sure," Carol said, unsure why, when trouble was in the air, butches thought they were the ones who had to check it out, when it was usually femmes who defused situations. Wouldn't it be better to send her to begin with, in a loose green skirt, her hair down, to say sweetly, "Anything the matter, officers?" Nope, dollars to donuts the buttoned-down crew-cut butch jumped for the door. Then, depending on the butch, she'd realize her mistake and signal to someone like Carol, or else she'd get her ego involved and tension would escalate. Dollars to donuts—what the hell does that mean, she wondered, raking in five-dollar bills while pouring sparkling water and cola. Someone she didn't recognize, with slicked back hair, in a flannel shirt, handed her a sealed envelope.

"This is a donation." The woman looked uncomfortable, a little embarrassed. Carol refocused, trying to put her at ease.

"Thanks. Everything goes directly to the women who need it."

"Yeah, that's what I want," the woman said, "and, um, a diet cola."

"We don't have diet drinks—we made a group decision not to support the diet industry. And those chemicals are worse than sugar." She was pleased with the decision but hoped she didn't sound too preachy.

"P.C.'ll bite you in the butt every time." The woman shook her head. "Give me a Calistoga, then."

"Here you go. And thanks!" As the woman turned away from her, Carol took stock of her distraction. Where was Ginny? Oh, standing in back of Myra, who was gesturing with the police outside. It looked like the conversation was under control. Femmes to the rescue.

She swiveled, noticing that Nash and Z.D. were also watching Ginny and Myra. Or the police. They were talking to that other woman she didn't know—how could she not know every dyke in Oakland by now?—but she couldn't hear them. Too bad she never learned to read lips.

♥

Z.D. looked away from the police as casually as she could, back to the woman Nash introduced as Laura. "Nice dance, huh?"

"Yeah. Hey, Carmen told me you had really good shit on sale."

"How do you know Carmen?"

"We work together on the Dyke March in the city."

"That March is a great thing," Nash said, measuring Z.D.'s mood.

"Thing is," Z.D. said, and now she felt the cops eyeballing every dyke in the restaurant, "I'm dry right now. Haven't been able to score anything even for myself in months."

The woman frowned. "That's not what I heard."

"You know how rumors carry. Listen, nice to meet you. If you give me your phone number, I'll call you if anything turns up."

"Well, OK," the woman said, scribbling her number on a matchbook cover pulled from her pocket. "Promise you'll call?"

"Of course." Z.D. looked at the number. "Oakland?"

"Uh-huh."

"I'm going to go help my girl sell drinks," Z.D. said as Laura squinted at her and went off to stand in the bathroom line. "Catch you later, Nash. Don't get any ideas about getting back together with Myra, now."

"Hey, is it not dyke etiquette to ask your ex-lovers for a dance?" Nash practiced her suave and debonair look on Z.D. before she crossed the room.

"How much for a glass of soda?" Z.D. grinned at Carol across the narrow table.

"For you? Ten bucks."

"Whoa! I thought you were all about supporting working-class dykes."

"This is about spreading the wealth—you don't feel my support?"

"You got me there, although it looks like our wealth is getting shut down." Z.D. nodded out the window, where a small group of dykes were now gathered around the squad car.

"Nothing that unusual about police in this part of town, especially when the dykes are having a party. Could be they think they're protecting us from stray dyke bashers. Feeling jumpy, Z.D.?"

"Feeling like jumping your bones." Z.D. reached over and grabbed the loose flesh on Carol's naked arm. Carol closed her eyes with pleasure. "Can you hand off this pop stand?"

"Yeah, hold on. Hey, Kaneesha, can you get someone over here to relieve me? Oh—and someone gave me this." She picked up the envelope she'd put under the money box for the drinks.

Kaneesha, who was in charge of their bank account, hefted it and broke the seal. She whistled—inside were ten one hundred dollars bills. "Who gave you this?"

Carol peered into the crowded room, but couldn't see the woman anywhere. "A white butch. She was wearing flannel. Not too many dykes wear flannel anymore."

"Only the old-timers," Kaneesha laughed. "This is something, isn't it. And there's a note—'from your working-class sister.' That's terrific. I'll hold on to this."

"It's sexy," Z.D. chimed in. "C'mon, don't you think raising all this money for dykes is sexy? You guys are doing a great job." Carol shot her a look, but Z.D. stretched out her arm in a gesture of gallantry. "I request the pleasure of your company at home. Great fundraisers need their own rewards."

Later, after, Carol was sitting on top of Z.D.'s pelvis, rubbing her hands under Z.D.'s undershirt, which she'd kept on, as she mostly did, the whole time. Z.D. stopped Carol's hand when it got close to her breast. "Come lie by me."

Carol curled up along her side, thinking how great Z.D.'s muscles were, and how maybe she should start adding some weight training to her weekly swim. "What are you thinking about, Z.D.?"

"You think a lot of Oakland dykes work on the San Francisco Dyke March?"

"Gee, I don't know. Since we don't have one over here, maybe a few. Why do you ask? You have a sudden desire to volunteer?"

"No, Nash introduced me to someone tonight who said she worked with Carmen over there."

"Short, pudgy white woman?"

"Yeah. You know her?"

"No. She was asking a lot of questions about LABIA, though, and I got a weird vibe from her."

"Yeah, me too."

"Z.D.?"

"Yeah, babe?"

"I know you like to keep your business private, but I do have a clue. You're careful, right?"

"More careful all the time," she said, as Carol snuggled in to sleep.

10

Molly called every Saturday morning at 9:30 a.m., if Carol didn't beat her to it. They competed in finding the cheapest long distance plans.

"That Lewinsky girl," Molly began, without saying hello.

"Woman, Mom."

"Get off it, cookie. I was a pioneer of non-sexist language in my day."

"Your day's not over." A rush of pleasure overtook Carol. Her friends all had such complicated relationships with their mothers, ambivalent at best. Not that Molly was all that easy, but she was fun, fun to talk to. Carol used her shoulder to cradle the phone while she folded Z.D.'s underwear.

"You better believe that! What was I saying?"

"Sounded like you were about to blame Monica Lewinsky for Clinton's messing around."

"I would never! But I think it's wrong how he's being persecuted."

"No argument here."

"I mean really. They're all—"

"Pricks?"

"If you must put it that way, yes. I bet you couldn't find ten men in the entire Congress who haven't cheated on their wives. It's not that I condone it, you understand."

Carol heard the familiar gulp, Molly's smoke intake, and tapped her nails on the wall. She'd given up pestering her about it, mostly. "I know. It's a weird way to divert attention."

"Exactly! You are my cookie, cookie. By the way, how's your Z.D. doing?"

"Fine, Mom. They keep her busy with that new mentoring program I told you about. And you?"

"Oh, you know, regular. I was thinking about taking flamenco dancing lessons, though. My mother always said we were half Sephardic on her mother's side, so it would be going back to my Spanish roots."

"You never told me that."

"The Sephardic thing? I guess it never came up. I'm not sure it's true. Anyway, we never ate like the Sephardic do."

"How's that, Mom?"

"Oh, apricots and prunes in everything, no gefilte fish. Anyway, what do you think?"

"About flamenco lessons? Why not?" Carol wished she could figure out a way to get back to Chicago more often. It would be a trip to shop for flamenco skirts with Molly.

A couple weeks after they'd parsed Clinton's dalliance, Carol heard her answering machine pick up a call in the back room, but since it was four on a Wednesday and she was in the middle of trying to explain algebraic variables to a confused seventh grader, she ignored it.

"You got a message, you know," Z.D. yelled several hours later from the bedroom, where she was changing out of her work clothes.

"That wasn't you?"

"No, I was jammed at the store all day—I had to train a new stock boy and I had purchase orders up the kazoo. Maybe you have a secret admirer?"

Carol was stirring spaghetti sauce. She always made hers from scratch—sautéing onions, five or seven cloves of garlic, tamari, mushrooms and peppers if she'd remembered to buy them, then browning some ground, free-range turkey or spicy turkey sausage with the vegetables. Plain organic tomato sauce, fresh basil, and a handful of dried oregano were added when she was pleased with the mixture's color. She licked the spoon. "Of course I have secret admirers," she said, dipping the spoon back into the sauce to give Z.D. a taste.

"Wow! You cook good. Did I ever tell you that?"

"You just want me to keep making dinner for you."

"That's why I married you."

"Z.D., you know I'm philosophically opposed to marriage—"

"C'mon, Carol, lighten up. Anyway, I'm not the marrying kind. Go listen to your message—I'll stir the sauce."

"Honey—," the gravely voice that was her mother's broke, separated by two time zones. "Honey. I've had some bad news. Call me."

Carol sat on the chair next to the answering machine. It would be almost nine in Chicago. She looked up to see Z.D. standing in the doorway. Carol kept her phone in what had originally been her bedroom when they first moved in, when they thought they should keep separate spaces, but which was now used mostly for guests and the overflow of her clothes. "What is it?"

"I don't know. I have to call my mom—she said she had bad news. Can you wait awhile for dinner?"

"You know what, I'll finish it up for you. I'm a pro at boiling spaghetti. Go ahead and call."

Molly still moved from apartment to apartment every couple of years, even though she was nearing sixty—okay, fifty-seven, which seemed like sixty to Carol. Molly'd probably been in this last place almost three years. Slowing down. They talked all the time, you'd think she'd know the number by now—312-549?-8? Even though Carol was adept with numbers, she refused to apply any mnemonic tricks to Molly's area code. Though she liked to say it was because she had enough numbers of her own, underneath she was dimly aware that, despite how well they got along now, she must be mad at Molly. She chose not to poke at why.

"Hi Mom. Are you still awake?"

"Carol?"

"Yeah, it's me, Mom."

"Oh, I was just drifting off, honey."

"I'm sorry—I was working when you called and then I forgot to look at the machine until now."

"That's okay, sweetie, I know how busy you are."

"Mom, what's wrong?"

"Wrong?"

"Mom?"

"Oh, I'm sorry. I took the sleeping pill the doctor gave me a little while ago. So, sweetie, I'm, well, I guess. I mean they—"

Carol waited, unaware that she was holding her breath.

"Your old mother is going to have to shuffle off this mortal coil. Or is that shuck off?"

"Shuffle," Carol said, suddenly unsure. Shakespeare; it must be *Hamlet* or *Macbeth*.

"Yes, that's right, shuffle. Shuffleuffelo. I remember now, Hamlet's soliloquy."

"Mom."

"Oh honey. I'm sorry, I am sorry. I thought that after you went through the change you didn't need pap smears anymore."

"Who told you that?"

"I was bored with Western medicine. Surely you can understand."

"Surely I can. But I still get pap smears."

"Of course you do. I've always admired how sensible you are for such a headstrong child."

"Mom." Carol wound the telephone cord around her wrist, and then unwound it. Z.D. swore by her mobile phone, but Carol was resisting portability. She liked the idea that sound came across the continent through wires until it reached her ear. Too many sound waves moving invisibly through the air means we are always making our way through clouds of phantom voices, she believed. Z.D. said in another time or place Carol would have been a spiritualist. A flashy, practical spiritualist.

"Oh, honey. So, I didn't get one. If I had, maybe they could have yanked my innards out and I could have lived as a withered hag with a bag for a few more years and seen the millennium."

"Mom, are you saying you have uterine cancer?"

"You are a bright child, aren't you? You always were able to follow an idea, even one of mine. All right." She took a deep breath, and Carol mimicked her on the other side of the Rockies. Finally

Molly found her voice again. "End stage. That's what he said. It's, uh, well, it's spread, they're pretty sure the lungs and maybe my liver. I'm glad your father's not alive to have to go through this, a lot of help that schlemiel would have been."

"Tell me everything the doctor said."

"Just a couple weeks ago I started feeling—oh, worse. It seemed dramatic—I was coughing all the time, and I had some kind of discharge—oh, you know. I didn't want to bother you with it. So I went to the doctor, they ran tests. I got the results today. He said—he was not optimistic."

"That's it? No treatment?"

"Now, Carol—I've seen enough people killed by the cures they shove down your throat for cancer. And I'm old enough to know what Stage Four means. Really, I've thought about this a lot, and being diagnosed hasn't changed my mind. I want to die at home. In my own bed." A muffled sound like mushrooms being shaken in a bag must have been Molly swatting at her mattress.

"Mom, you need a second opinion." Carol stood up, resolved. "I'm coming out there."

"Wait, honey—I'm so sleepy. We'll talk about this tomorrow. Call me in the morning, OK?"

"OK."

"I'm so glad you called. Goodnight, honey. Don't worry. I mean it. This is just another part of life."

"Yeah, the part that sucks."

Molly laughed. "You bet, kiddo."

Carol hung the phone up and stared out the window. The long day was washing out, a cool slate blue September evening, with fifty birds singing in the yard. Z.D. was putting plates on the counter, one shlup two shlup, and rummaging in the silverware drawer. She said, "Z.D." but her voice wasn't carrying. She straightened out the pens on the telephone table and went into the kitchen. The electric lights were overwhelming, making her blink.

Z.D. turned and watched her. "Your mom?"

90

She fidgeted with napkins on their white enamel kitchen table. Hadn't they intended to replace it with a wood one the next time she had a big win or Z.D. got a raise? "I think my mom is dying."

"Oh shit."

Carol laughed. "Yeah, you could say that. Shit fuck asshole piss damn. Death reduces you to swearing like a ten-year-old. Feeling like a ten-year-old. I want to kick someone in the shins."

"Here, punch me."

She made a fist and started to swing at Z.D.'s shoulder, but her arm faltered before contact and fell to her side. She let herself collapse into Z.D.'s hug, as much collapsing as she'd ever allowed herself.

Z.D. reached to turn off the gas burner with one hand while she stroked Carol's back with the other. "What did she say?"

"Let's go sit in the living room. It's too bright in here."

On the couch, Carol slumped and tightened in one gesture. Z.D. stroked her arm but kept a distance, wary, sniffing for the quality of her lover's anguish. A mean anguish? A let's-ignore-this-and-go-for-a-ride-to-the-nearest blackjack table anguish? An anguish that opened its animal eyes wide at the headlights bearing down on it and shattered the hearts of anyone in hearing range with its ululation?

"I have to cancel with my students and find out the best rates to Chicago. The students have to wait until the morning, but we can start calling the airlines now. We can do it from both phones."

"All right." A practical anguish, Z.D. thought.

"I'm sorry, Z.D. You must be hungry."

"Don't worry about that."

"I mean—I don't know what's happening, what's going to happen. She'd taken a sleeping pill and she wouldn't tell me any details. She said, 'in the morning.' I can't do anything for her tonight. But you can at least have dinner before we start making phone calls."

"Not you?"

"I'm not hungry."

"You made a great dinner—eat a little with me."

"Okay—if I can make a list while we eat."

"Anything you want."

Reservations made, dishes washed, suitcase packed, they lay together. It was a warm night. Carol felt the lump of muscle in Z.D.'s arm, where her head rested. Musculature. Even the strongest muscle melts, falls off the bone, becomes powder. She felt for the bones above her own fleshy breasts, clavicle, underneath, deep under fat, ribs. Do bones have sensation after you're dead? Are the bones lonely in the grave for their missing flesh? Does the flesh of children carry atomic memory of their parents' cells? Does my dad make contact with Molly now through me, do I have to be a stand-in for my dad? What am I supposed to do, to feel?

Z.D. heard Carol's sigh and shifted to rub her head with her free hand. This is the big time, when you've got to go through death with your girlfriend. This was what she signed up for, she guessed, but she didn't have to like it. Her four brothers formed a wall that separated Z.D. from her dad—and she expected they'd take care of him when his time came. When her ma's time came, on the other hand—she wasn't an only child like Carol, but she was her ma's only daughter. She was the one who "didn't have a family" in her family, except for Amos, whom she figured for an extreme closet case, and Jake didn't count. Anyway, they'd expect her to drop everything and show up. At least, if they bothered to call her at all. No, they'd call. Would she be as willing to go as Carol? Oh man, who the hell prepares you for this?

Carol landed at O'Hare late the next night, having told her clients she didn't know when she'd be back, perhaps they ought to find someone else for the semester. She wondered how she was going to manage without the income, but of course Z.D. would help if she needed it. She'd drummed her fingers on the tray table for half an hour, adding and subtracting the money in her checking account, the payments still owed her, the bills due, until the man in the middle seat's throat clearing penetrated her consciousness. "Sorry," she said, "I'm a little distracted." She wasn't one to tell strangers on planes her business. This morning, Molly hadn't had much to add to the conversation they'd had the night before— some sighing, some: "I'll be fine dear, you don't have to come."

Don't have to come is code for if you don't show up in the next day, your mother's curse will rise up from the sewage lines that skirt the Great Lakes and enter your veins with the howling sludge of the entire continent. What's a mother's blessing after all but a promise never to curse you? The delicate tethers tremble. In the old days, if you left home you couldn't go back; news of a parent's death reached you months later by steamer or horse. In two hundred years, we have invented freedoms that keep us more closely tied to our origins than we were before the railroad spikes were driven. You can never leave your mother's village now, because her village is everywhere.

Does every daughter feel this anxiety? Z.D. had offered to come along, although Carol knew it was a gesture made in the hope of being refused. Z.D. liked to be left alone when she got sick. Carol wanted homemade chicken soup, fluffed pillows, someone to wheel the TV into her bedroom and watch Oprah with, filling her water glass as soon as it was empty.

"Only-children think they're the center of the universe," Z.D. said.

"Stoic butches don't understand how companionship heals."

"You're afraid to confront your own sickness."

"You call sweating in the dark confrontation? Having the damn flu is not what I'd call a spiritual opportunity." Z.D. had to agree with that last sentiment.

Carol weighed the comforts of her lover's presence against the sickening gurgle in her bowels, presage of the trials to come. She decided it would be wise to have Z.D. stay home, collect her pay-check, be the soothing voice on the other side of the phone rather than a daily observer.

◆◆◆

93

She rolled the suitcase down the hall, trying not to make too much noise, wake anyone up. This was not the apartment building she expected—she was thinking chrome, yuppie stucco, gentrification. But this was old Jewish, or old Polish, brick built between the world wars. Sure, it had been renovated into the new form of condominium which had no more community in it than an expressway, less, probably. But they couldn't knock the chicken soup and garlic smell out of the walls. Probably everyone who lived here was keen on that, nostalgic.

"I liked it when I moved in," Molly said the next morning. "Now it makes me want to puke. You know what, let's look at the rental ads."

"Mom, you can't move now."

"Why not?"

Carol looked around. Three full book cases, five boxes of books in cartons stacked in a corner with a black magic marker gash uniting them, giving them the appearance of a column, perhaps Molly's attempt at a post-modern art joke. What could be more ironic than to mock your own instability with a tower of moving boxes? Still, Carol appraised the couch, armchair, TV/VCR combo, a dining room set, pots, pans, a waffle iron—and the bedroom, the guest room, and the clothes... "I'm not packing this up."

"Who asked you to? C'mon, kiddo, I only want to look at the ads. We have moving companies in Chicago, you know. Grownups use moving companies, not their kids. I need you for other things."

"Try and be realistic—"

"Listen, offspring, don't lecture me. You don't think I'm realistic? I got you through college. I own an apartment building."

"You own an apartment building?" Carol was incredulous. "This one?"

"Of course not."

"Where?"

"We'll talk about that later."

"What? Mom—"

94

"Look, I just want to see what's available."

"I can get you some incense. We can burn sage. You don't have to move just because it smells like chicken soup."

"Sage." Molly considered. "That might be a good idea. But it's not only the smell."

"What then?"

"I figure if I keep moving, the angel of death won't be able to find me."

Molly meant this as a joke, or a half joke. "I saw this movie once about a Jewish anthropologist who changed her name when she was dying of cancer—was it cancer or leukemia?—does it matter?" She paused to cough. "Anyway, she was hoping to outwit the Angel of Death. Do you think the AOD could be female? A her-angel would be almost comforting, especially if she looked like, oh, Angela Lansberry or Bessie Smith, but that doesn't seem right—you know, accurate."

"Accurate according to whom, Mom?" Carol pulled at a loose thread in the armchair where she sat.

"Exactly right. We don't need to get all Old Testament-y about it. But the anthropologist even went to a mikvah and dunked herself in some stagnant brine in the name-changing ritual. Didn't help, though. She still died." Molly looked up at the ceiling. "Did you ever notice how the acronym for Angel of Death sounds like an ancient Armenian musical instrument. The Aoouuuddd." She made her mouth a small circle and pushed the word out.

"You're hopeless." Her mother's sense of humor relieved Carol, even as she protested. When did Molly get old? The last time she saw her she was middle-aged, going for miles on the path along Lake Michigan. Vigorous. Now she was stooped, overcome by a hesitancy that seemed to generate wrinkles every time she moved. Maybe it was Carol's fault, maybe she had stopped looking.

"Yes, I suspect I might seem so. Though actually I have a lot of hope."

"For what?"

"For you."

"No fair, Mom. You cheat."

"And I hope you'll learn a thing or two from my cheating. So settle in, we'll talk, we'll look at the apartment ads. It couldn't hurt."

Carol was driving along the lake in the rain. Nine is a good time to steer through big cities—the evening commute is done, most of the late movies are just beginning, sophisticated city eaters are finishing up or starting dinner and the drunks have only scratched the surface of their fear of the dark. Swing shift hasn't let out yet, lobster shift hasn't started. Lobster shift, could that be right? Someone told her that graveyard was also called lobster—and it wasn't any damn fisherman's daughter from Maine. Whose idea was it to call the darkest, latest night a lobster—because it had claws, could crush you, crush your hands in some factory that never shut down if your eyes grew weary at 3 a.m.?

But lobsters weren't only for the rich, and they might taste good right about now. The dying can have extravagances that the living shun, and she would do almost anything to indulge her mom. Could Molly keep a lobster down? Where can you get lobsters at night in November in Chicago? Lobster season must be over, winding to a halt up north when the wind closes in the harbors and the pots have to be hauled out of the coves lest they freeze. Does the debris off shore freeze in the winter? Fresh water freezes at 32° Fahrenheit, but she should remember how salinity effects the equation. Clearly the whole sea doesn't turn to ice, and somewhere there's an interchange with the tropic waters, some place the Atlantic melts. Stunning, what a small grip she had on geography, even though she loved to look at antique maps and had driven from Chicago to Oakland twice in her twenties.

She licked her chapped lips and pumped the brakes to avoid skidding as the traffic, which had been moving along at around 40 miles an hour, jerked into a twenty mile-per-hour zone. Two months she'd been dancing attendance, and every day her mother looked grayer, farther away. She hadn't been able to save her dad from his flaming wreckage, but she wanted to believe in some magic, some ancient mother-daughter exchange, that would give her mother life, breathe the fight to live into her lungs. I want a word to rise out of the wind and aim its lettered finger up—I want a yod, that silver pointer the old men use in synagogues to keep their place in the holy book, a silver pointer shaped like a hand. I want a yod to break through the grimy sky and write with its fingertip, a word, the word I'm supposed to say to save my mother's life, Carol said out loud in the car, her mother's ten-year old Camry. It can't be lobster.

"Where did you get this?" her mother said, looking suspiciously at the package.

"At the grocery store."

"I don't remember—"

"Grocery stores in fancy neighborhoods carry lobster tails, mom. I can put in it the broiler, I can melt some butter—do we have lemon?"

"Lemons for lemonade. 'Lemonade, lemonade, stirred with a spade, good enough for any old maid. Oopps, I baptize myself!'"

"What?" Carol had the momentary sensation that the solid parts of life were melting, had been melting for a long time, but she hadn't bothered to notice.

"Your mother is not, I repeat not, having drug-induced hallucinations. Unless free association is hallucination. Is it?"

"No, but—"

"It's Tennessee Williams. God, don't they teach anything in school anymore?" Molly made a melodramatic sweep with her hand that reminded Carol briefly of her old gay buddy, Philip. She wondered what he'd do if his mother was dying. Then she wondered if he was still alive. But after a few seconds of calculating how many Philip Goldbergs were likely listed in the Seattle phone book, his last known abode, she suppressed those tangential anguishes. "In fact, I played Amanda Wingfield in eleventh grade and you came to see me."

"So I did. You should have had a stage career."

97

Carol suppressed an urge to crack that the modern stage wasn't big enough for both her and Camryn Manheim. It would take fifteen minutes to explain what she meant. She deflected by asking, "Did they teach you Tennessee Williams in school, Mom?"

"Point well taken. But then, I'm a self-educated woman. I only brought it up since he's one of yours."

"I don't think either of us would say that."

"What?"

"What you said. What did you say?" Carol was staring at the lobster tails, wondering if she really was going to cook them.

"Oh," her mother gave a weak, ratchety semblance of a laugh. "I said he was one of yours."

"Well he's not one of mine. Don't you think it's kind of weird how everyone assumes gay men and lesbians have all this stuff in common?"

"You don't?"

"Not really. It's as if no one can imagine a corner of the world where women don't want to hang out with men. It's like heterosexuality all over again. Gay men are gay because they want to be with men, not because they wish they could spend their lives on panels with dykes. And vice versa."

Her mother pushed her bottom lip out and nodded, considering. "I suppose you would know."

"Lemons?" Carol turned her back and started toward the kitchen.

"Maybe some of that bottled stuff in the back of the fridge. But Carol—I don't want lobster. I don't think I could handle the stink."

"Lobsters don't stink, mom, they smell good."

"Everything stinks now, cookie. You wouldn't believe how everything stinks." Molly pulled her bathrobe tight around her shoulders and made a face.

So Carol put the lobster tails in the freezer, poured a couple glasses of ginger ale, all that Molly wanted most of the time. She sat on a chair by Molly's bed. How small my mother looks, how shrunken. That whirlwind she was has become a puff of smoke.

Molly bit her lip, and held out her hand, which Carol took. Molly cautiously covered it with her own, let Carol's hand rest between hers before she spoke. "Everyone makes a big deal about this, honey. So I want you to be honest and tell me how you feel."

"About what, Mom?"

"You know."

"How I feel about your being so sick?"

"For such a smart girl, you've been unusually dense lately." Molly tongued her lips, which were dry and brittle, chapped. "Where's the lip balm?"

"I've got some here." Carol extricated her hands, stood up, and fumbled in her coat jacket until she found it.

"Vanilla. I like that. Doesn't make me want to vomit. So?"

"So? C'mon, Mom, give me a hint."

"Are you going to help me or not?"

"Oh," Carol said softly, understanding finally what Molly was talking about. My mother wants me to kill her. No, no, no. Say it this way: she wants me to help her die with dignity. That's what the brochures said, the ones from the Hemlock society she'd found under the heap of old magazines next to Molly's favorite reading chair. The room quieted. Even the street held its breath. Carol counted the veins that looped over the bones in her mother's hand and waited.

"You know, the doctors say I have a five percent chance of remission. That's a ninety-five percent chance of dying. Painfully. Distended, bowel obstructions, liver failure. In a hospital—" she spat the word out as if it were urine. "—surrounded by strangers, hooked up to machines. You know what? Let's not go there. You won't like it anymore than me." Molly cleared her throat.

"Than I," Carol whispered.

"Pssh," Molly smiled weakly. "Enough with the English lessons. Seriously, you must know I've been thinking about this. I'm still able to do it myself, and I will. You can leave first if you need to. But I'd rather you were with me."

99

"Do we have to decide this tonight?"

"No. You sleep on it."

"I'll try. Call me if you need anything." Carol went into the guest room where she'd been camping out. Where were the guests? The friends, the aunts and uncles who would tell her what to do. Molly would only talk to them on the phone. The angel of death was sitting at the door, comfortable in a lawn chair like that old guy who used to live across the street from them when Carol went to Senn High. The old guy—what was his name?—Constantine? amazing to remember it now. Constantine, first Christian emperor. History sends up its debris, all the great dead men. And their namesakes, holding onto to dwindling powers, claiming pavement territory among the evenly spaced trees. Molly used to call them the prisoner forest. "You can't lock up trees, Mom," Carol had complained. "Oh yeah?" Molly said, blowing smoke up between their leaves. "Take another look, kiddo."

When Molly went, it would only be Carol left, to make a difference, to light a candle. She'd learned to light yartzheit candles from her bubbe, squat glasses full of white wax that Jews use to mark the anniversary of a death. At some point, she couldn't remember when, though she had a vague memory of doing it in a college dorm room, she started lighting them for her dad. When did her father die? Sometime in late July of 1970, while she was away at camp. She had picked July 22 for the symmetry, 7-11+11.

Her rationale seemed frivolous now, but you had to pick something. She'd be the one to remember her mother, her father, her grandparents, and then after her, the wick would burn out. Damn, this is morbid, she thought. But a candle would be good, if they were really going to do this thing—one of those big seven-day candles they sell in Santerias, to pray to the Virgin to change your luck, not a wimpy yartzheit candle, which anyway you can't light for the living. We could use a change of luck. Carol fell asleep, finally, around 3 a.m., and dreamt of drapes catching fire from a candle a child had knocked over.

◆◆◆

"You know what we should do?" Her mother was having a good day—a faint rose crept into the cinereous flesh of her cheeks, and she had actually gotten down a grilled cheese sandwich.

"What, Mom?"

"Have a little game of cards. Poker—no, I've lost my interest in bluffing. Rummy."

Carol found the deck in a drawer by the window. "500 or gin?"

"Gin. Who knows how long I'll last."

"Molly, do you have to bring everything back to death?"

"Of course I do, now that I have your attention. Get me another ginger ale and then deal."

"Dying people get very bossy, I've noticed." Carol slapped the cards into two piles, arranging her hand for a run of spades, with two fives.

Her mother clicked, sighed, wheezed, drew. "We're entitled. So listen, you know where the will is?" She peered over her reading glasses to squint at Carol.

"Bottom drawer of your bureau, under the underwear. Where you used to keep your sleeping pills."

"I knew you stole them, you know." She looked back at her cards.

"Sorry, Mom—it was the thing to do back then." Take anything, find anything to take—raid your mother's pharmacopoeia when you visited from college, trade seconal for acid, amphetamines for ludes. What was so great about that? The only really good day she had stoned on anything stronger than pot was when she got kicked out of the university museum for yelling at the guard about the Arp sculpture—made for the blind, the label said—that was kept under a plastic cube.

"It's always a miracle to me that any children survive adolescence these days. You're like those baby sea turtles—what was that movie?"

"The one where Katherine Hepburn locks up Elizabeth Taylor? *Suddenly Last Summer*. 'Suddenly, suddenly last summer, Sebastian—'" Carol did her best Hepburn impression, clutching

101

at her chest, and shaking her head. Molly started to cough spasmodically, but waved Carol away when she hovered over her with a glass of water and a sedative.

"I'm fine. You're just too damn funny."

"I'll be more serious."

"Please." Molly grinned at Carol, regaining her composure. "What was I talking about?"

"Sea turtles?"

"Oh, the sea turtles. You kids. Exactly."

"Exactly what, Mom?" Carol drew another heart. Useless.

"We've got such a sanitized view of them—cute baby sea turtles. But in the movie it was more like it really is—horrible, the hatchlings desperate to get to the ocean before they're eaten alive. And then the ocean, teeming with danger. I'm amazed anyone makes it past the age of five anymore. Danger is everywhere and probably you've skirted it by a second here or there. Of course, my number's up."

"Mommm."

"The dying are expected to tell the truth. Is it my turn?"

"I guess. That's a pretty depressing view of things, Mom." Carol passed on the six of clubs her mother laid down.

"I'm allowed to be depressed once in a while now, am I not?"

"You got me there. Can you use this?" Carol discarded a seven of diamonds.

"Yes, thank you very much. Anyway, I meant to tell you, I have a file drawer in my desk—it's marked 'baby photos,' and it should have the statements—"

"What statements, Mom?"

"Stocks and things—you know."

"Stocks?" Carol peered at her mother over her cards.

"Okay, so I became a capitalist in my old age, and a landlord, so sue me. The deed, too."

"Where is this mythical apartment building?" Carol was not at all sure she believed Molly. What business would Molly have, fixing someone's leaking plumbing?

102

"On the South Side, not too far from the University."

"How can you own an apartment building in an African American neighborhood?" Carol put her cards down and frowned at Molly, who managed to fix her with a cold stare.

"You think I haven't considered what I'm doing? Don't you pull that morally superior act on me. I had morals long before you discovered—what is it you call it these days?—social justice?" Molly took another swig of ginger ale while Carol frowned. "That place was a slum before I bought it. Now everything's up to code and clean, and all the apartments have new appliances. There's a problem, I take care of it. Shvartzes gotta stick together," she drew a card and cackled. "Gin."

"Mom, that's terrible."

"What, that your old mother should beat you at cards?"

"Molly, sometimes—" Carol slapped her cards down on the mattress, although the sound of cards hitting blanket was hardly satisfying.

"You know what Sartre said? If there were no Jews in Europe, Europe would have had to invent them. You know, in order to have anti-Semitism. In Europe, we were the Black people—even you would have been, with your blond hair, and your healthy little double chin. That's how you got your name. Schwartz. Shvartze."

"I know that, Mom." Carol ignored the dig and stared at her useless cards, remembering her first love, Eileen, how they'd spent what seemed like hours running their fingers along the colors of each other's hands. She'd never seen the colors of her flesh until she saw them through Eileen's eyes, never tasted the fear and wonder in the skin she'd simply carried around, until then. What had Eileen done when she'd smacked her head on the wall of No Future for Women Athletes, especially Black? Maybe she took her University of Colorado degree and became a gym teacher. Maybe she lived in Molly's apartment building now. "But it's not the same in America."

"Maybe it isn't, and maybe it is. My parents never talked about the war. Harold's parents, on the other hand, hardly ever shut up about it. Maybe that's why he was so keen on Vietnam. Anyway, nobody in my apartments ever complains."

Carol leaned her head into the palm of her left hand. An apartment building on the South Side. What was she going to do with that? Sell it? Give it to the tenants?

"Listen you. I know you've got a big heart, and that good socialist feminist streak, because I brought you up right. You listening to me, Carol?"

"Yes, Mom."

"Oh, give me that damn glass of ginger ale, cookie; I've run out of strength," Molly sighed. She took a gulp, and lay back against her pillows. "A woman alone—and that's what you are, don't start with me about your friends and lovers, that's all very nice—but you have to think about your old age. And you have to have one, for me. Don't interrupt me. I want you to be able to travel, have some fun. Sure, give some of my money away, could I stop you? But keep enough for yourself. Promise me."

"Okay, Molly," Carol let out the air she was holding in. After all, she'd have no daughter to sit with her at the end. "Okay, I promise. But I don't have to keep the apartment building, do I?"

"It's a good investment, you'll see. Land is the best, but I guess you won't want to come back to Chicago when I'm gone. That's the other thing."

"Don't you need to rest yet?"

"I'm going to have all the resting in the world soon enough." Carol winced as she watched a wave of pain course through her mother's face. When it passed, Molly said, "So I want to be cremated. I know it's not Jewish, but Harold—"

"Oh," Carol bit her lip. Plane gone down in the jungle. Ashes to ashes. "You feel that close to him after all this time?"

"It's not that I'm such a big romantic, don't get me wrong. But he was the father of my child. And I've always been a sucker for symmetry; you get your geometric proclivities from me, not that schlemiel. So it's okay with you?"

"Why wouldn't it be? I'll arrange it."

104

Molly sighed for the hundredth time. It was hard to distinguish sighing from breathing now. "Arranging is what I wanted to spare you. I meant to take care of it myself but I—I never got around to it. Hell, I'm only fifty-seven. I figured I didn't have to worry much, since everything would go to you by law. Turns out dying's got as many details as life. Take a hint, OK?"

"Don't worry about it, Molly. I can figure it out."

"You're a good girl, you know? It's a big comfort to me, how I can count on you. You remember that movie, *Chocolate Water*? That can't be right."

"*Like Water for Chocolate*?"

"That's the one. Everything's getting so jumbled up. Movies, books, the stories my mother told me." Molly closed her eyes and held her hand up, making a trembling signal for Carol to hold on. "In that movie when the mother dies, she comes back as a ghost to haunt her daughter. She was a nasty character."

"Oh, yeah, I remember that." Now what, Carol thought.

"When I die, I'm going to come back to bless you. You'll see. So if any ghosts show up, say hi. I'm serious, sweetie."

"That's nice, Mom." Carol ran her tongue over her teeth, and started to cry.

"Hey, no tears. My mother didn't say anything to me at the end, so I want you should know you have my blessing. Now do me a favor."

Carol was wiping her eyes with one of her mother's tissues. "Sure, Mom."

"I don't have the energy to shuffle. You do it."

"You want to play another hand?"

"One more."

December shoved November aside with a stinging wind. Carol called Z.D. three, four, sometimes seven times a week, but insisted she not come. "Molly's waiting for her birthday. She thinks it will be poetic to leave on the same day she came in."

"Your mother's something else," Z.D. said, watching the ash

105

grow long on the joint she'd put down on a bottle cap. "Don't you want me there for this?"

"Maybe after. Definitely after. I've got a crematory lined up, and we'll have a small service there—she's got some friends, people from work, a couple of the women from her old CR group who she finally let visit last week. Next Thursday's her birthday. She wants a cake and balloons, hard to believe, but that's it. Come Friday, OK?"

"You really think you can be there alone after she—"

"I want to be, Z.D. It's like a—I don't know, a rite of passage."

"I can respect your need for ritual, but if you change your mind, babe, just say the word. I know how you like company. I'll be there Friday otherwise."

"You're being a good friend, Z.D."

"I hope all this time away hasn't made you forget what else."

"Not forgetting, I promise. Thanks." The idea of sex created an odd shiver that yanked at the muscles in Carol's belly. She cupped her flesh in her hand and hummed after she hung up the phone.

Molly's skin was as gray as the sky outside. She wasn't able to do more than smile when Carol brought in the cake with the wax numerals five and eight burning, and gestured for Carol to eat a piece. It was 11 a.m. Carol picked at the chocolate icing on her plate, watching her mother breathe. Breathe in, breathe out. What spirit fills the lungs? Now she's living, soon she'll be dead. In old comic books, Superman could stop the planet from turning in order to prevent catastrophe. Catastrophic, Carol thought, the word moving through her face. Molly was beyond noticing.

"I'm ready now," Molly said, but her hand shook when Carol placed the pills in her palm.

"You don't have to do this. It's okay to change your mind."

"I can't bear having you wipe my ass one more day, kiddo. I'm weak, not afraid." Her voice sounded scratchy, one of those old black vinyl records they had when Carol was a child, warped, skipping. "Give me the water."

Carol held the glass and her mother swallowed, one pill after the other. Her neck was so thin that Carol could trace each tablet's journey. Some last supper. Carol put the glass on a coaster and sat on the edge of the bed, having a momentary sensation of plunking down on a teeter-totter, her greater weight about to send her emaciated mother flying. Molly only sighed.

Then they waited. For a while, Carol stroked Molly's hand, lightly. This will be the last day you are warm to my touch, she thought. She pressed her teeth together. After some time had passed, an hour, maybe, Carol said, "I love you, Mom."

Molly smiled, and moved her hand faintly in Carol's, a motion that could be interpreted as a squeeze. Molly's lips twitched, and Carol bent over. "I want you to know—"

"What?"

"This isn't hard." She breathed with difficulty for a few more minutes. Carol realized she was matching her, gasp for gasp. It hurt. Oh, don't hurt, little mom, please don't hurt. Then Molly's chest flattened and rattled, and her hand went limp. One moment breathing, gone the next. The hour, the minute, of her death.

"Oh, Mom." Carol bent her head over her mother and wept.

When she was done, she went to the window. At first, all she could see were the years when weeping would continue in spasms of the grief she felt now. Then she noticed a wet snow was falling, big flakes outlining the limbs of the trees outside, planted in the small circles of dirt drilled in the concrete every twenty feet.

11

At 3:50 p.m., Carol is standing by the crap table in the Isleta Casino, fifteen minutes south of the Albuquerque airport, with three other players—a tall, Native American guy in a blue suit, shifting a stack of five-dollar chips from one hand to the other as if they were a slinky; a mid-western white guy wearing a bolo tie; and a small woman in her fifties, near as Carol can figure, who looks like a tough Chicana grandma—the kind who won't let her granddaughters wear lipstick until they're twenty.

Before Carol's father went to Vietnam, they played the globe game, one of her few clear memories of him. He'd say, "Close your eyes. No, close them for real." Then he'd spin the globe and shout, "Now!" Carol stuck her finger out and felt the bumps of the whirling continents that signified the Urals, Alps, Rockies. When she opened her eyes, her finger would be pressing on Switzerland or Venezuela. "Aha," he'd say and pull out the atlas. "How should we get there?"

"Boat." She always wanted to go by boat, although at that age the only boats she'd seen were toys and paddle boats on Lake Michigan.

"I could fly you there," he'd say, since he was already a pilot.

"Boat."

"Alrighty then, tramp steamer it is, to Caracas."

Maybe it was the tramp steamer, the word tramp. At seven, she was already Disney-fied, falling hard for the anthropomorphized gray cartoon dog Tramp. A tramp steamer sounded like adventure under the watchful eye of a big-hearted, smart dog guardian. Dog star, she'd heard that too. At night, when her dad had first gone, she prayed to the dog star and Tramp himself, begging them to bend the rules so she and her dad, off they could go to Caracas, the mountain city near the sea. She believed each star was a mind, a face, listening. Were they too far away to hear?

Now everyone was dead. Molly, Harold, probably Tramp, although what Disney wrought never seemed to die. Caracas must still be there. These days, it was hard to be sure—perhaps Exxon had bought all of Venezuela and renamed the cities for its board of directors. Venezuela has oil, right? She had trouble enough following politics in the Middle East; South America and Africa—people were dying there, for lack of her attention, that was all she knew. The old robber barons and the new techno-imperialists carved up the world—she'd seen the documentary where the second generation Rockefeller brothers had split the globe into quadrants between them, remaking the map in a room off of Fifth Avenue. But ordinary Americans like Molly profited too. All the old binaries—profiteers and the exploited—didn't make the clear sense they once had. What did it mean when the exploited learned how to turn a profit, make a deal?

Carol figured tycoons should be overwhelmed by their own abundance—money, power, things—wearied by shouldering the bushels of numbers that signified ownership. Now that she had money, well, promise of money, she thought it more than ever. There had to be a number that would be enough for anyone. Give the greedy their greed and let them have oh, say, twenty million, hell, fifty million. Wouldn't that create enough rich/poor divide, give the wealthy all the cars and houses and horses—all the superiority—they wanted?

Molly left everything to her, including the damn apartment building. Carol was surprised to find no favorite charity nor old friend named in the will, nothing feminist, Jewish, political. Of course, the will was twelve years old, and Molly had been expecting to live—forever, most likely. Death flossed its teeth with out-of-date paperwork, crammed poorly planned wills in its shoes to keep

109

those bony feet dry while the tears of penitents flooded death's law offices. The dead were a chorus outside the glass doors, wailing, "But I didn't mean ..." What a jerk, Carol thought, unsure whether she was talking to Molly or herself. Or Death. At the end, there's so much to ask and no one to answer. Not like that's news.

She was tired of questions, didn't want to talk to Molly's lawyer, bored with Oakland in January, so she hit the ATM, then put her finger on a map of the U.S. and closed her eyes. Her father's ghost breath sent a shiver through her nerves, which made her finger skitter across the page. "I'm going to Albuquerque, where I've never been," she told Z.D., who was walking into the living room with a beer.

Z.D. wiped the bottle's condensation off on her jeans. "What's wrong with you, honey?"

"Why are you bothering to ask me that?"

"Let me come with you."

"You know I love your company but I need to be alone when I see Route 66 for the first time."

Z.D. downed her beer in a gulp, went to the bookshelf where she kept most of the Auto Club's free tour books for the states west of the Mississippi, and tossed Carol the guide to New Mexico and Arizona. "Well, you can find someplace to stay in there—only a year out of date. You know, you're not letting me in on much lately."

Carol looked up, surprised. Wasn't her despair as recognizable, ordinary as cockroaches scattering on kitchen linoleum in sudden light? She'd never felt more transparent. It occurred to her that Z.D. might be in pain too, and a line from Baldwin's "Sonny's Blues" came back to her—something like, "my pain made his real." But her pain was having the opposite effect. Plastic sheets of pain through which she could make out the dim outlines of others, moving in slow motion, were thrown over everything. My mother has died and you're still driving the car, going to work, paying the bills. How can you?

Z.D. patted Carol's shoulder as she went back in the kitchen for another brew. "All right, baby. It's okay. I'll be here when you're ready to talk to me."

Carol's plane got into Albuquerque at 1:19; she rented a Chevy something—little, with roll-down windows. Who's going to roll down the windows in New Mexico, anyway, unless they're getting burgers at the drive-thru? It's either too hot or too cold. That it was too cold interested her—she imagined New Mexico would be warmer than California in January, but the air shone in the low 50s. Go cheap when you can. She'd read somewhere that millionaires got to be millionaires by saving money, not by spending it. Was she a millionaire? She should be able to count that high. Maybe, maybe almost after the Southside building got sold. She shook her head as if money were water trapped in her ear after doing somersaults in the pool.

She figured discovering Route 66 could wait, and left the car in the parking lot of the Airport Best Western, which advertised a free shuttle to Isleta until 1 a.m. Best Western was a big step up from the Motel 6, or the rustic cabins on women's land they found out about in *Lesbian Connection* when she and Z.D. took road trips. She bounced on the bed for all of five minutes before she headed out, feeling rich. What is rich, what is free? The questions seemed like the lyrics to a song she'd forgotten most of. By 3:45, she'd had a piece of pizza and a coke at the casino snack bar. The craps table didn't open until 4 on weekdays, and it was a Tuesday afternoon.

It *is* Tuesday afternoon. The guy in the blue suit has a heavily pocked face—adolescent acne, probably, though it's gone now. Grandma lights a cigarillo. A couple croupiers, old white guys, come to the table and take up their positions, looking weary. Her feet are flight-swollen, hot in her pantyhose, even with the air-conditioning, and her eyes feel like they've been packed in brine. Most of the time, she carries a bag, partial to black leather shoulder purses with a little rhinestone trim. But in a casino, a bag is a

111

liability—you have to watch it, and that's distracting. What butches taught Carol was the value of pockets. She fingers the wallet in the pocket of her red slacks, the ones that drape so nicely and don't need a belt—the idea of having to take off a belt going through airport security made her nervous, although she'd never actually seen anyone have to do it.

Her mother's money. Who would have figured Molly for a saver, let alone an investor? She must have seen opportunities, though. Secretaries for businesses—the people you drop secrets in front of without thinking, the hidden ears. For a moment, she sees her mother as a mouse, scooping up cheese crumbs that come her way, scurrying them off to a hiding place, frightened by the statistics about women and poverty in old age. Not getting old now.

Molly's staking me, Carol thinks. I hope that gives her pleasure wherever she's looking on from. The Grandma narrows her eyes, and then says she'll be back to no one in particular. As she heads to the bathroom, the pit boss and a security guy with a tray of chips come up. The pit boss unlocks the bank in the center of the table, counts what's there, and watches the security guy unload fresh chips. Counting, counting. It's all numbers from here on. Pit boss waves and the third croupier, the stick man, who is a woman this time, comes over to take her place. It's one minute to four. Carol buys in for five hundred dollars, taking hundred-dollar bills out of the stack in her wallet. Seriously scared, not wanting to show it, moving up to the big time, she takes a deep breath.

The croupiers have name tags—Al from Phoenix, Marty from Denver, Kylie from Sante Fe—the most local of the three, and apparently the only Native person among them in this Native casino, although she has to admit she can't always tell. People of intermediate, unidentifiable color sometimes bond, though often enough take umbrage at the sight of each other, not all that unlike the way fat women are wary of each other in public. Mestiza, probably, in New Mexico—Spanish and Native and who knows, maybe Converso, those Jews who fled the Inquisition, who still light candles on Friday nights because "it's a family tradition." Anyone could be anyone out here, where only the artifacts of gambling are familiar to her.

"Players card, hon?" Al from Phoenix asks. When she says "not yet," the pit boss, a pasty-faced middle-aged guy whose collar is too tight, asks if she wants one, and she gives him her driver's license. If Carol plays long enough, they'll give her a free steak and pair of fuzzy dice.

In the casinos everything converges—money, sex, and race. For a moment, Carol can see Native dancers swing a great braid of confusions in the face of all the immigrants, the children of immigrants. At last, the dancers chant, we have your attention. You remember those stories about Manhattan Island being sold for $24 worth of beads? Those foolish Indians, you were taught in school, who didn't know the value of the place they lived, who didn't understand that land could be sold and bought. But look, we've kept those beads all these centuries, and they're valuable antiques. Want your bead back? Here it is, under one of these three shells. Quick! Which shell is it? Oh, wrong again. Now who's the sucker? The bought and sold? Carol hears mocking voices that no one else gives any indication of listening to, bounces on her toes, staring down at the green felt.

People, men, start to come over; the Grandma comes back and takes her place in the last shooter position, next to one of the croupiers. Blue suit guy rolls first, choosing his two dice so that they add up to eleven from the five he's given. Carol's standing next to him. "Coming out," calls the tall, doughy croupier, whose name tag says Marty. "Yo bets, horn, C&E?"

"C&E," Carol says, throwing down a five-dollar chip to cover the ten she has on the line, yo high. Really it's for suckers, to respond to the croupier's chant for opening extra bets, the craps and eleven, but she usually takes it anyway, always when it's her turn to shoot because she has a tendency to roll craps once or twice before she gets going, which pleases her because it disarms all the guys. Oh, they think, just a girl shooter, crapping around,

113

ha ha—but then she'll roll a couple sevens, get them out of the way, and make her point three or four times before she sevens-out. At least, when it goes well.

"Yo elev!" Kylie calls, smiling at Carol sideways. Carol nods, as if hitting eleven on the first roll is her due, even though it's never happened to her before. Everyone betting with the shooter—right now, that's the whole table—gets even money on the pass line. "42 to my second," Kylie says, nodding to Carol, and Marty pushes a stack of chips toward her. Not a bad start. The shooter rolls a nine. Carol likes nines, and puts twenty buck odds behind her pass line bet. Funny how you can have an emotional relationship with numbers.

"Hardways for a nickel each," she says, "and a nickel horn, twelve high," throwing a $25 chip toward the center. Horn bets— the one-roll, craps, and eleven against-all-likelihood of coming in—are mapped out in the middle of the table. More long shots— but after nines, craps often roll. That's her theory, anyway. Everyone at the crap table has a theory, including the croupiers. Really, only number theory covers this: she saw the exhibit on the odds of how often numbers will roll in a craps game in the Chicago Museum of Science when she was in high school. You used a lever to throw a pair of electric dice, and a pellet would fall into a giant pyramid corresponding to the number you rolled. Sevens made up the wide base, and twos and twelves made up a slightly flattened tip—it's simple probability over time. A pair of dice's numbers add up to seven more than anything else; then sixes and eights, then fives and nines, then fours and tens, threes and elevens, twos and twelves. You can get a short-lived spike, the pyramid out of line on the nine or the three, you can roll five tens in a row, but over time, it's always going to be the same damn slope.

The trick is to know what time you're in. Even if the odds favor the seven, the three is going to roll sometimes. Are you in some-time? Carol watches the guy rolling. He picks up the dice and sighs. The croupiers always watch the shooter, although Carol

114

can't imagine someone trying to substitute loaded dice in a casino. You'd get found out in an instant, and never be allowed back in. He rolls a twelve. The pit boss frowns at her, since her two buck twelve high pays thirty to one.

"Nice bet," he says, adjusting his tie.

"58 to your second," Kylie says, all business this time. Clearly Kylie doesn't want the pit boss to think she knows Carol, even though there's no possible way she could be telling her how the dice are going to roll. In blackjack, sometimes dealers can give players hints about their hands, giving them a small advantage in whether to draw a card or stay. If the cameras pick that up, the dealer's fired faster than a chain-smoking mid-westerner can yell bingo. But when the dice are in the air, only psychokinesis can change their path. And getting them to do your bidding would take a lot more skill than bending a spoon. Not that Carol could bend a spoon by focusing on it, although when she was in her twenties, like everyone else she knew, she tried.

"Nickel on hard eight for the dealers." She throws a chip in, emulating the way she's seen guys with big bankrolls tip the dealers by making long-shot bets for them, and Kylie places it carefully.

"Thanks, Carol," Marty says, getting her name from the players club card the pit boss hands Carol back with her ID.

"Nine's the point, nine to pay the line. Neener neener," Al intones.

The shooter rolls a three.

"Crap dice. Fourteen to your second," Kylie says. Carol gets paid again because they keep her horn bet up as long as craps and elevens are rolling. A player could theoretically take it down, but no one ever does.

The Grandma stares at her. "Bruja," she whispers, sneering. Carol doesn't let on that she knows she's being called a witch. But she's thinking about it as she picks up her chips, throwing a nickel on the Come line. Maybe now is the time to claim whatever witch lives in her mind.

115

"C'mon shooter," the guy in the bolo tie yells, "let's see some action." Like most of the guys at the table, he's put place bets on all the numbers—6, 8, 5, 4, and 10.

The shooter rolls a hard eight. "Wow," Carol says. All the regular eights get paid. Then the hard eights—Carol's, the one she put up for the dealers, and a couple others around the table—45 bucks each. Her five on the Come line goes to the eight, she puts ten-buck odds on it, but her horn bet is gone.

The shooter rubs his forehead with the back of his hand. "Eight again!" Marty calls. She gets five dollars on her eight Come bet and twelve more on the odds. But it was a two and six—"hard eights are down," Kylie says. Although Carol doubts another hard eight will roll for a while, she calls "back up on the hard eight," throwing in a nickel chip, a kind of offering to the table gods.

Most people think a six will follow an eight, a five will follow a nine, a four will follow a ten, as if there were a cosmic symmetry in the way dice fall. Carol's theory is that the nine and ten roll together as often as the nine and five. So while the betting's open, she says "place the ten and five," purposefully snubbing the six. Ten's a good bet if it comes in—3 to 1. Of course a six rolls. The pit boss smiles at her now, more serenely. This Carol person had a short lucky streak, starting out, nothing to be worried about.

Then the shooter gives her a ten. The hard ten is down this time. "Press it five, and put me back on the hardways." She's getting only five back, but the shooter rolls another ten, hardways this time, and she's handed 95 bucks. Pit boss sighs.

The Grandma has been doing all right, betting the field, with twenty bucks on the five. Still, Carol clearly annoys her for an unseeable reason—the only other woman at the table—because she's fat, fair, younger, lucky today? The men are getting noisy—the shooter's doing well and chips are flying. He rubs his hand against the felt, picks up the dice, and throws a nine, making his point. A big cheer goes up—everyone gets paid, the odds bets behind the line make three to two. One roll and Carol's up well over 200 bucks. What was that Kenny Rogers song?

Carol goes for the C&E again on this same shooter's new come-out roll, but this time he makes a seven and the C&E is cleaned off the felt—the line gets paid, everyone likes sevens coming up before the point; they think of that as "getting them out of the way." The new point is five. Carol bets it the same as the nine, she still has her hardways and ten bet, and the croupier moves her five to the nine, checking with her to make sure that's where she wants it to go. Hard four, and Carol collects another $35. When he rolls a soft six, her hard six goes down, and she shakes her head, no, when the croupier asks her if she wants to replace it. Another nine comes up; she gets paid and says, "take it down." Most of the time, players leave their place bets up even if the number comes in four times in a row—especially when it does. But she has a feeling. The shooter rolls and the dice bounce high, off the table. Right, that's it. When the dice hit the floor, nine times out of ten the next roll is a seven. Well, maybe seven times out of ten, Carol smiles to herself, wanting to be honest with the odds. While the pit boss inspects the die, she quietly passes Kylie a nickel and whispers, "seven." When her chip goes there, the Grandma gives her a laser look that could ignite an oil refinery.

Seven it is. All the money goes down, but Carol makes her last bet, which pays 4 to 1, $20.

"Good roll," everyone says, with the undercurrent of "shmuck, you got me to put all my chips on the table and then you go and seven-out."

Now it's Carol's turn. She asks for new dice and chooses, like the guy before her, the two that combine to make eleven points out of the ones Kylie offers in a bowl. Pieces of ancient ritual infuse games of chance, Carol realizes, holding the red dice in her hand. In another life, I might have been offered a still beating heart in a wooden bowl, and been judged by how I picked it up.

The Grandma puts her five dollars on the Don't Pass line— betting that Carol will roll craps and not make her point. Carol smiles at her as generously as she can muster in the casino. The guy with the bolo tie takes the opposite tack, and plunks a black chip on the pass line, a hundred bucks. Carol bets ten, her C&E, and rolls a two. "Crap dice, snake eyes," the croupier calls. All the line bets, including that black chip, get swept away. The Grandma, whose nostrils flair briefly, gets paid, as does Carol for her C&E.

This is how I start, Carol mumbles to herself, rolling something that's 30–1. Let's halve those odds. "Press my eleven," she says, throwing a nickel down, so that she has seven dollars on the eleven now. The guy in the bolo tie chants, "Okay sweetheart, be good, give it back," puts another hundred on the line and twenty-five on the eleven. She plunks the dice in front of her a couple times, the way she's seen old men do, getting a bad roll out of the way. Then she picks the dice up and throws them hard against the egg-crate cushioning of the table's back wall.

"Yo elev! Yo, yo! Pay the line!" Marty from Denver calls out, excited. Payouts are good for the croupiers, they bring in better tips when the table's hot, and everyone knows the casino will make its money back. Mr. Bolo gets even money on his pass line hundred, and another $375 on the eleven, for which Carol gets $105. The Grandma loses her Don't Pass bet, and mutters something under her breath. Bolo tie throws Carol a 25-dollar chip, but she shakes her head, doesn't touch it. "No thanks, I'm fine."

"Just wanna tip you, darlin'."

"Give it to the croupiers, then." She flashes a smile, trying to keep the table energy bright.

"Never argue with lady luck. Here you go, boys—I'll put it on the line for you." The croupiers thank him.

The table is full now, and guys are making horn bets and hopping hardways, which are the biggest one-roll sucker bets on the table—unless, of course, they happen to come in. Carol feels the pizza thunking in her belly. She likes the crap table because you get these guys with their piles of black chips next to anxious young dudes betting five dollars in the field, the rich and the pretenders all co-mingled, jacked up for the same statistical fate. It's not like blackjack where the big betters are segregated to their own $25 and $100 minimum bet tables, or the high-roller slot rooms where you have to bet a minimum of fifteen bucks a pull, and that goes fast. At the craps table, old Duponts with nothing better to do stand beside Native engineers, Black computer whiz kids, Jewish dykes, the Grandma of one of the waitresses, Romanian drug dealers looking to clean their cash. Not only greed, but a kind of hope passes among them—something beyond money—a wish to be right, in the right place at the right time, calling the right shots.

The gambler's religion of ego. Can you set up a Buddhist calm in the midst of that fervency? A non-attachment to the outcome, a happy, disciplined curiosity on statistical outcomes? Are Buddhists ever statisticians? Maybe what you are looking for, Carol thinks, is Jewish, or lesbian—a well-developed sense of irony, irony as spiritual practice. Tonight I come to the costume party as the Oracle of Irony. Nothing better than a casino for spiritual symbolism. It was Marx, after all, who defined money as a system of symbolic values, and he was a Jew. But not famous for his sense of humor.

She rolls an eight, and exhales. Eight is an easy point, although not her favorite. The numbers have personalities. Three is the butch that runs away from home during adolescence; seven is a dentist, smug for having picked a profession that always pays. Sixes are housewives, reliable, secure, with a hint of danger underneath. Nines are the swaggering dykes she always falls for: smart, cool, hands in their pockets and trouble in their eyes. But what's an eight? Even less dramatic than a six—a banker, a banker's number.

The Grandma is betting she doesn't make the eight, but that she rolls a five before she sevens out. The Grandma has sixty dollars riding on the five now. Carol looks straight at her. She hears the old woman say "bruja" again under her breath, and it bothers her. Then she hears Bonnie Lockhart's lyrics, "Who are the witches? where did they come from? maybe your great great grandmother was one," a song written for children. She smiles, and rolls a five.

All the five betters get paid, the Grandma gets $72 on her bet, which is still up. But she hasn't quit glaring at Carol. Carol picks up the dice, and rolls another five, and then a third. Finally the Grandma smiles, but into her stash of chips, not at Carol. Jeez, she could at least spare a little nod in my direction. "C'mon shooter," someone cheers. Carol has a nickel on all the hardways, and rolls a hard eight to make her point. A hard eight isn't a banker, it's a bookie—she grins at the image of two fours stacked on top of each other, in a double-breasted suit, with a fedora cocked over its tiny dice eyes.

Everyone's happy. She's happy. Even the Grandma, who lost her Don't bet, is happy. The Grandma decides to bet with her now, still without eye contact, and Carol makes two more points, rolling many numbers, making some inspired horn and field bets along the way. A flush enters her limbs, a long fork of heat pricking at her skin from underneath. By the end of her roll, she's up $785 dollars, and the afternoon is young. By the time the afternoon is old, and her feet are killing her, she's up well over $4,000. The dice were hot, then got cold or her instinct was off once the Grandma left the table, without saying another word. Sometimes, Carol thinks, you need an evil eye to keep you honest. But eventually she gets the rhythm back. On her last turn as shooter, she keeps fifty dollars on the pass line, staggering herself with bravado, taking double odds and hitting all her Come bets, rolling a sequence of fours and sixes toward the end.

Several men have tried to tip her, two offered to buy her dinner. "Do I look like someone in need? Tip the dealers," she always says, and the dealers like her. Kylie has gone to other tables, gone on break, and is back as the stick person when Carol rolls her final seven-out. "Color," Carol says, laying her stacks of chips on the table, getting back pinks—$500 chips—nine of them along with three blacks, two twenty-fives, and three fives. Four thousand, eight hundred, and sixty five dollars. She leaves a nickel chip for each of men, and a twenty-five for Kylie, who grins. Is Kylie a dyke? Does Carol care tonight? She asks the pit boss, "Who do I see about getting dinner?"

He smiles at her for the first time in hours. She'd be back, or do something foolish with her winnings—most people did, figuring it was the casino's money anyway. And it is. He writes something down, passes it to her, and tells her to go to the hospitality center after she cashes out.

The chips are heavy in her pocket, circles of plastic that mean she could have anything she wants tonight—a lobster, if a lobster is to be had out here in Isleta, New Mexico. She has a quick image of the lobster tails she threw away after Molly died. Of dumping every single thing in Molly's fridge into a green garbage bag, and shoving the damn cake in on top. The cashier's voice wakes her up, makes her realize she's famished. "Good night?"

"Kinda," Carol replies.

"You want this in hundreds or a casino check, hon?"

Carol calculates the thickness of forty-eight hundred dollar bills. She wants to experience that weight. "Hundreds, please. Let me keep one of those pinks for now." Forty-three hundred dollar bills.

"Your call. Be careful with all this cash," the woman says, slapping hundreds onto a pile.

Carol never held so much money. People will think I'm packing, she laughs to herself as she crams it into her pants. But she determines to be cool, and anyway, what safer place to carry money than in a casino, unless you're careless enough to get pickpocketed. Z.D. always said, carry your money in your front pocket. Z.D. had experience with cash that Carol still tries to be oblivious to.

The guy at the casino rewards counter takes her card, looks at the note, and smiles. "New player? From California, huh?" He's looking at her data on a computer screen. "Welcome to Isleta. I'll give you a comp for anything you want at the Tiwa—that's our best restaurant—but it's closed Tuesday. Can you come back tomorrow? Good. So here's the slip for tomorrow, and here's another for the buffet tonight. It's open for another hour—doesn't look too busy over there. Enjoy!"

Ah, the buffet—guilty pleasure. Is seeing how much tamale pie, fried chicken, and chocolate pudding you can eat a measure of

121

mourning? Grief tangled up inside her with all this increase. Money was coming at her from every direction—she used to go to the buffets in Reno because you could get very full for very cheap. She used to budget, knowing how much vitamin C cost at the natural foods stores versus the discount outlets. The appearance of Says Who, a fat woman's clothing store across from Mama Bears Bookstore, had delighted her when she was at Cal—a short bus ride down Telegraph Ave. providing her with an afternoon's distraction, flouncing before mirrors in clothes she actually liked. But she'd been startled by the prices and rode back to campus calculating the difference between the sweatshop wages of children in Malaysia with local women doing piecework and groaned. Whose poverty should she wear on her back?

Mostly she shopped at Goodwill, and later, when Says Who opened a reused and discount outlet, Seams to Fit, she was more comfortable there, hoping the seamstress sweat wore off if you bought secondhand. Carol still got the cheapest dental floss and batteries at the dollar store, skimming whatever she could for the dares that were her luxuries. Economy was habit. But now, what was economy? A difference of two, or twenty, or fifty dollars? All those years Molly saved, put away, planned, bought stock five shares at a time—that apartment building Carol had already instructed the lawyer to sell—to give to her, thirty-seven years old, childless, restless. Solipsistic to think it was all for her, wasn't it? Maybe Molly planned to tour the Yucatan, or see the Great Wall. Oh Molly. How she would rather have Molly than a plate of éclairs—the sensation washes through her, and she pushes the plate away, full, rich, thrilled, and in misery.

She looks at her watch when she emerges from the Ma-Tu-Ey buffet—only ten-thirty, nine-thirty at home. It's early, but she's feeling slightly sick from over-eating and excitement. She's not ready for the shuttle back to the hotel—what hotel was that? Best Western, she remembers, placing a hundred-dollar bill in the currency holder for a dollar poker slot machine. The video poker

122

hands are mesmerizing—animated trumpets blow in the face cards—and the machine seems friendly enough for a while. Her hundred becomes a hundred and thirty five, then ninety, then a hundred seventy, then sixty, and from there drops to three. On her last hand, she shows a ten, jack, king, ace of hearts, and nine of diamonds. She holds everything but the nine and whispers "queen of hearts" out loud, pressing the "deal" button. Three of clubs, and just like that, no more hundred dollars.

"Don't feel bad. Hard to get the queen of hearts," someone says behind her. Carol turns to see Kylie, her favorite stick woman, sans nametag. "Sorry if I startled you," she says.

"Are you making sure I give back the casino's money?" Carol smiles at her.

"They can't pay me to worry about them. Don't let me interrupt you—"

"You know what, I'm done. But I'm confused—I thought tribe members got back a share of the casino profit."

"Yeah, some casinos, some tribes. But not mine. I'm just part of your authentic Southwest experience, ma'am."

Carol juggles the bitterness of that practiced observation with the clear warmth coming from Kylie. Maybe it's a test. "Oh yeah—I forgot. It's you who makes this slot machine different from the ones in Reno." Kylie nods and looks Carol over, apparently approvingly. "Well, thanks for being my own personal atmosphere. I was just putting off getting on the hotel shuttle."

Kylie frowns. "It's after eleven."

"Don't they run until one?"

"Only on the weekends."

"Oh. Well, I guess I can afford a cab—cabs come out here, right?"

"Sure, but I'm off now and heading home—why don't I give you a ride?"

"You're allowed to do that?"

"They don't like us fraternizing with guests in the casino, but what I do on my own time is none of their business."

123

Yes, definitely, Kylie is flirting with her. Something encouraging is coming off her. And then she hears her mother saying, You're gonna get in a stranger's car with four thousand in cash on you, kiddo? What, I didn't raise you right? Leave me alone, Molly, she answers back, this is dyke life, and you're not living it. Oh, sorry, Mom.

Kylie, watching Carol's face, says, "Are you all right?"

"I'm sorry—something I ate is disagreeing with me. Maybe salsa and éclairs wasn't the smartest choice."

Kylie laughs. "Well, let's get you back to your room, then."

Kylie insists driving Carol home is a welcome diversion in her seventy-mile commute, and regales her with how much better Santa Fe is than Albuquerque, although it is ruined by the damn tourists, no offense. By the time they get to the Best Western, they've charmed each other. Of course, the twenty-five dollar tip started it for Kylie, and having a stranger show interest is enough for Carol. "So, um, you want me to just leave you here?"

Carol looks at the hotel, looks at Kylie. "I'd like you to come up."

"I thought you might." Kylie's grinning.

"Why don't you drop me off here and park—I'm in room 548— give me a couple minutes." When Kylie squints at her, Carol reaches over for her hand and kisses it, slowly, lingering. "Maybe I drew the queen of hearts after all."

"What a terrible line!" But Kylie's laughing.

"Welcome to all my personal failings. Still want to come up?"

"Not much of a failing for a one night stand," Kylie strokes the side of Carol's cheek with her kissed fingers.

"Okay, then. See you in a few." Carol hops out of Kylie's banged-up Jeep.

At the front desk, she asks for the manager, and puts the roll of hundreds into the hotel safe. Now you're using your noodle, Molly says in her left ear. Then Carol orders a bottle of their best champagne sent to the room. Oy, Molly says.

She hadn't even unpacked her toothbrush when she checked in. Grit, travel, dizziness, anticipation, longing, guilt—oh no, what would Z.D. do if she finds out about this? How could she have not considered that? Well, Z.D. doesn't have to find out. It's a goddamn one night stand in a hotel in Albuquerque, where I've gone to mourn my mother. Oh, that's good. Definitely, she'll say, oh, poor you Carol, you're so impulsive, such a Leo—always have to shine for someone. Shine it on, sweetheart. What the hell am I doing? She's brushing her teeth when Kylie knocks.

"I wanted to get cleaned up—come on in."

Right behind Kylie is the waiter with the champagne. "Nice touch," Kylie says, once the cork has been popped, the guy tipped, the glasses poured.

"Queen of hearts," Kylie toasts.

"Queen of hearts," Carol answers. Carol drinks the champagne quickly. Who knew that when you ordered "the best" from room service in New Mexico it was going to cost $130? Is this what rich people do—drink money? She pours herself another glass, not noticing that Kylie is barely sipping hers. Kylie shuts the shades, turns off the overhead light, leaving one bedside lamp on. Carol pours herself a third glass and puts it on the table.

Kylie has a beige polyester shirt on that must be regulation casino. Underneath she has a simple sports bra, and under her pants, a pair of men's boxers with a Cat in the Hat print.

"Now that surprises me." The little Cat in the Hat faces seem to swarm in the air. What was she doing?

"They were a present for my 30th birthday," Kylie offers. "Don't let them fool you. I mean business."

"30 this year?" All of thirty. Thirty and thirsty. She takes a long swallow, draining the glass.

Kylie gets up, refills it for her. "This year." Then, as if challenged, Kylie pushes Carol onto the bedspread. "You did want this, didn't you?"

"I do. I do want this." Yet Carol looks sideways, not at Kylie but at the print of Native American horsemen on the wall. Whose country is she in? Surely, not her own. Kylie's country? Where croupiers wear Dr. Seuss boxers?

Kylie is strong, quick. Quicker than Carol expects, she is in her mouth, on her arms, grinding into her belly. An old, momentary body shame sweeps Carol. "I'm so big—"

"I like big." Kylie's voice is husky with her hunger now. "Right away, I liked you. You're a winner."

That's what it takes, huh, winning. She's a winner, a sinner, a beginner, beginning again, again, winning all winter, that's good, move your finger, oh, almost, you've almost got it, "More," maybe she'll get it, sense her way in, increase the pressure—Carol wiggles to position Kylie's motion.

"That's a good girl, you can take more, you're a big, greedy winner, aren't you?"

Greedy? That's what Z.D. says. Is it something butches learn to say in their secret training camp, or is it something about me? Is this greed, what greed is, abandoning your lover, your mother, your home, everyone who wants to soothe you—grabbing instead at strangers, at money, at—what—what was she—oh.

She's convulsing; the pulse starts in her clitoris and shakes her, inside her uterus shakes, a tomato on a vine in a terrible storm. "Kylie!"

Kylie rolls on her side, three fingers still inside of Carol. "Good?" She peers at Carol's face, her bravado slacking.

"Kylie that was—great—but please don't take this the wrong way—I think I have to—I think I'm going to—" Carol makes it into the bathroom, flips the seat up moments before the éclairs, fried chicken bits, half-digested broccoli, tortilla chips, bean, cheese, fry bread, baby shrimp forge a path back up her esophagus and she pukes.

"Damn," she hears Kylie mutter in the other room, and then the TV clicks on. Kylie's watching midnight *M*A*S*H* reruns as Carol continues to heave up the remnants of her day, breathing hard. Possibly as much as a year later, Carol crawls back to the bed. Now the room is spinning. The pain, which had threatened to cut her in half as she was throwing up, is now a series of small daggers in her belly, back, and legs. "Could you turn that down, please," Carol begs.

"Yeah, fine. You going to be OK?"

"Please stay a little while. I know this isn't what you signed on for. But I need you to help me."

"Help you how?"

"I don't know." Carol knocks the dregs of the champagne off the nightstand and Kylie picks up the glass, puts it on the room service cart. "Please help me." She can hear Kylie pacing.

"You going to be sick again?" Kylie asks.

"I don't think so. But the room—"

"I always thought big girls held their liquor better. Don't drink much, do you?"

"No, not usually—I don't feel good. I'm sorry. If you could just help me."

Kylie's quiet for a while, rocking on her heels, looking at Carol. "I am helping you," she says, finally. Her voice is soft, and Carol hears it again—"I am helping you."

"Oh. Oh, thanks. Thanks, I really appreciate it." Then she hears a door close, thinks she hears a door close, as she passes into dream.

A nun motions for me to enter the room. It's my cell—white from corner to corner, a tiny, clean cubicle, a bench, a small barred window. I have been brought here for my moral crimes. If the nun knows which ones, she won't give me a hint. The sister locks the door. We are in the middle or at the edge of a vineyard. I can just get my arm through the bars and reach a clump of grapes. I am hungry. I know they will not give me enough to eat. As soon as I have the grapes, I understand I have committed the crime of theft. Tillers of the soil appear to me as holograms projected in my cell, tall dark women wiping sweat from their foreheads with gnarled hands. Very Disney. I eat the grapes. Then I know I

must hide the stem, and there is no place in my cell that can-
not be inspected with a quick roll of the eyes. Except beneath
my clothes. Or back out the window where anyone could find
the evidence. A deep voice enters the dream, saying theft is
one thing, but concealment is another. The sin is not being
able to show even a sister/jailer my crime, my need, my
shame. I am in the right prison.

Carol wakes, her head in a vise, her throat parched. 9:47 on the clock radio by the bed. She never sleeps that late—where is she? After images of, what?—a room in a nunnery, a vineyard, linger behind her eyes. When did Z.D.'s Catholic school childhood start infecting her dreams? She smacks her lips, hauls herself up. In the bathroom, a sour, rotting seaweed smell assaults her, and she remembers everything. Kylie. Must have left. Carol rubs her breastbone in a circle. She drinks three glasses of water quickly— for the dehydration, hangovers are all about dehydration, she heard that someplace, though the water hits her empty stomach in a hard surf that makes her belch. She showers, finds clean clothes, a light pink lipstick, which she gingerly applies. Her lips feel greasy. Her eyelids feel greasy too, even though she knows she's clean. Did she shower? She goes to check the bathroom—the shower curtain is wet. Yes, showered. Finally she pulls the drapes open. Outside it's bright, and mountains glint to the north. Z.D. would go for a ride. That's what she'll do, get some coffee and some protein, and go for a ride.

She finds yesterday's slacks in a crumpled ball near the desk. Fishing in the pocket for the keys, she remembers that $500 chip she had left. Not there, not in any pocket. Did she put it in the safe? No, she only put the hundreds in the lock box the manager offered her, she'd been in a hurry. Anxiety grips her. She goes to her wallet—none of the cash she'd kept out—a couple hundred in tens and twenties—but all her credit cards—all? yes, all of them, her bank card, her license, the brand new casino card—that's all

128

there. And the coupon for a free dinner at the Tiwa Steakhouse.

"I *am* helping you," Kylie's voice floats back to her.

Molly, fortunately, is silent.

Great, I've cheated on my lover, thrown up my dinner, and been rolled by a croupier. Think of it as reparations, the cut the casino doesn't give her for being the wrong tribe. But does that mean she should take it out on me? She sits down in the desk chair and closes her eyes. A hundred half-thoughts about race, country, who gets paid back for what was taken, how women whose grandparents experienced attempted genocide should figure out relationships, hover in a jittery haze punctuated by the after-image of the Cat in the Hat, that ridiculous red stove pipe concoction. When she finally opens her eyes again, she notices a folded over piece of hotel stationery on the desk. Inside is the pink chip, the cash, and a note: Looking for this?

Carol rubs her forehead. So many ways to get revenge. Damn white girls always needing to be taken care of, wasn't that what Kylie thought about her? Maybe it makes no difference what Kylie thought. Maybe it makes every difference. What can she do with the damn $500 chip anyway—she's not going back to that casino. She should have just given it to Kylie. But that would have made her look pathetic, as if she was paying her, as if they weren't acting like women simply attracted to each other, an island of honest sensation in the midst of a surreal landscape. Carol takes a deep breath through her nose, feeling confusion, shame, and fear.

Downstairs, she gets three hundred dollars out of the hotel safe, has a couple of scrambled eggs, dry toast, and three cups of coffee. Then she straps herself into the rental car, and heads north, beyond Santa Fe, past Route 66, toward the cold mountains that ring Taos.

12

Z.D. slid up to the curb as Carol walked out of the terminal. "Perfect timing," Z.D. beamed. Even though it was in the high fifties, the Oakland sun was shining, so she had the top down. She'd remembered to put a throw blanket on Carol's seat, who was never thrilled about convertible rides in winter.

"Thanks for coming to get me." Carol threw her roll-on bag into the trunk, got in next to Z.D., whom she kissed quickly on the cheek, before she started to play with the contents of her purse.

"At your service, ma'am. Don't you want the blanket?"

"Oh, yeah. Thanks, honey." Carol got out to adjust herself while the traffic cop jerked his hand, signaling for them to get out of there.

"Oakland's a great town, but it's got the most uptight airport in the world," Z.D. mumbled as she merged into the exit lane. And Carol seemed as wound up and locked down as the security guys. Z.D. decided to ignore it. "How is out there?"

"Nice. Colder than I expected. Pretty." Carol turned her head to look at the Black neighborhood that ringed the airport, after the commercial zone. Least desirable property, fewest trees, tiny houses shoving at each other. "Sangre de Christo Mountains above Taos—you'd like that."

"Yeah. Good name, Sangre de Christo. Wonder who bled there." Z.D. had taken a couple Spanish classes at State, after she started hanging out with Nash. "Good to be able to speak the true language of the state you live in," Nash laughed, deflecting Z.D.'s gesture of camaraderie. But Nash was right.

"If you drive through the town of Taos, you don't have to wonder. They can call it Christ's blood all they like, but I don't know, it feels like the U.S. is still fighting the Indian wars there—only with dollars. Every motel is called Kiva this and Pueblo that, and you know the Indians aren't getting the money—except minimum wage for being maids." Carol paused, and decided to omit discussion of Native casino economics. "Here, if anyone bothers to think about it, it's history. But there—" Carol found her lipstick, pulled down the visor to look at her face while applying it.

Z.D. glanced over at her. "I like that in a girl."

"Politics?"

"Lipstick."

Carol punched her arm lightly.

"Maybe you and I should take a road trip next summer. My assistant's coming up to speed—I could take two or three weeks off. What do you think? I'd like to see the Southwest with you."

"You want to appropriate Native culture too?"

"I want to appreciate it. Like you just did."

"Fine, but not with me in the summer." Carol stared at her face in her compact mirror. Are there special wrinkles that signal deceit? "The Southwest goes up to 116°, Z.D. You'd want the top down and you'd give us both heatstroke."

"Well, Yellowstone then. How about Yellowstone?"

Carol didn't answer. They were passing near the elementary school where Carol had volunteered with first- and second-grade girls, teaching them to read, helping them with their first math sums. She'd flip over a box of pencils, and have them count ten. What happens now if I eat five of them? You can't eat five pencils! Want to bet?

"Where'd you go?"

"I was thinking about Girls, Inc."

"Oh yeah, you used to volunteer for them over here, didn't you?"

"Just over there." Carol pointed to the left, past the fried chicken and Salvation Now! signs.

"How come you stopped?"

131

"Got busy. LABIA, my own tutoring—you."

"Am I only part of your busy-ness, then?"

"You know what I mean, Z.D. I'm kind of hungry—can we stop somewhere?"

Z.D. checked her watch. Middle of the afternoon. "Low blood sugar, is that what's making you so cranky? Taco Bell's coming up on the right here."

"I'm buying."

"Oh, in that case—how about the Chinese place over on Grand?"

"Across from the movies?"

"That's the one. They'd be open now. Sure you don't want to go home first?"

"No." Carol bit her lip. Maybe she could figure out how to tell her more easily in a public place. Maybe it would be safer. Not that she was scared of Z.D.

They disagreed on whether to have chicken or fish. "Let's get both, then, and take home the leftovers," Carol said.

"Someone's flush."

"I did alright." Carol paused.

"How alright?"

"I'm ahead—" she stopped a second to consider the pink chip that lay, uncashable, in the bottom of her bag. Of course subtract that, it's part of your gambling losses, kiddo, a high-priced souvenir. Was that Molly's or her own voice? "—twenty-eight hundred seventy six dollars."

Z.D. whistled. "You must have been on fire."

"The first night I was up about forty-three hundred, but then I stopped at a couple casinos on the way to Taos and got sloppy."

"Not too sloppy. Maybe you should quit your day job."

"You think?"

"No," Z.D. shook her head quickly. "No—in fact, I was wondering when you were going to get back to tutoring. You should call up your clients while the semester is young—otherwise they're going to find new tutors."

132

"I guess. But maybe I should take the rest of the year off."

"It's not only about making money, honey. I think you need some structure."

Carol blinked. "Look who's suddenly Ms. Responsible."

"Just looking out for you, that's all. Nash is doing a new play over at Theater Rhino—*The Lesbian Brothers* or something. You could always volunteer to usher."

"That's cute." Carol shook the last remnants of her four-day old headache off, and played with her chopsticks.

"Yeah, that's me, cute all over." The waiter came by, and Z.D. ordered onion cakes, fried snapper with bok choy, eggplant, and kung pao chicken, no MSG. "For someone who came out so far ahead, you don't look very happy. And don't tell me it's about your mother." Z.D. put her hands palms down on the table.

Carol took a drink of water. "Flying is very dehydrating."

"Carol?"

"Z.D. I—" she looked down at the tablecloth, which had a soy sauce stain to the right of the paper placemat. "How long have we been together?"

"Nine years last summer, but you know that. You never forget an important number. So what's up? You have the nine-year itch?" Carol fidgeted with her chopsticks. "Shit. Shit, Carol. You do have the fucking itch."

"I don't think that's why—"

"Fuck. You expect me to sit here and eat with you while you calmly tell me that you're sleeping with someone else? In fucking New Mexico?"

"Z.D. Please keep your voice down."

"Oh, now you want to be all civilized."

Carol sighed. "I'm not sleeping with someone else. I did—"

"You did what? C'mon, cough it up."

"I let myself get picked up. By a dealer."

"You fucked some guy?" Z.D. pressed her palms on the table and rose halfway out of her chair, leaning toward Carol.

"Don't be such a sexist, Z.D. Lots of dealers are women."

133

"Oh, well, in that case—" Z.D. slumped down, curling her fists into tight balls.

"You could let me finish."

"You could be finished. All right, all right. Go ahead." Forbearance, isn't that what the nuns say? What the hell is forbearance anyway? Fucking self-control. You'd think Carol might give it a try.

"The shuttles had stopped running, and she offered me a ride back to my hotel."

"Oh, so you got her off as a kind of tip?"

Carol clenched her teeth. "I know you're mad."

"You bet."

The waiter came with the onion cakes, plunked them down, and disappeared as fast as he could. Carol put a piece on her plate and proceeded to shred it into tiny bits.

"Everything happened really fast. I threw up, and then she left me."

"At least she had some sense."

"This isn't coming out right."

"There is no right way for this to come out. You're an idiot."

"Idiot" meant that Z.D. wasn't going to walk out on her, at least not now, not in the restaurant. But scorn was like hydrogen peroxide, stinging, a punishment for wounding yourself. "Okay," Carol said, "you're right. It was idiotic. I let this twenty-something year old stranger come up to my room—no, she was thirty, I think—and I got drunk and puked my guts out." And then Kylie mocked me, Carol thought, but didn't add.

Z.D. snorted, and stroked below her nose.

"Philtrum," Carol said.

"Don't think I'm going to let you charm your way out of this. I know what my fucking philtrum is by now. You're leaving out the sex part."

Carol closed her eyes. "I think we had sex. I'm pretty sure that's what made me throw up. Well, what triggered it."

Z.D. was quiet for a while. She picked up a triangle of the

onion cake, dunked it in hot mustard, and chewed it slowly. Carol was still shredding hers. "So did you puke on her?"

"I don't think so. God, I hope not." Carol felt a stab of heat in the back of her neck. "But I was seriously sick for—days."

"Serves you right."

"Since when are you into Old Testament retribution?" Carol winced as she said it. Better that Z.D. should think she got what was coming to her, that the universe immediately stomped her for her sins, that infidelity doesn't pay. Was she being punished? For helping her mother die? She started blinking.

"Oh, now you're going to hold back tears. You're a piece of work." Z.D. threw the remainder of the onion cake down on her plate and motioned for the waiter. "We're going to get the rest of the order to go, please." The waiter looked relieved. Z.D. stared at Carol. "Listen, I know your mother just died and you don't know what to do with yourself. But you don't have to be such a fucking asshole. You won't let me near you, but some punk dealer—"

"It's not like that, Z.D.," Carol whispered.

"Then what's it like? And stop closing your eyes. Look at me."

In the reflected glow of the fish tank, Z.D.'s irises were moss, dark moss, sequoia moss, muddy after a hard rain. You could slip in the forest, break your leg, and what would be the sound of a tree clapping then? Zen homilies couldn't be more unyielding than those eyes.

"You don't have anything to say? I trusted you—"

Trust? What does trust have to do with this? Carol realized that would be the wrong question to ask, and took another tack. "It was selfish of me, Z.D. I was only thinking about myself."

"I didn't even cross your mind?" She sounded incredulous.

"Of course you crossed my mind. Of course. It was like—a fast break in basketball. The ball gets thrown to you and you just run."

"Not to your opponent's damn basket."

"Please, Z.D., it wasn't about opposition. It had nothing to do with how I feel about you."

"Oh great."

"It was how I felt about myself. Someone was interested in me and I used her to change my reality. Or, at least I tried to. What I ended up feeling was ashamed."

"Don't give me that crap. Women are always interested in you, and you're always flirting with them. I never paid any attention before. Now what am I supposed to think? Fucking A. Nothing is worse than jealousy. Didn't we agree about that?"

"I still agree. That's why I'm telling you."

Z.D. shook her head. The waiter brought the bagful of their order, and put the check in front of Z.D. Carol grabbed it and paid.

"At least you threw up."

"For hours."

"You're not getting any sympathy from me, so can it. I'll drop you off at home—I'm going back to work for a while and try to calm down."

"I really want to get through this, Z.D. I don't want to hurt you."

"A little late for that, don't you think?"

They didn't say anything in the car, and Z.D. didn't get out to help Carol with her bag. Carol turned to look at her.

"I love you, Carol. But I'm not promising anything right now."

"I can live with that."

"Yeah. You'll have to." Z.D. backed out and drove off.

13

"Everyone goes to therapy," Carol complained when Myra suggested it over breakfast at Mama's Royal Cafe the next week. "It's—I don't know—so retro." She ignored Myra's snort. "So me and Z.D.—Z.D. and I—" she amended, quickly, turning away from Molly's ghost, shaking a finger for all the times she self-righteously corrected her mother—or maybe she was disapproving about something else, in which case Carol didn't want to know. She shut the menu and stared directly at her friend, "So we have problems right now. Everyone has problems getting along. Adjustments must be made!" She giggled at her pronouncement and got serious again. "At some point we develop the insight to get through it, or we don't."

"C'mon, Carol. What makes you think you're the only lesbian too special to admit you might need help?" It was an ordinary Thursday and they'd scored one of the four prized booths with faux leather pads over wooden benches and high, dark-stained pine dividers, which afforded them the illusion of privacy. Myra, whose first psychotherapy client wasn't until two, ordered the mushroom jack omelet, with extra fruit instead of potatoes.

"That's why we have friends." Carol wanted the tofu rancheros, her favorite breakfast at Mama's. When her stomach asked her what she thought she was doing, she told it, hey, it's tofu, not eggs. You can handle a little salsa and black beans. That's what you think, her stomach said, but Carol was not in a receptive mood.

"Your friends will get tired, and you'll find yourself repeating the same story over and over, an endless feedback loop. You go to therapy to change the story's pattern—and to give your friends a break." Myra poured a generous stream of milk into her coffee.

"See, I don't think we ask our friends hardly enough," Carol said, settling in to be patient for her breakfast, since the kitchen usually took its time. "That's the trouble with this idea of community we throw around—if we were really a community, we'd sit down with folks having a hard time; we'd see them through, and not put up with the same tired excuses. We'd risk questioning each other's realities instead of going, 'yup, uhuh' all the time. We wouldn't professionalize caring about each other."

"What the hell do you think I'm doing right now? I'm not here out of some warped 'professionalization'—it's because I am your friend, and I take that seriously." Myra sat up straight and glared.

This gave Carol a moment's pause. She studied Myra, whom she'd known tangentially since they'd met at the second Jewish feminist conference in 1984, when Myra had a gardening business and Carol was still a student. A slipped disc had forced Myra back to school. Now they'd worked together the last four years raising money for LABIA. Myra was on the thin side—well, thinner than Carol—and had a slightly creased, open face and the kind of wide mouth that she'd lately noticed most movie stars had. Myra usually wore sweaters or overshirts a couple sizes too big over tailored slacks and was about six years older than Carol. If you went to Central Casting for the welcoming, white, warm-glamour, mother shrink almost anyone could wish would put her arms around you, soothing the fibrillations of a spirit out of synch with the body, Myra would be it.

"But how would we ever find a therapist like you?" Carol was surprised she'd said that out loud.

Myra coughed to cover her laugh. "The Bay Area is stuffed with therapists like me." She held up a hand to stop Carol's protestations. "OK, maybe not all of them are as kind, clean, and brave as I am, but I could give you a list of six good ones to start with—you'd interview them, see who fit."

"Nice idea, going to the therapy supermarket, picking out the best organic brand, but Z.D. is going to have to agree—and she's always been dead set against it."

"Then go alone."

"I don't need therapy in order to be alone—I'm alone just fine."

At that Myra cocked her head and raised her eyebrows.

"OK, so my mother died and left me more money than I can cope with, and I cheated on my girlfriend with some croupier whose license plate number I still remember—but I would say that equally qualifies me for a financial planner." Carol was relieved to see the waitress coming with their orders.

Myra smiled and thanked the waitress before answering, "Yeah, you probably could use a financial planner—too."

Carol played with the salsa on her rancheros while Myra buttered a piece of sourdough bread. "Yeah, maybe dealing with the money is what I should be paying attention to. Therapy—I don't mean this as any kind of personal criticism—"

"Uh-oh," Myra said.

"No really. You know I think you're probably great at what you do, and I trust your feminist analysis—"

"Big of you."

"You know what I mean. Therapy must have taught you a lot, since you've been able to deal with Nash again after what she put you through the first time."

"A relationship is not a rodeo ride where you cling for dear life after the bull dyke has thrown off all the other cowgirls." The creases around Myra's eyes filled with unmistakable pleasure.

"That's funny." Carol relaxed enough to start rolling up a mixture of tofu, cheese, salsa, and black beans in a flour tortilla. "And that's what I mean. We spend so much time trying to get our own personal dramas fixed that we don't have any attention left for—"

"For the revolution?" Myra said through a mouthful of mushrooms and egg.

"Yeah," Carol nodded, not sure who was making fun of whom; took a bite and then another, because it tasted good. "It's not just therapy. It's dieting, it's fashion, it's electoral politics, it's Newt

Gingrich, it's—spending an hour figuring out what kind of stupid toothpaste to buy. It's amazing we ever get anything done."

"Granted, modern life is full of distractions." Myra wiped her mouth, sighing. "But in order to prioritize—if that's what it is you want to do—you can't avoid your own problems. When you feel settled, relatively secure—I know, if you feel secure there's something wrong with you—I mean, comfortable in your skin, in your being—then you'll be that much more effective."

"You think Winston Churchill was comfortable in his skin?"

"Winston Churchill?" Myra appeared incredulous.

"The last century's most famous manic-depressive if I remember correctly. He was effective."

"We call that bi-polar disease now."

"Fine, I apologize to all the offended bi-polar people who might have overheard us." Carol didn't notice the tattooed waitress near the coffee pots squinting in her direction. "But my point is, if everyone waits to get their psyches all tuned up, nothing would get done. At least half the productive energy in the world is from a good neurosis."

"Are you really arguing for the greatness of the world that Winston Churchill—and all those other unbalanced men—made?"

"I'm arguing for the power of the shadow side," Carol said, swirling the melted cheese in her cup of black beans.

"Therapy doesn't make you give up your shadow side—it's not like getting a lobotomy, which is what you seem to think. If anything, it gives you access to your shadow side. It lets you—align your energies from all the resources you have, instead of fighting with yourself. Why do I have to give you this speech again? It's like stroking iron filings with a magnet so you create an image, instead of leaving them in some disordered heap."

"Like one of those Uncle Wiggly toys we had when we were kids? Put hair on the bald guy?" Carol mopped up some salsa with her tortilla.

"Let's hope you can be a little more creative once you're not in conflict."

"You think I'm in conflict with myself?" The food on her plate gone, Carol started doodling on her napkin, rows of binary code, zeros and ones. She liked the pattern.

"Looks like it to me. As your friend. Since you asked. And at the very least, you're in conflict with Z.D."

"It might distract her to fight about therapy instead."

"There you go." Myra pointed her fork at Carol.

"But I already like my shadow side—I don't want anyone messing with it."

"No one's going to change you but yourself." Myra ate the last slice of orange on her plate.

"See, I could get one of those postcards with the ten favorite phrases of psychotherapy and hang it in the bathroom. Number 3: 'No one's going to change you but you yourself.'" Carol mimed taping a card to a mirror. "It would be a hell of a lot cheaper."

"Very funny. What did you mean, you like your shadow side?"

Carol gazed blankly over Myra's shoulder, remembering how she felt in the Isleta casino, rolling the dice a long way from her home with Z.D. Then she remembered something else. "The second or third time I was driving from Cal to my mom's in Chicago for the summer, I stopped in some western town, maybe Laramie, Wyoming, for the night, a college town off of 80." She licked her lips absently. "I used to pick college towns purposefully, because I had some idea they were safe." She shrugged, looking at Myra as if to apologize for her naïveté. "Anyway, it was still light, so I was driving around, scoping out the diners, the Goodwills. I was on some secondary road, and a boy was walking a puppy—a little black puppy, maybe some kind of lab mix—on the shoulder. I remember that there weren't any sidewalks and the puppy wasn't on a leash. All of a sudden, the puppy ran out into the road." Carol paused, looked down at her empty plate.

"There wasn't a lot of traffic, but a car was coming, and the boy yelled at the dog, which seemed to get confused, and stopped. I could see these guys in the car barreling toward it—I was going slow in the opposite direction. They were young, maybe still in their teens. The driver got this look on his face, the nastiest happiness I ever saw, and then he deliberately speeded up—deliberately— and mowed that puppy down. Crunch, then a hose of blood. He didn't stop. I could hear the boy screaming—I think I screamed too. I pulled over to the side of the road and wept."

Myra waited for a couple seconds before she asked, "You didn't help him?"

"What was to help? His dog was dead. I was a Jewish lesbian alone in Wyoming in 1980-something. I wasn't about to chase two teenage killers. The boy needed his mother and I've never been the motherly type."

"We call that rationalization—but if that's it, that's not much of a shadow."

"Not me, Myra—that guy who ran the dog over. That's evil."

"No argument, but I'm not sure I'm following you." Myra signaled the waitress for more coffee.

Carol waited while the plates were being cleared away before she continued. "Look, I think everyone has an impulse to destroy or at least to get violent when they're angry, but that kind of glee in it—there has to be a difference between that and the kind of pleasure I get from breaking the rules."

"What kind of rules?"

"Playing with money, for instance. We know so many women close at hand for whom a couple hundred bucks makes a significant quality of life difference, not to mention women in Africa or locked up by the Taliban. You and I spend half our free time on fundraisers."

"Half is probably an exaggeration, but it's not only about getting the money," Myra said, "it's making connections between women."

"Yeah, okay. But I found myself perfectly willing to have two hundred bucks—I think five hundred at some point—spread out over the craps table. I loved it. I mean, I was mostly winning, so it made me feel powerful. But even when I wasn't winning, I didn't care—it was a tremendous adrenaline rush. Like being in the center of your own ego, finally, without apologizing for anything. Is that a shadow side?"

"It sounds more like the beginning of an addiction. I'd be careful with that." Myra blew on her coffee to cool it.

"I'm not interested in talking about addiction."

"No?"

"No. I'm interested in the intersections of number theory with morality."

"OK, now I'm really lost. What the hell are you talking about?"

Carol shook the last bit of caffeine out of her tea bag. She hadn't been able to get the waitress' attention to put more hot water in her pot. "I'm just making that up. But really, I want an equation for right and wrong—like an odds table. And don't start with me about moral relativism. Everyone calculates a hundred instances of right and wrong everyday, like staying in the merge lane during rush hour until the last second or even whether or not to order fruit instead of potatoes."

"Got me there. Guilty of making a moral decision over the menu," Myra cocked her head and grimaced.

"So that's why I want a chart—you could keep it in your purse, like one of those cards that tells you how much to tip. The odds that gambling a little is wrong are, say, 15–1, but the odds that stepping out on your girlfriend is wrong, even when you're drunk in a strange city, are 2 to 3."

"That's worse, right?"

"Way worse. But is it worse than killing a spider? No, seriously. I have to admit that I have sometimes felt a weird kind of pleasure stomping on snails in my friends' gardens, like I enjoy that icky popping sound they make. Is a snail's life worth so much less than a puppy's? I ask forgiveness for this on Yom Kippur."

"I thought you weren't religious." Myra glanced up to meet the glare of a woman poking her head around the corner, clearly willing them to vacate the booth.

"Even those of us who think that god is an illusion are sometimes compelled to invent imaginary friends to discuss our spiritual ailments with."

"Which brings us back to—"

"How therapy has taken over the role of religion in modern life?"

"You don't let up, do you? But I want you to notice how much you care about what's right and wrong. Seems like evidence not only of a shadow side, but—what's the opposite of a shadow side?"

"Being a girl scout?"

"No one would ever accuse you of being a girl scout." Myra reached over and patted Carol's hand. "But I'd say you come down on the side of the angels."

"That's me. I'm angelic. And I'm getting breakfast."

"You do have your angelic moments, Carol. It's why I stick around."

"And all this time I thought it was because I was an interesting case to you."

"Well, that too." Myra checked her watch.

"Our hour's up, huh?"

"You can be a royal pain in the butt, you know that?" Myra balled up her napkin and threw it Carol.

Carol laughed, and left a ten-dollar tip.

14

"I'm out of here," Carol said, got in the car, and drove into a cool, early June night before Z.D. could do it first. How many times was Zenobia going to bring up her indiscretion in Albuquerque, anyway? Z.D. had refused to consider couple's counseling, as Carol had predicted, but she didn't want to do anything else, either. When Carol suggested maybe she would move out for a while, Z.D. actually started to cry. To cry! Since she was crying, she'd let Carol hold her, and they had a sweet, easy night, watching TV, making popcorn. But that was almost two weeks ago. What had she done tonight? Teased or wiggled, trying to get Z.D. jazzed for her, but Z.D. stiffened, got remote, and the argument was all over them again, like the powdered sugar from a donut, splotching your blouse no matter how carefully you eat it.

"I know I should let this go," Z.D. shrugged. "I wish I could. Besides, you threw up on her. You never threw up on me. But god-dammit, Carol—" And they were in the thick of it, powdered sugar in their hair, in their eyes.

Out driving, Carol realized what she wanted was a lesbian bar. Her friend Ginny liked to talk about how Ollie's was, back in the day, how they never closed as long as a woman was alone at a table. "You know, not to squeeze drinks out of her, but to make sure she had someplace to go." Ginny gave her a tour once, but the building didn't look like much in the daylight—a squat rectangle with padded, torn vinyl doors down on Telegraph Avenue near the paint stores. The rumor was that it was about to be remodeled into a church. That appealed to their sense of irony—old dyke ghosts haunting the hymnals, the faint sound of billiard balls as a soft underscore to prayer.

No dyke bars in Oakland now, just a club scene that took over various dance floors around the Bay—you had to really want to shimmy or make a splash in order to keep track. What about those of us who want a quiet place to go on the spur of the moment when you can't be home and you don't want to interact? Carol found herself downtown, near Jack London Square, and spotted a sports bar, Lil's Diamond. She circled the block—the area was recently spruced up in one of the periodic Oakland downtown revivals. Lil's Diamond had glass windows along the front, which seemed welcoming enough. She never liked to go in bars that didn't have windows. Something claustrophobic—or worse. As if without windows men could do whatever they wanted—piss in the pickled egg jars, throw darts in strange women's backs.

She never went to the White Horse for exactly that reason—the windowless exterior—even though it was the only gay bar in Oakland and god knows women were always suggesting a drink after some Mama Bears concert they'd gone to across the street. She didn't go to many concerts anymore, anyway, finding the girl and guitar format tiresome. Was that woman-hating? If she loved women and praised them, wasn't she allowed to be cynical about them too? Maybe she was getting cranky—coming up to the onset of menopause, a hormone storm watch posted along the edge of her nerves. A place for every rationale, and every rationale in its place.

Lil's Diamond Sports Bar and Grill reminded her of joints on the side streets in Reno, the ones she passed while walking between the big casinos. It was Naugahyde, hokey, and homey, full of electric beer signs with revolving colored lights that illuminated trout streams, and strategically placed TVs tuned into four different games at once. Men joked and gossiped over the electronic buzz, and the place had an almost pleasant smell of beer with something fake-pine scented underneath. Lil, or someone pretending to be

Lil, was behind the bar, and at least three or five of the guys had brought their dates. A couple single women on bar stools nursed drinks and watched the game. The A's fans bunched up and talked about statistics. She liked that in men—how they got all convivial and mathematical around sports, like they'd spent the last five generations together. Guy energy put to innocuous competitive use. It wasn't exactly charming, but she let herself be amused.

The first time Carol hung out at Lil's, she ordered a martini and nursed it for an hour, retreating into her best unapproachable haze; long enough, she figured, to make Z.D. conciliatory when she got home. But she discovered she liked it at Lil's—a place no one expected her to be. She'd turn off her cell phone, buy the racing papers or sports betting magazines, and relax. She liked corner tables, a booth if one was empty and the place wasn't too crowded; she craned to watch whatever screen was closest to her, marked up the forms, drank a couple glasses of house red wine, and went home.

After her third visit, Carol began telling herself she "frequented" Lil's Diamond. "Frequented" sound like an old black-and-white movie. Rita Hayworth would "frequent" a bar, she bet. Dames, her mother would have said, dames hang out in bars, not nice young girls like you. "Yeah, Mom? How nice do you think I am?"

"Don't get smart with me, cookie. Kids always think they've invented sin, just because the old people around them have gotten bored with it. You'll see. Sin isn't all it's cracked up to be." Molly would have laughed at her own wisecrack, laughed deep into her chest until she started coughing, one of those dry, hacking coughs that make you think, oh god, she's going to heave up her intestines. If they had had that conversation. It would be nice if Molly would let her know the truth about sin in one of her nocturnal appearances. On the other hand, it would be nice if Molly stopped showing up in her dreams altogether—no more singing the score of *Bells Are Ringing* ("That Judy Holliday, she was a great comic talent. Too bad she died so young."), no more cutting up American flags and sewing them into socks—could that be right?

When did she dream that? It would be a good idea for Molly to take a cosmic hike.

Z.D. was on a new good-citizen kick, going to some kind of civic or political meeting a couple nights a week. Carol only paid attention to the fact that if Z.D. left first, she couldn't complain about how Carol chose to amuse herself. Oakland's pretty safe if you're not an African American man under twenty-five in your own neighborhood. Pretty safe. Carol knew how to hold herself precisely on the street, to give off an "I'm just coming back from the Judo class I teach" vibe.

One night, the man at the next table surprised her. "Bet you ten bucks Tejada strikes out."

She appraised him—darkish white guy, with the first signs of receding hairline, clean-shaven. An ordinary sports fan, with a yellow tucked-in L.L. Bean catalog flannel shirt, whom you might have mistaken for a late-night talk show host if not for his medallion—St. Christopher's? How would she know? Maybe fifty saints grace the faces of bronze medallions. How many could she name? St. Francis of the birds, St. Jude of lost causes, she thought, remembering wading through *Jude the Obscure* in 9th grade, and St. Sebastian, the guy with arrows piercing his body. Was that it? Jews are supposed to know more than that about Christian cultures. Maybe the wine had washed all the saints out of her.

Tejada had just come up to bat. "I like Dominican shortstops. You're on," Carol said.

"Whoa—maybe I just lost ten dollars."

Carol turned from the man to watch Tejada connect with the ball and hit a double. "I guess," she said.

The man stood, pulled out his wallet, and made a gesture, indicating he was ready to sit down.

"No, I don't want company, thanks."

"Why'd you take the bet, then?"

"I like to bet."

"Yeah, I've been watching you study those racing forms. Who do you like tomorrow at the county fair?"

The ten-dollar bill in front of her ameliorated her misgivings, and she checked her papers. "Honest Able in the third—" although the horse looked all right, she'd picked it partly out of home-state allegiance, "and Gloved Fist in the fifth."

The man looked over her shoulder, scratched his head. "Interesting picks. You go down to the track to place your bets?"

Carol had been in Golden Gate Field's club room with its bank of TVs showing races around the country that you could bet on when the track was idle. She was less comfortable there, in the bright afternoon, usually one of only two or three women, not counting the ones behind the counter selling tickets to the sweaty men whose whole attention was riveted to win, place, and show. They were different than the sports bar guys, many of whom had played the same sports they were absorbed in—at Lil's, the guys cared about the players, knew their problems, were sometimes inspired by their good deeds. Jockeys don't spend their vacations as the favorite visitors on kids' leukemia wards. Besides, she was not impervious to the arguments about animal abuse some of the women she knew advanced about horse racing. On paper, it was easier to think of them not as animals but as equations. "Not often," she said. "Mostly I keep tabs on how well I do in my head."

"And how well do you do?" The guy, still standing, smiled.

"Pretty well," she said, feeling confused, unsure of whether she was being patronized.

The guy bit his lip. "Want to see how well your picks would do tomorrow?"

"What do you mean?"

"If you let me sit down, I'll explain. I'm Henry, by the way." He extended his hand.

Carol took it, skeptical, glad none of her friends could see her. But wasn't that why she was in Lil's in the first place? She gestured to the seat opposite.

"And you?" he asked, making himself comfortable.

"Rita," Carol gave him the first name that popped into her head. Rita Hayworth—she wasn't the one who beat her children with hangers, was she? No, that was Joan Crawford. She was pretty sure her mom had liked Rita.

Henry chuckled as if he understood her alias and lowered his voice. "Okay, Rita. Here's the deal. All I'm offering is a chance for a little side wagering. I've seen you in here before, and it seems like you know your stuff."

Oh, Carol thought. What do you know? Turns out Mr. Catalog Guy is the friendly local bookie. And all this time I thought he was a dentist on the make. "So you'd write my bets, pay me off when I win?"

"That's the general idea. I get a little vig of course."

"Of course." Carol wasn't exactly sure what a vig was, but she believed it had something to do with skimming something off the top.

"So your horse, Honest Able, it's a long shot at 8 to 3. Go to the track, you'll get 8–3. If it wins, naturally."

"Naturally." Carol was studying him carefully. He flicked at the fingernail on his left hand while he spoke.

"I'll give you 7 to 3. Still a good bet, and of course you save the expense of gas and parking—not to mention wasting a perfectly nice afternoon at the track. Besides, I bet a woman like yourself has a day job."

She noticed that he said woman, not girl. "Yeah. I teach calculus at Mills." That was a good lie, she thought. And not that implausible.

"Wow. So you're way ahead of me on this."

"Well, I've never made a bet with a bookie before."

"We don't really like that term," Henry said.

Carol wondered who the "we" was. "So what should I call you?"

"Call me your friend."

"I hate to tell you this, Henry, but I don't call people 'friends' lightly. How about, um, 'associate.'"

"I guess that would be okay. Sounds like something out of a bad gangster movie, though. I bet you'll be calling me your friend within a month."

"I wouldn't put money on that. But I will put twenty bucks on Honest Able."

"Just twenty? How about that other horse, Gloved Fist?"

"That's a favorite."

"I'll give you even money on it, as a first time special."

"They call that a loss leader. Although, now that I think about it, maybe your bet on Tejada was the hook."

He smiled at her, showing bright, even teeth. "Hook, maybe, but I never lose intentionally. Listen, if you'd like to bet on tomorrow's ball game, I'd prefer to write that."

"I'd like to do a little more studying up on the team stats."

"Take your time—I'll cover almost anything. And I'm reliable."

"How would I know that?"

"This first time you'll have to gamble." He winked at her, which she found more amusing than annoying, though it was close to fifty-fifty.

"Well, that is the point. Okay. Why the hell not? Put thirty on Honest Able and twenty on Gloved Fist." She fished in her purse and found a fifty folded up behind her license, which she was careful not to let him see. "If I win, I'll be back tomorrow night around nine."

"I'll be here," Henry said.

And he was.

Z.D. was off to a dress rehearsal of a play Nash had designed at the Berkeley Rep—an intricate, long Zen masterpiece with complicated sets.

"You could come along—Nash won't mind."

"Are you inviting me?" She looked Z.D. in the eye quickly, and then glanced back at her shoes.

"I guess. We've been spending a lot of nights apart, huh?"

"I'm not feeling patient enough for a long night at the theater. Maybe the next time, though. Maybe we could go out to dinner or something this weekend?"

"Yeah," Z.D. said, "yeah, maybe dinner would be okay."

She kissed Z.D.'s cheek and, although Z.D. took a sharp breath, she didn't go rigid. Time, Carol reflected, moves us along. Wherever we're going.

Gloved Fist, like most favorites, punked out. But Honest Able beat the field by a length. Her fifty-buck investment had turned into $210. "Not bad," Henry said. "You've got an eye for the long shots." He paid her—they were in a booth out of sight of the windows. "Anytime you want, we can do this again."

"You always here at Lil's?" Carol put the money in her purse without counting it.

Henry gave her a steady look and fished a card out of his back pocket. "Henry's steam cleaning," it said. "Pet stains—our specialty!"

Carol laughed. "I don't have any pets."

"Not even a fish?"

"Not even." She shook her head. "Is there some kind of code so I don't end up having my carpets cleaned?"

"It never hurts to get those cleaned, you know. I can give you a special rate. But all you have to do is ask if Henry's busy, and say it's Rita. No big cloak and dagger."

"How do you know your phone's not tapped?"

"I got a lot of friends," Henry grinned.

Carol was in bed reading *The Chronicle*'s sports section when she heard Z.D. unlock the front door. She slid the paper under the nightstand and picked up a book.

"Oh, you're still up," Z.D. said.

"How was the play?"

"It went on forever. Guy with a goal gets side-tracked by demons or something, journeys here and there, monkeys steal his amulets, turns out he's been dreaming—three hours of that. It'll probably be a hit with the cultural masochists. Nash's sets were great, though. Only thing worth going to it for."

"You should write theater reviews."

"I sure have seen enough plays by now. It's like a secret life. I could be like those Siskel and Ebert guys on TV. Wouldn't that be a kick?" Z.D. stripped to her undershirt.

"Siskel died this year."

"Oh yeah. Brain tumor, right? That's what comes from using your noodle too much, being the big expert."

"That's mean."

"I know. Maybe I should go to confession?"

"I'm trying to be serious, here, Z.D."

Z.D. turned and looked at Carol carefully. "What's up?"

"Speaking of secret lives—" she saw Z.D. take a step back and realized what she was thinking. "Not that, honey. Honest to god, I will never step out on you like that again. I love you more than—"

"More than what?" Z.D. moved closer to the bed.

"More than blueberries."

"Blueberries, huh?" She relaxed, blinked with fatigue, and looked at the alarm clock. "Jesus, it's after one. I'm going to have to drink a gallon of coffee tomorrow. Okay, then what's your secret?"

"I made a bet with a bookie."

"A bookie? They still got those guys? Where'd you find him?" Z.D. turned around with a deep, relieved breath. Maybe that New Mexico business was really behind them. She emptied her pockets onto the bureau, took off her pants, ran her hands through her hair, and suddenly thought to be puzzled. She wasn't sure how she was supposed to respond to this.

"At a sports bar down in Jack London Square."

"What were you doing there?" She turned to face Carol.

"Hanging out."

"Since when do you hang out in straight bars?"

"I found it one night when we were fighting. It's not really that different than a coffee shop—except it's night and liquor."

"And bookies."

"The bet I made on today's horse race paid over two hundred dollars."

"Man, I can't take my eyes off you for a minute." But Z.D.'s admiration was clear. "He paid you?"

"Yup. So dinner this weekend is my treat—that new restaurant on Grand they say is owned by dykes."

"Autumn something?"

"Yeah, that one. What do you say, Z.D?"

"What do I say?" Z.D. looked up at the ceiling, and then bounced onto bed beside Carol. "I'm a little confused here."

Carol ran her palm slowly down Z.D.'s shoulder. "How is this so different from your dope business, honey?"

"I don't got much dope business anymore."

"Really?"

"Yeah. You remember that woman that was hanging around LABIA before your mom died?"

"No. You know the last year has gotten kind of hazy to me."

"Yeah," Z.D. looked at Carol. A cascade of emotions ran through her tired muscles. She wondered if she'd take it so hard when her own ma died. Probably not. Being an only child is different five hundred ways. "Well, anyway, turns out she was a Fed."

"How'd you find that out?" Carol pulled the bedsheets over her, as if the idea of a Federal agent—of what? The FBI, narcotics?—hanging around dyke dances made her colder.

"I made a couple friends with the cops downtown—they were looking to find these guys, real amateurs, who were stealing truck-loads of damaged goods out of freight yards and trying to unload at stores like mine."

"Z.D., your own secret life never ceases to surprise me."

"We haven't been talking a lot, have we?" Z.D. watched Carol's mouth twitch. "Anyway, I let them know when I got offered this fishy deal. Helped the cops, got a raise, now I've been going to these weird Chamber of Commerce meetings. I'm still not sure how I got roped into that. And the cops tipped me off about the Feds. Local cops don't care much about dope, and they're pissed about how the Feds are all over the medical marijuana clubs."

"When did all this happen?"

"It started while you were in Albuquerque."

"Oh."

"Yeah. So." Z.D. tugged at her undershirt. "So I figured I'd cut back. I'm making good money now. Dealing's beginning to feel like kid stuff to me. And besides, I've got a rich girlfriend."

"So you'd love to go out to dinner with me, right?"

"Ok, yes, I'd love to go out to dinner with you. But I'm still worried about this bookie thing."

"It's Oakland, honey, not an episode of the *Sopranos*. And anyway, I didn't give him my real name."

"What name?"

"Rita."

"Like in that Beatle's song about the meter maid?"

Carol sang the lyrics she could remember while taking the opportunity to snuggle up. "But I was thinking about Rita Hayworth."

"That sounds like you. My movie star." Z.D. turned and stroked Carol's hair. Carol held her breath. "I know I've been hard on you, baby. And caught up in my own stuff. You don't have to spend your nights in some bar, though. Stay with me more."

"Yeah?"

"Yeah," Z.D. said, "I've been missing you."

"Me too. Missing you." Carol whispered.

"Let's make it a real date Friday night. I'll be your gentleman caller, and I'll pick you up at seven, OK?"

"I'll expect flowers."

"Don't press your luck," Z.D. laughed, flipping the alarm on and turning out the light. Carol ran the sole of her foot over Z.D.'s calf, and Z.D. moved closer. In a minute, though, she was snoring.

Carol couldn't sleep. Something about money, something about the bookie. Henry. Oh. Harold. Molly was close, she was always a dream, a bank statement away—keeping the mother-daughter internal dialogue in gear, engaging Carol from a hundred directions unless she pushed back, said "I'm doing this on my own" to her mother's ghost. She'd read an article about Jewish rituals around mourning. Children were supposed to have a good eleven months after one of their parents died when they didn't have to go to parties, weren't expected to engage in community life. At first, she'd thought it quaint. Now it made sense. Would that we lived in a world that left us our grief. But her father—

Carol reached to touch her lover's body. Z.D. sputtered a rhythmic, comforting snore. Turning on her side, she ran her palm over Zenobia's shoulder—dry, muscled, soft, throwing off heat that warmed her. She had an image of herself for a moment as a vagrant, wandering from shadow to shadow, and Z.D. as her steady trash can fire under the bridge. Then she saw her mother again, lighting the flag in their Chicago back yard. She rolled over and stared at the ceiling. How could she still miss the rough stubble of her father's cheeks, or him making omelets on Sunday mornings? So many armies, filling the nights of the people they leave behind. Violent conflicts never end; they burrow through our muscles like parasites, waiting to strike. War. Oh Dad, how could you have thrown your lot in with the men who make up wars?

15

Z.D. insisted on stockpiling twenty plastic gallon jugs of water and a case of canned tuna, but they survived the millennium, Y2K, although Myra re-injured her spine dancing at the big New Year's Eve party LABIA co-sponsored with the Fat Overground. Got carried away, she said to her doctor, when, five months later, she had exhausted herbal remedies, ice packs, and acupuncture.

"Disks are tricky," her doctor said, studying the MRI on his light box. "You can be a professional wrestler and be fine, or turn around at the movies and that little motion does it. I'm surprised you're still walking around."

"I'm glad we agree." Myra glanced at Nash, who had taken to spending the night four or five times a week since Pride weekend last June. She'd cleaved to fidelity for nearly a year now, but accompanying Myra to the exam turned Nash's face the color of a dried-out tea bag with a green tinge underneath. Myra was glad to have Nash there, though, and Nash would probably do a great job scheduling help after the hospital. Even if she wasn't always emotionally available, she was reliable.

"At least you're still young and healthy. We'll get you up dancing again in no time."

"When a doctor says 'we'll have you up in no time,' he means no time for him, because he won't be around. For you, eight weeks." Carol shook her head at the twelve bouquets of flowers that filled Myra's semi-private room at Alta Bates in Berkeley. "You told your clients you were having surgery?"

"Word gets out," Myra said, turning from Carol to the window.

157

"But I think only one or two are from clients. At least two are from Nash. The rest are from, oh, I don't know." She waved a hand toward the vast world outside.

"I figured you'd get flowers, but I'm floored by your popularity. Who can compete?"

"Carol." Myra turned her head slowly back. Her legs were pulled up in a traction device that reminded Carol of pictures of the Spanish Inquisition.

"I'm sorry, Myra. That was dumb. I'm not competing with you for anything. I promise I won't go completely narcissist on you. But I did bring you a present." She rummaged in her bag and pulled out a small box.

"Please unwrap it for me." Myra pushed the button that dribbled more morphine into her intravenous drip.

Carol pulled a chair close, and held up the box for approval.

"Nice wrapping job."

"Thanks. We all have our small talents." She pried up the scotch tape, folded back the paper, took off the top, and proffered it. Inside was a blown glass sphere the size of a lime, in which spirals of purple, blue, and green intertwined.

Myra extended her free arm, picked it up, and held it under the light. "I like this."

"You don't have to sound surprised." Carol took the big marble from Myra's hand and set it up on the night table on its small plastic stand. "Nash isn't the only one who knows how to give good presents. You can reach it here whenever you need a change of scenery."

"Very thoughtful," Myra yawned.

"Where *is* Nash?" Carol wasn't quite ready to leave.

"Oh, Nash," Myra sighed. "Nash isn't big on hospitals, though she does come for an hour or two every day. Something about her parents being doctors, I think. Butches can be such babies sometimes."

"No kidding," Carol agreed. "But you're still—"

"Oh, we're fine, I guess. She brought me an armload of books

158

on tape so I wouldn't be lonely for her in the night." A very small laugh trickled out of her. "You have no idea what it's like here at four in the morning."

"No, I guess not." Carol flashed to Molly calling her for a bedpan in the middle of the night. "Actually, I hope I don't have to find out."

"That's my pal." Myra tried to shift her weight sideways without much success.

"Can I help?"

"Maybe ask a nurse to come in on your way out."

"You have a button for that."

"Yeah, but it works better when someone asks."

"OK, sweetheart, I can take the hint. You rest. Call me if I can do anything."

"Thanks for the marble. It'll be something nice to look at when they wake me for my morning blood draw."

By August, six weeks later, Myra was hobbling around fairly well, and could sit with her clients for three or four hours a day, which wore her out, so her friends did whatever they could to entertain her. Myra puttered around in a small house on the Oakland outskirts, bought in the early '90s while the market was slumped, much to most of her friends' envy. Carol wasn't envious, though. She'd told Myra about the apartment building in Chicago, but not how much she got for it. "I did get a financial planner, like you told me to. I want you should know I pay attention and follow your advice," Carol had said. Myra just laughed.

Carol knew that Nash had twice declined to move in, and Myra insisted that business about the third time being a charm was superstition. She was not going to offer again, even though Nash was there nearly every day since Myra got out of the hospital. "Nearly," Myra said, raising her eyebrows.

Carol and Z.D. joined Myra and Nash to watch a women's basketball game on Myra's brand new 30-inch TV, bought especially for her recovery—LA Sparks versus Sacramento Monarchs on ESPN, the Monarchs being as close to a home team as Oaklanders could have. Z.D. and Nash were pitching cards into a hat, finishing off a large bottle of Belgian ale Nash had picked up ("pretty nice for bougie beer," Z.D. allowed), talking about DeMya Walker's muscles, and the cute way she stuck her rear in the air when she shot.

"Must you?" Carol asked.

"They are kind of cute." Myra, who was sprawled out on the couch, nodded to Carol.

"Those two or DeMya?"

"Everyone. Relax, Carol," Myra picked up a pretzel from the bowl in her lap, broke it into pieces that she let fall back in.

"Yeah, Carol, relax," Z.D. turned to give her a quick glance. "Look. Don't you think that's sexy?"

Carol sucked her lips. The woman's blue jersey flapped loose beyond her shorts. She was running toward the key. Passed the ball to Penicheiro, who threw it back to her; DeMya lifted it right above the defense, plunked it in.

"Nice shot, girlfriend," Nash said.

"Nice assist, Penicheiro," Myra added.

Nice skin, Carol thought, like brown bottle glass with the light shining through it, even though it hasn't been dusted in awhile.

"Hey, Carol, I'm talking to you," Z.D. said. "Where'd you go? What do you think, DeMya or Lisa Leslie?"

"Now Leslie, she's an athlete," Myra slapped the side of the couch for emphasis, shifting to her hip to change the pressure on her spine.

Carol tried to imagine Myra before she became a therapist, when she was a rowdy young outdoorsy femme. "You want another beer? I'm getting a beer," Carol said. "It's no use being sober around all you maniacs."

"Don't give me that," Z.D. said, "you know you love us. And the Monarchs."

"Beer?"

"Yeah, sure."

"Me too," Myra said.

"Me three," Nash looked at her for the first time in ten minutes, and checked out Myra, who seemed alright, lying back, enjoying herself. "But Carol, you have to admit DeMya's got something going on there."

"She may have it going on. But the Sparks are hot. I'll give you eight points on the Monarchs."

"Eight points?" Myra looked puzzled.

"You have to watch out for her," Nash said. "She's betting that the Sparks will win by more than eight points."

"So if the Monarchs lose by three, I'd still win?" Myra considered Carol.

"If you want to take her bet, that's how it works."

"I'm not sure I should be encouraging this, Carol."

"Oh don't be such a damn therapist, girlfriend." Nash got up and perched on the sofa arm, since the game had gone to commercial. She ran her palm down Myra's blouse in what could pass as a caress.

"Enough with the therapist cracks, honey." Myra caught Nash's hand in a light grip.

"You know you're a fine woman by me," Nash replied.

Myra turned back to Carol. "All right. What the hell. Five bucks on the Monarchs. They're going to fly all over your Sparks." She put a five-dollar bill on the coffee table as Carol disappeared into the kitchen.

Carol came back with a tray of Rolling Rock. "What's this stuff?" Nash wanted to know.

"Ah, beer of the masses at last," Z.D. mumbled.

"I bought a case for Myra last week when it was my turn to shop. It was on sale, and bottles are better for you than cans— aluminum can give you Alzheimer's, they say."

"I heard that too," Myra vouched.

"Anyone want a glass? I didn't think so," Carol said as they all shook their heads no. Carol would have preferred a glass, but she didn't want to get stuck washing dishes—she certainly wasn't going to leave them for Myra. Z.D. turned up the sound as the game came back on for the second half.

"You need to stop reading those newspapers," Nash said, after taking a long swallow. "Every day they say something new will kill you, and a month later they're all, oh we're so sorry, we were wrong about that. But watch out for strawberries."

"Nevertheless—" Carol started.

"Stop yapping. I can't hear the TV," Z.D. grinned at her, turned to Nash. "When she says 'nevertheless', it's time for drastic steps."

"OK, I'll behave." Carol plunked down next to Z.D. and put her head in her lap. Z.D. sucked in a breath, and then stroked Carol's hair. "Oops—here comes Leslie for a three. I don't know, Myra."

The Sparks won by eleven points. "I told you so," Nash said, watching Carol pick Myra's five off the table.

On the way back from Myra's, they stopped at Everett and Jones for barbecue—ribs for Z.D., chicken and links for Carol. Carol watched the aproned man and woman in the kitchen—just visible through the plexi-glass shield through which customers ordered—engage in a practiced choreography, plopping down potato salad, baked beans, meat, sauce, throwing two slices of brown bread in wax paper into the bag. Hot back there—they probably dripped sweat into the sauce all the time. Maybe they were careful, maybe they were the nieces and nephews of Dorothy Everett and her eight daughters who started this enterprise, and had an investment in each meal. She hoped so. Hoped it wasn't only rote labor for them, but some promise mingling with the barbecue smoke.

At home, Carol popped open another beer. "This apricot ale goes nice with barbecue—want to try it?"

"Sure." Z.D., who was arranging their meals on plates, looked over her shoulder at Carol. "You're drinking a lot today. Are you okay?"

"C'mon, Z.D., you can down a six-pack in an afternoon."

"Yeah, but that's me. And I've been cutting back some. You didn't notice?"

"You feel okay?" She took a long sip of the ale, and considered Z.D. Tired, she thought. I'm tiring her out.

"Okay, I guess. You know, with everything that's been going on between us, I didn't want to be confused about what was me and what was—random shit sloshing through me."

With her free hand, Carol picked up the plate Z.D. had put together and kissed her quickly on the cheek. "I like that, random ions sloshing through you."

"I didn't say 'ions.' Anyway, I was asking about you. We know you don't hold your liquor so good."

Is she really bringing that up again? Carol forked a slice of the spicy, grainy links slathered in hot caramelized brownish magenta goop, and chewed. Then she grimaced, letting her fork clunk against the ceramic edge, careful enough not to splatter. Z.D. put her dish down and stood looking at her.

"I'm not getting on your case, honey. Really. I thought maybe we could talk if something's bothering you." Z.D. slid into her chair.

"Eat your ribs while they're still warm." Carol looked up and met Z.D.'s eyes, deciding to relax. "Really, the beer is good with this—and it helps you forget that the meat is full of hormones that will kill us."

"Oh man, you're on a roll today." Z.D. sucked the sauce of a rib and then inhaled the meat. "Everything in the world's going to kill us—you know what I heard last week?"

"What?" Carol was alternating chicken, links, and potato salad, trying to get them to come out even, with the links for the last bite.

"The orcas up in Puget Sound—they have all these laws protecting them—but they're dying from PCBs in the water."

"Orcas are going to be gone?" Carol put her fork down.

"Looks like it. You're right, this beer is good with ribs. C'mon, Carol, I was just trying to make a point."

"Which was?"

"We got to take these little pleasures. Okay, maybe next year

163

we'll become vegans. But it's always some kind of balancing act—being responsible and enjoying the lives we have. We'd go nuts if we could hear the voices of everything that was suffering."

Carol pushed around the lumps of potato salad. "Everything that screams," she said, under her breath, anxious for the hundredth time about keeping money in the stock market. What's responsible about that? But Molly would approve, would say women gotta plan for old age, for emergencies. They looked at their plates quietly for a minute, and then continued eating. "You know what I'd like to do?"

"No, but I hope you'll tell me."

"I'd like to look at mom's photo albums after dinner."

"Really?"

"Yup. If you'll sit with me."

Molly left two albums—one a 1950s antique, with black pages and photo corners that had to be pasted on to hold the pictures. They started with the newer one, which had plastic pockets and was filled with pictures of Carol from high school on—her first love, Eileen, was there, holding up her prized basketball shoes, on the third page.

"You've always gone for us strong types, huh?" Z.D. squeezed Carol's arm. "Give me a break," Carol said. She flipped though the pages quickly, slowing down for a second at images of her and Z.D. at the beach that Nash had probably taken. Nice of Molly to put them in. "We did make a good-looking couple, though."

"Whadya mean, did?"

"In the picture. Pictures are always past tense." She paused, staring at the page. "We still are a good couple, huh?"

"Looks like it." Z.D. nodded, comforted to be sitting next to Carol, doing something so ordinary, so intimate. What is a photograph? Chemicals that fix the past in place, or a representation of the future, of hope for possibilities, all the lines that move forward and back, criss-crossing, creating their stories?

"I want to see the other one." Carol ran her hand over the brown, textured front, caked with Chicago dust. She turned past pictures of Molly's parents, whom she knew only from the photos, past a studio portrait of Molly when she graduated from Teacher's College, in a cap and gown. She stopped when she came to Harold in a striped t-shirt, pushing her on a tricycle. On the opposite page, Harold was leaning on a guy by the side of a plane.

"He looks like a fag," Z.D. said.

"What?"

"Okay, gay. But, really. Look at the way he's got his hand draped around that guy's shoulder. And here, just after he's pushed you, with his hand on his hip."

Carol grabbed at the album and frowned at the photos.

"And what about that curl in the picture you keep in your sock drawer?"

"Why were you looking through my sock drawer, Z.D.?"

"For some socks. Jeez. So what if your old man was gay—why is that making you so touchy?"

"I'm not touchy." She wiggled her feet and Z.D. put her hand on Carol's knee. "And I don't like to be touched on my knee—it tickles. You should know that by now."

"Damn, Carol. Okay, okay." Z.D. took a breath, ran her finger under the edge of the photo, dated February, 1970. Carol put her hand on top of Z.D.'s

"You're right. I'm being touchy. Sorry. This picture was taken the year he died." She tapped the black album page with her fingernail. "Maybe he was gay. But guys in war—don't they always screw each other when women aren't around?"

"I guess." Z.D. took a small sip from her beer can. "Yeah. Whenever you hear about guys being together for more than two weeks, you always figure they're going to go after each other. It's like they can't live without it. Two women can spend years going around the world, and no one even suspects they might get it on, unless they're wearing dyke march t-shirts or something. Like, even that dyke who went to the North Pole with that straight woman—"

"Ann Bancroft. I remember because of the actress, you know, who was in *The Miracle Worker*."

"Yeah, I remember now—it's funny how they have the same name."

"They didn't really. Anne Bancroft—the actress—changed hers. She's Italian, I think. Bancroft is about as WASP as a name can be." Carol stopped to meditate on the phenomena of name-changing. "You think dykes changed their names to erase their ethnicities?"

"Maybe some of them. Of us." Z.D. considered whether going by your initials was changing your name or not. "Not like actors, anyway. Actors wanted to be more acceptable. Dykes wanted to—well, I can't say what every dyke wanted, but not to be more acceptable, that's for sure. Were we talking about sex?"

"Sex and Ann Bancroft."

"Right. So what was the name of that straight woman she went to the North Pole with?"

"Liv? Liv something. We saw the documentary. You could google her if you really want to know."

"No, that's just my point."

"Which was?"

"No one thought that they would get it on with each other."

"Well, hell, they would have froze solid, wouldn't they?" Carol laughed, and turned the album page. It was another page of guys at a base somewhere with palm trees, posing in front of barracks and bombers.

"Nah, I don't think so, at least if they were in a sleeping bag. Anyway. I'm just saying that we all expect men to get horny, especially young men doing dangerous things. Maybe he wasn't really gay. A Kinsey scale three or something."

Carol looked at her father's image, staring at another guy, a white guy with a crew cut and a big chin. That could be a reason why he signed up for Vietnam, at least subconsciously. It could explain why so many men were eager to go. Maybe patriotism was a cover story for sexual opportunism, especially since America had gone so co-ed, and people weren't partitioned from the opposite sex anymore, the way they had been for all those centuries. Homosocial—she'd learned that in college. The army would have been the place, the hot ticket, for guys who couldn't make the football team but who'd secretly longed for their butts to get patted in the end zone, the camaraderie, the muscular bodies stinking man funk in the locker room. Throwing your body over a buddy to keep him from harm's way would have been a noble fantasy, not tawdry like cruising around Chicago hoping to get laid while your wife and daughter thought you'd gone out for milk.

"What's that face for?"

"I was thinking about gay men. About my father."

"It's only a theory, Carol."

"But maybe you're right. Maybe he was scared and thrilled and—I don't know. I never think of Jewish men as having lust—no, that's not right—as having the kind of lust that's part of militarism. But the Israelis have it—I've seen it on the faces of the guys in the films at the Jewish Film Festival. So why wouldn't my father have had it?"

"We like to think of the dead as holy." Z.D. stood, pitched her beer can through the doorway into the kitchen recycling bin, and plunked back down.

"Good shot."

"Yup. I got aim."

"Did you ever want to be a soldier?"

Z.D. cocked her head to her right shoulder in a gesture that always reminded Carol of a retriever being puzzled by the command to go fetch. "Hmm. Nah. When I was young—oh, in tenth or eleventh grade, maybe—this is embarrassing."

"What, honey? You don't have to be embarrassed with me."

Z.D. stared at the wall. "You know how you are then, all hormonal and not knowing what your life is going to be, so impatient to be grown-up you can't stand it? I wanted to ram my fist through the sky until it broke and god's secrets rained out. Remember that?"

"I wouldn't have put it that way, exactly, but actually, I do remember." Carol stroked Z.D.'s sleeve.

"Sometimes I thought of myself as one of the conquistadors."

"Really?"

"I told you you wouldn't like it."

"No you didn't. You said you were embarrassed. But that's not embarrassing."

"No?"

"Uh uh. It's fascinating."

"Yeah, great. Fascinating."

"Oh stop. You're not some specimen to me, you're my butch. Tell me more about it."

"Your butch, huh?"

"No doubt about it." Carol wiggled her butt closer to Z.D.'s.

Z.D.'s shoulders relaxed. "It was about—I'm not sure now. Being bad. Pillaging. Taking what didn't belong to you—to me. I wanted stuff. I wanted a silver helmet that gleamed, I wanted bags of gold and rubies, I wanted women to swoon when they saw me coming, tremble with fear and longing."

"Swoon's not a word I've heard you say." Carol chewed on her bottom lip. "You wanted women to fear you? Did you want to force them?"

"It was a fucking fantasy." Her shoulders went back up. "It wasn't, I don't know, explicit. I'd think about it when I'd go to the park by myself, climbing up a hill or something."

"An outdoors fantasy, huh? Most of mine I have in bed or at the movies."

"Yeah, you're a dark corners kind of girl, aren't you?"

"Don't change the subject. Your conquistador fantasy, it was about power."

"Of course. I was fifteen, sixteen. And it's not like I didn't know that the Spanish did terrible things, you know, that they are not really to be admired, even if they did it all in the name of the Church. Or especially because they did it for the Church, Holy Mother colonialism. But I was jealous of what my brothers had."

"Dicks?"

"Nah. I always thought dicks were—weird. Kinda silly looking and out of control. I wanted their swagger. You know, the way they walked around our neighborhood as if they were God's gift. Even Amos, who didn't exactly swagger, but still acted like—"

"Entitled?"

"Yeah, entitled. Working-class boys can get their entitlement on the same as anybody. Any guys. At least in their own realm. It's not easy to do if you're the one who always gets roped into washing the dishes."

"Aw. You don't have to do the dishes tonight."

"You're just saying that because we hardly have any."

"Busted. But maybe we can do something else."

"You hold that thought. You ready to put this album away?"

Carol's father lay in her lap, still dead. She took a deep breath. Even explanations don't explain anything, do they? We're always lost in how life rushes at us, its dirty waves full of historical flotsam, sexual juice, and the hunger for importance. She folded the album shut, and turned into her lover's mouth.

16

Z.D. raised her voice so Nash could hear her over her downtown gym's general clank and groan, and noticing that she was puffing slightly while she spoke, dialed down the incline on her treadmill to foothills. "The realtor promised me that the house we're renting belongs to Donna Summer."

"Donna Summer who sang 'Hot Stuff' and then became a born-again?" Nash had her treadmill set to a stroll on city streets, which was, she figured, exactly right. "You think Carol will like being in a born-again's house?"

"Man, these people don't actually live in those houses in Tahoe. They stay in penthouse suites at Harrah's if they come to town. The house are investments to rent to shlubs like us."

"Where'd you learn a word like shlub?" Nash tried to ignore the muscley African American guy on her right who seemed fascinated by their conversation.

"Hey, I pay attention. Me and Carol, we've been together now, what? Like twelve years. I had to learn something. Anyway, Carol will think it's camp. She likes camp."

"I've noticed myself that camp is making a big comeback. You can even hear a little disco under the house beats," Nash said, hopping off her machine. "It's a nice plan, Z.D."

"Yeah. They said the hot tub fits up to twelve people." Z.D. experienced a twinge of envy at the ease with which Nash stopped working out when she got tired. Maybe she could slow down some, herself. She wasn't going to be street-fighting Carol's bookie, and her brother Jake was in prison somewhere in Colorado for pistol-whipping a 7–11 attendant during an armed robbery two years ago—with any luck, he'd get himself killed in jail.

"Maybe we can get a little orgy action going," Nash said. Mr. Muscles smirked at her before moving on to the free weights. Maybe he was gay. Probably. She hoped so. Z.D.'s gym had enough free-floating testosterone to pump up every trans-fantasy in the East Bay. She didn't care for it, herself, and besides, the place smelled like fancy cheese you were saving for a special occasion and forgot about six months ago.

"In your dreams, Nash. You want me to invite Myra or not?"

Nash toweled the sweat off her neck and forehead. "I don't know. Who else is coming?"

"Lots of enthusiasm for your girlfriend there. Okay, you, me, Carol, Cordelia's coming down from Seattle—"

"That's nervy, inviting your girlfriend's big ex."

"They haven't even seen each other for five or six years, and Cordelia's three months pregnant. I'm not exactly worried."

"Pregnant? How old is she?"

"Must be the same as Carol, pushing forty."

"I can't figure having a kid at forty."

Z.D. shrugged. "One thing Carol and I always agreed on was we didn't want kids. But Cordelia told her she could be the godmother, and she's all excited about that." Z.D. picked up a couple of five-pound hand weights and went to work on her biceps.

"Easy to be auntie for a kid who's a thousand miles away." Nash sat on a green exercise ball, pretending to practice balancing.

"Exactly the right distance, if you ask me. So, Cordelia's coming, and Ginny, Sandra, Tourmaline, Jan, Denise—"

"Denise Galt?"

"Yeah, her. She's the one who got Carol started in tutoring. Why?"

"We had a little thing in-between Myra."

"Is that why you two split up the first time?"

"No, it was because of Kendra. Or, este, 'I used Kendra to extri-

171

cate myself.'" Nash affected a German accent, which she thought reflected the formality of therapeutic language.

"Is that what you think?"

"No, it's what Myra thinks. I had the hots for Kendra. It doesn't have to be a big psychodrama every time. Attractions happen. What can I say?"

"You can say you're a dog," Z.D. put down the weights and whipped her towel at Nash's shoulder.

Nash nearly fell off the ball. "Ease up—I'm a good dog these days. Yeah, invite Myra. Don't tell her I hesitated."

"You won't get distracted by Denise?"

"No, that's over." Nash brushed her palms. "Fini."

"'Cause I don't want any scenes at Carol's fortieth birthday party."

"You're the one taking us to Tahoe—you don't think she's going to spend the whole weekend in a casino?"

"Not the whole weekend if I can help it," Z.D. grinned.

Indeed a giant black hot tub with a D emblazoned in the tile work filled the basement of the disco diva's digs. The house was a nightmare of competing architectural visions—not just visions, but angles, as if the builder of the second story was having a fight with the builder of the first, crying, "My exposure will be to the south, you dummy! Whatever made you face your windows west?" The house twisted on its axis, a misaligned spine. The only thing that united the four levels was the padded wallpaper in every room.

"This is what you get for renting someplace sight unseen," Carol observed, pressing her hands to the dusty, flocked wallpaper in disbelief as she, Z.D., Nash, and Myra made their first trip in from the car.

"It sounded great—anyway, everyone gets their own room." Nash explored, and Z.D. claimed the master bedroom on the second floor. "We get this jungle-motif one with a canopy bed and its own bathroom. Not too shabby."

Carol took a breath and forced a smile.

172

The bathroom was done entirely in black and gold—black toilet, black sink, black tiles, gold trim, gold finished faucets, gold mirror rim. In this black sink Carol spit on the morning of her 40th birthday after a quick trip to Harrah's the first night when all the guests were accounted for. She couldn't do more than come out fifty dollars ahead. In the old days, that would have been winning; now it was breaking even. Since the stock market had tanked, Carol spent her swimming time wishing she'd sold her Cisco and Oracle stock at the top, then bought it back. Money had evaporated while she'd been thinking that the big pension funds, the DuPonts and Rockefellers, couldn't let the market go down anymore—it was their goddamn money. Eventually she realized she didn't know the first thing about it. Well, the first thing, maybe, but not the second, certainly not the inner circle third. How many circles in the world of money? As many as in the *Inferno*, she guessed, and deep in the center, a tortured priest, speaking in Italian tercets. Maybe she should have applied herself more to foreign languages—at least, to the ratios of economics. She still could, she could even go to graduate school and get an MBA, her mind was still sharp enough to figure out profit. An MBA! What are you thinking about, girl?

Everything about money changes when you have some, she decided for the fiftieth time, and got distracted, noticing her spit was hard white. Since when wasn't spit clear? She wasn't sick—she felt her head, pressed the base of her throat. Thick white morning spit—the body gives you its own little gifts as you age. Why hadn't Molly told her about the part of aging that wasn't death? Weren't moms supposed to prepare their daughters for the stages of life?

No one tells you you're going to have to live with decay every minute—that the things you turned your head away from—varicose veins and warts and scars and spit and scabs, creases and tears and shit—will be your inheritance, the joke of aging, the thing beneath the usual gags about being "over the hill" and "it's not so bad if you consider the alternative." Alternative to getting used to leaning over the basin and washing down your spit, alternative to the limp and buckle, the increasing need to stretch, the hundred new small interventions you make with your body that take up the space of a day, fill the hours in which you might wonder why the medical profession is so intent on lengthening life span. Not that long ago, forty was the beginning of old age. But we are here and still young, her generation asserts. Carol was not entirely convinced.

How could Cordelia even consider getting pregnant? Cope with her body knocking her sideways, hormone rebellion, challenging all the hard-bought peace you come to as your skin changes, inch by inch? It takes a lifetime just to be comfortable with how you eat. And the food! They'd had to haul up food for fifteen dietary needs, and there were only nine of them. You'd think they came from different planets. This weekend was turning out to be a test run for Lesbian Nation. Only organic for Cordelia, although, she confessed, she mostly wanted saltines (organic saltines, check); no sugar for Ginny, but honey and rice syrup were okay (it wasn't easy to find a sugar-free birthday cake, so they compromised with diabetic cookies, about which Ginny complained because she wasn't diabetic, just trying to keep from becoming one, but it was Carol's birthday after all, so okay, they could have the chocolate cake from Ladyfingers that Carol wanted); Tourmaline had always been a vegetarian—even her hippy parents were, but Denise had recently converted and given Z.D. grief about having a turkey. She eventually gave in as long as they made stuffing she could eat, but when they wanted to put walnuts in the stuffing, it turned out Myra was allergic. Not to pecans though, pecans would work. "Some birthday party," Carol grumbled to Z.D.

"You know you love your friends."

"But I had no idea what it was going to be like to live with them for a weekend."

"And it's not over yet," Myra said, fishing out containers of olives and cheese for their lunch. "Isn't anyone here lactose intolerant?" She held up a package of Brie in one hand and a container of sour cream in the other.

"Not that they said," Z.D. answered, taking her seriously, slicing whole grain organic bread.

"How far is it into town?" Myra asked.

"3.7 miles to the casinos," Carol said.

"Oh, that's town?"

"Leave her alone, it's her birthday," Nash joined in.

"I clocked it last night. Everything's in a two-block radius. There's no Whole Foods up here—maybe not even in Reno, and that's over the mountain."

"There's a natural food store in a strip mall in Truckee." Cordelia appeared in the doorway wearing gray sweat pants and a yellow corduroy shirt, her hair buzz cut. "I had to pee, so Ginny stopped. And then I had the munchies. Pregnancy is weird. One minute, food is disgusting; the next, you feel like you're stoned and can't get enough chocolate chip mint ice cream."

"My favorite!" Carol said, turning to her.

"Is it? Oh yeah, I guess." Cordelia looked dubious. "Happy Birthday, sweetheart." She gave Carol a quick kiss on the cheek.

"Aww, you remembered." Carol ran her hand over Cordelia's belly. "I can't get over this."

"So Cordelia," Myra closed the refrigerator in resignation that she wouldn't find what she wanted to eat, "sit down and tell us the baby story."

Z.D. rolled her eyes at Nash.

"It's not a long story. When I met Linda, we realized we both really wanted a whole family—"

"You have to have kids to be a whole family?" Z.D. looked annoyed as she spread mayonnaise on her toast, scraping it as she went.

"Don't take it that way, Z.D.—it's not what I meant."

Carol wrapped her arms around Z.D.'s waist, and whispered in her ear, "We're a family, honey."

"We're all family, here," Myra added.

"Yeah, one happy lesbian commune," Nash mumbled.

175

Cordelia sighed. "Clearly that came out wrong. I apologize. I got to be thirty-five and I wanted—it's hard to explain. My father used to say there were three ways to be immortal: write something worth reading, do something worth writing about, or have children. I don't really believe immortality is such a big deal, but I've sat through a hundred women's rituals where we all named our mothers and grandmothers. I wanted somebody coming after to name me. And I want to know that kind of love you can have with a child."

"That's kind of sweet," Myra said, finding a bunch of celery in a paper bag on the floor and starting to wash it off.

"Linda was the one who was supposed to get pregnant, but she couldn't."

"Couldn't?" Nash asked, settling back in a kitchen chair against the wall, surveying the scene.

"You don't want to know how complicated it is."

"How complicated what is?" Tourmaline came in barefoot, wearing a tie-dyed shirt two sizes too big and loose gauze pants.

"Getting pregnant," Cordelia said.

"I thought you just got a donor and a turkey baster," Tourmaline yawned.

"We all know about turkey basters," Carol said, turning back to Cordelia. "It's hard to imagine you, though, getting—basted."

Z.D. snorted, piled her sandwich with ham, swiss cheese, and sprouts, grabbed a ginger ale, and went into the living room.

"Is she mad at me?" Cordelia asked.

"Unless she thinks you've broken the sworn rules of butchdom by getting pregnant, I doubt it," Myra said, looking through the doorway.

"She could be a slightly jealous," Nash added.

"Jealous? We were lovers a hundred years ago," Carol said.

"I'm not that old," Cordelia said.

"Jealousy is not a rational animal." Nash winked at Myra, but Myra waved her off with an expression of disgust.

◆◆◆

176

Nash went to watch the A's and Mariners game Z.D. had found on cable.

Myra watched Nash's back, fidgeting with the celery. Then she looked over to Carol. "So, birthday girl, I figure from your mileage calculations, you were out gambling last night. How'd you do?"

"'Sometimes you're the windshield, sometimes you're the bug,'" Carol sang, swiveling her head to show off the ruby earrings Z.D. had given her in bed that morning. Breakfast in bed, a vase with a flower, a present beside her scrambled eggs. That Zenobia was still a charmer.

"Come again?" Cordelia asked.

Tourmaline picked up the Brie and sniffed it. "You guys actually eat this?"

"It's a Mary Chapin Carpenter song I like," Carol said, ignoring her. "Although I've often wondered what it's supposed to mean. The bug part is clear enough, I guess—if you believe that there's some great ledger where the reincarnated souls of karmic losers get theirs by being splattered against a windshield."

"But what kind of lesson can a bug learn?" Cordelia asked, tracking Carol's idea.

"Exactly my point. You know, I always liked you." Carol got up and ran her palm over Cordelia's fuzzy head. "It's the whole problem with the idea of reincarnation—if you're coming back to learn a lesson, I think it gets lost on you if you're a sea urchin."

"You have a very magic kingdom idea of reincarnation," Myra observed. "Like the fairy godmother's magic wand—poof—you're a sea urchin."

"What do we know?" Cordelia got up, opened a package of crackers, and poured herself a glass of club soda.

"Can I have some of those crackers?" Tourmaline asked.

"Help yourself." Cordelia put the crackers on the counter by Tourmaline's elbow.

"We don't know much, apparently. But it's the windshield part that confuses me—what's that a metaphor for?" Carol took a bite of the sandwich that Z.D. had left for her. Not bad, she thought, though it needed a little—onion, that's it, onion. No, too early in the day for onion, and besides everyone had been kissing her. She didn't want to discourage that.

"And thus has the parsing of poetry come to this, the desultory examination of empty popular song lyrics of the late 20th century." Denise came into the kitchen, still in her pajamas, looking sleepy.

"Okay, professor, you tell us what the windshield is."

"Is there any coffee?" Denise followed the motion of Carol's hand to the coffeemaker and poured herself a cup. "A windshield. What is it? A moving, transparent wall against which things splatter that have the misfortune of being in the way. It represents, therefore, ruthlessness. Perhaps a metaphor for the neo-colonialist experience. A ruthlessness you can't see coming."

"Women aren't ruthless," Cordelia said.

"Oh ho, if you sat and listened to my clients, you'd think twice about that." Myra took a noisy bite of her celery for emphasis.

"You wanted exegesis, I gave you exegesis," Denise said, disappearing the way she'd come.

"Exe-who?" Tourmaline asked.

"It's a ten-dollar word for explaining a text, I think," Carol said, fishing out a bottle of wine from under the sink. "Hard to trust anyone who talks like that."

"More what she doesn't say you have to watch out for." Myra waved the celery in the general vicinity of the doorway.

"Now who's jealous?"

"Jealous of what?" Cordelia looked confused.

"Nash had a brief fling with Denise a while back," Carol explained, rummaging through the drawers for a corkscrew.

"Brief is the operative word," Myra said. "I can't picture Nash putting up with that vocabulary for very long."

"Maybe it reminded her of her Jesuit education. Or she was over-compensating for dropping out of college." Carol splashed a little wine on her shirt as she wrestled the cork out. "Damn."

"Isn't it a little early in the day for that, Carol?" Myra squinted at her.

"It's my fucking birthday. And I only want one glass."

"Hey, hey! Play nice, everybody." Cordelia looked up from the neat pile of cracker halves she was stacking. "Nash dropped out of college?"

Myra gave Carol the you're-not-supposed-to-spill-those-beans look, but explained. "Yeah. She's always talking about finishing up. Her family's all professional—doctors, architects, lawyers—my theory is she left to piss them off, although I'm not sure she ever told them she didn't get her B.A." She got up. "It's so nice outside, I'm going for a walk. You going back to the casino, Carol?"

"At least there they want you to celebrate with a drink."

Myra came over and hugged her. "Whatever you do, I celebrate you."

A Rabbi Moshe Liberow of Colorado Springs was quoted, in a Reno paper that someone had brought back to the house, as saying, "One tiny mistake won't invalidate all of the work. It can be fixed. God is strict, but he is not cruel." Carol, surprised to see a Rabbi from Colorado quoted in Nevada, in the middle of July, no less, not anywhere close to a Jewish holiday, wanted to take it as a sign. The Rabbi was talking about transcribing the Torah, the first five books of the Bible, how the work of scribes must be allowed to stand, since the exacting work of the copyists was never meant to be like Buddhist sand mandalas, patiently shaped for months only to be blown away. The Jews have an entirely different conception of how things should be put to use, of what use is, Carol decided.

"Jews have morals for every occasion," her mother had said sometime in those last couple weeks, "but when the chips are down, where are they?"

"Don't I count, Molly? I'm the only one you let in." Her mother had—what? tried to laugh? Go away, Mom. It's my birthday. And don't tell me that's why you're here.

Carol decided she ought to play hostess before indulging her desire to check out Caesar's Palace, where she hoped her luck would be better than at Harrah's, and rounded up a hot tub group.

179

Ginny had driven Myra to an easy hiking trail she knew. Sandra, Tourmaline, Jan, and Denise agreed to go tubbing, but Cordelia wasn't sure it would be good for her blood pressure, which was already showing signs of pregnancy elevation.

"She's gotta bring that up every minute," Z.D. muttered to Nash.

"You invited her," Nash whispered back.

"Do I have to be naked?" Z.D. asked to cover their conversation.

"You can soak in your undershirt and boxers if you'd be more comfortable," Carol assured her. "You too Nash."

Nash looked miserably at Z.D.

"Come on, Nash," Sandra said, "I'm not going to be the only color in the tub. Besides, who can resist soaking where Donna Summer may have lain."

"You wish. The divas only buy houses like this for investments— they party in penthouses in town. I got it straight from Z.D., or maybe I got it crooked," Nash said. "But since you make it an issue of women of color solidarity, I will valiantly take up the hot tub cause."

They stood around the hot tub, wrapped in their towels. Although it was in the high 80s outside, the basement, built into the side of the hill with a slice of meadow view, was cool enough for tubbing comfort. But the water ran cold and rusty.

"Hey, what's the deal here?" Tourmaline asked.

"It was perfectly adequate last night," Denise said. When they looked at her, she added, "Jan, Nash, Myra, and I took a tub around midnight, before Carol returned."

"Traitor," Z.D. said to Nash under her breath.

"Okay, I secretly like hot tubs. I confess to my tropical blood," Nash laughed. "But she's right, it worked fine last night."

Carol noticed the wistful smile Denise flashed at Nash. Had they been playing footsie under Myra's toes?

"Something's busted now." Z.D. was on her knees, scoping out the plumbing. "Maybe an obstruction, or something rusted through."

"Overnight?" Jan asked.

"I'm not a plumber. I'll call the rental agency." Z.D. straightened up.

"So much for the disco orgy," Carol shook her head at Z.D. "Don't worry, honey, you found us a wonderful—well, interesting—house, and we're all having a great time, right?" Yeah, yup, exactly, sure, the women chorused. "Those of you still amorously inclined can make use of the padded cells upstairs or the decks. I'm going to the casino."

"Naked?" Z.D. reached for her butt.

Carol swatted her away. "I'm going to put on the beautiful silk vest my friends gave me for my fortieth birthday. Want to come?"

"Only if the vest is all you're going to wear. But, nah, I always throw a hundred dollars down the mouth of some poker machine, and there's another game on in an hour. Unless you really want me to come, since it's your birthday—"

"I want you in the jungle print bed when I get home." Carol said, pulling the towel around her cleavage.

"I bet you do." Z.D. smirked.

"OK, we get it. You two have somehow avoided lesbian bed death after all these years and we're very impressed," Sandra said from the stairwell.

"I'll come. Always fascinating to watch operant conditioning in action," Denise said.

"What she said," Nash laughed. "I'll keep you company too."

What fun, Carol thought. Us lowly bettors are about to be observed. O god of the Main Chance, of the avalanche of millions betting tonight, holding their lottery tickets in their hands, strict god, how are we to interpret your signs? Belief is the two of swords—with each hand we are smitten and cleaved, yet we return to the game every time, because we believe. Gambling is hard for people who don't believe. Certain kinds of gambling, certain kinds of bets. Belief or no belief, the cards are dealt in the order they're shuffled. And what a relief—a clear outcome. No waiting once the numbers come up. The world of possibilities is actually shrunk to a manageable size in casinos. You have nothing to decide but whether to play and how much to bet. Nothing humans can do rearranges their hands and yet nothing distracts us from the hands we're dealt—no nightmares, no headlines, no love. What is it we feel when we think we feel luck?

"Hey, Carol." Tourmaline came into the bedroom while Carol was dressing.

"Having a good time?" She checked herself out in the full-length mirror. Nice vest, she thought, running her hands over her hips.

"It's pretty up here—I'm going to take a few cuttings from the rhododendrons outside. You don't think they'll mind, do you?"

"I don't think they'll notice. Want to come to the casino with us?"

"You know that's not my style." She took a deep breath. "Listen, I have this friend Sophia who I've known since the '80s back in Northampton."

"Whom," Carol said, trying to decide which necklace would go with her new earrings. Molly raised her eyebrows in the mirror. "You gonna do that even to your friends, cookie? It was bad enough you were always correcting me. Knock it off."

"Whom, okay," Tourmaline agreed. "Whom I've known. Anyway, she's a psychic now. I was thinking you might want to get a reading from her."

"A psychic reading? Me?"

"I thought it might help you deal with, like, this stuff about money."

Carol sat on the bed and faced Tourmaline. "Why do you think I need help dealing?"

"Hey, who wouldn't? You never had money before, and now you're throwing this big party—"

"Actually, Z.D. got a big raise this year and she's covering most of it."

"That's cool. But still, it couldn't hurt."

"I believe in psychic readings about as much as I believe a space

182

ship is going to arrive and beam up all the lesbians, taking us to a gynocentric paradise." Carol traced the skull of a tiger glaring up from the bedspread.

"That would be fun," Tourmaline laughed. "I've never seen a space ship, though, and I have had psychic readings. They're cool—you can think of them as conversations with your best inner self. And what's the worst that could happen if you went?"

"A, I could waste my time. B, I could be convinced to do something that makes no rational sense."

Tourmaline tucked her chin down and peered over her square eyeglasses. "The stock market makes sense? Casinos make sense?"

"Well, if you accept certain premises."

"Patriarchal premises," Tourmaline nodded, as if she had just won the argument. "So why not try out some other premises—Sophia's not a scammer. Hell, she can't even afford health insurance, so she's not doing this to get rich."

"Why does she do it?" Carol was distracted by some chipping nail polish on Tourmaline's big toe.

"She told me once that when she first started hearing this voice, she thought she was crazy. She took all kinds of drugs to stop hearing it. But at some point she realized she was channeling another reality, and when she did, she flushed all her drugs down the toilet and let it do its work. She's been remarkably centered the last couple years. There are other realities all around us—don't you think?"

"Mmm. Maybe." Carol had to admit she had an active relationship with Molly's ghost—but she believed that was simply a process of internalizing her mother's voice, following the logical trajectories of how Molly would have responded to situations. Sometimes driving at night she saw hitchhikers on the side of the freeway, but when she passed the spot, her headlights picked out only signposts. Were they apparitions or mirages? Quadratic equations and the laws of thermodynamics can't explain everything, but maybe that's only our limited ability to apply our minds to the problem. And figure out what the problem is.

"Logic is useful for a lot of situations," Tourmaline said, "but don't you think it's a very male—masculinist—conception, that everything follows linear paths? What about intuition, hunches?"

"A lot of physicists think space is curved—wrinkled even," Carol said, considering the possibilities.

"All right. So hidden in those wrinkles are other worlds, brushing up on ours. Maybe the membrane between them isn't so rigid. Why not give Sophia a call?"

"But what's it like? What does she do?"

"First, she pours blood over your shoulders—"

"Icch!"

"I'm joking, Carol. It's not a big deal. You sit in a room with her, she closes her eyes, and after a while she speaks in a different voice."

"What do you mean, different?"

"Just different." Tourmaline shrugged. "You'll see. It's the voice of the being that she channels. It seems to know things we don't have access to."

Carol looked back at Tourmaline's feet. Certainly she'd like more access. To how she felt, to how it was going to work out between her and Z.D., to whether or not she should give away money. But suppose this voice of Sophia's told her to bet everything on Zombie's Revenge in the third race at Golden Gate Fields, or to give it all to the National Center for Lesbian Rights and take a vow of poverty. Or buy Sophia health insurance. Would she do it? Sophia would probably pick up and reflect what she wanted to hear. How much of a sucker could she really be?

"I want to give you a reading with her for your birthday present, if you'll go."

"If you put it that way, I guess I'll give it a try. Give me her phone number."

"It's hard to give you anything, you know," Tourmaline said.

"I apologize, sweetie. I'm feeling a little out of sorts this afternoon. It will probably be the most interesting present I get, and I appreciate it."

◆ ◆ ◆

184

Carol, absorbed in imagining what a psychic might say, startled when she realized Denise was coming on to Nash in the front seat of Nash's car, something about postmodern anxiety expressed in secondary meta-fictional narratives that take in the working class and people of color. Could that possibly be flirting? But the under-current was clear. She decided, for everyone's sake, to ignore it.

Feeling impinged on by their energy, she left them as soon as they got to the casino. In the Sports Book room, she figured she'd make a small legitimate bet on the game between New York and Houston, which was about to start, even though she'd called in a bet on New York for two hundred twenty to Henry before they drove up here. She considered New York a sure-win proposition. Can't have too much of a good thing.

Both five-dollar crap tables were crowded—she watched two young African American men trying to impress each other, the taller one winning by throwing back-to-back hard sixes, a quick ninety bucks. She decided the energy was good enough in the room to play at the ten-dollar minimum table, also almost full. She squeezed in at the last position next to the croupier. She started with her usual pattern, double odds behind the line, come bets with odds—but after the point, craps rolled twice, and then the shooter seven-ed out. Fifty bucks gone in a flash. She pursed her lips. The next shooter, a little white guy who had the face of an opossum, made his point quickly—an easy eight—but before two hours were up, she'd lost four hundred dollars.

"How you doing, birthday girl?" Nash came up behind her.

"I've had better nights."

"Sorry to hear that. You'd think the goddess would be on your side when you turn forty."

"Maybe that's when she leaves. Hold on." She took a five-dollar chip and threw it toward the center of the felt. "Boxcars," she called.

"Five on the twelve," the stick woman replied.

"You bet the twelve?"

"It's thirty-to-one if it rolls."

185

"Seven out!" the dealer called.

"And nothing if it's a seven." She stared at her last four chips—down $480 now. Carol put the twenty she had left in the field, a bet she rarely made, especially on the come out roll.

"Five, the point is five, fever five, no field." The croupier scooped up her chips.

"You know what, Nash? Let's go back to the house. Where's Denise?"

"I left her over there making eyes at a blackjack dealer. A good-looking Korean butch."

"How'd you know she's Korean?"

"Actually, she's from Michigan. Her parents are Korean. Unlike you white girls who are afraid of your shadows, I asked."

"I am not afraid of anyone's damn shadow."

"My apologies, señora. It's absolutely true, you're the bravest femme I know."

"I'm too out of sorts to take the bait tonight, Nash. Let's just check the game scores before we leave." Houston beat New York by three.

"How'd you do, honey?" Z.D. was watching an old movie with Cordelia, eating popcorn, which they were getting all over the couch.

"Not so good. But I'm glad to see you two getting along."

"It's because you weren't here," Cordelia said, reaching for the remote that Z.D. had left unguarded.

"Very funny." Z.D. appraised Carol. "How not good?"

"I'll tell you later."

Z.D. whistled. "That not good."

Upstairs, Carol said, "Seven hundred seventy five dollars not good, counting what I owe Henry."

"You going to pay him?"

"Always."

"Honor among thieves," Z.D. checked out her arm muscles in the bathroom mirror, frowning.

"We're not thieves. We're gamblers."

"So you think of yourself as a gambler now?"

"Well, among other things. Many other things. And you knew that when we moved in together."

"Carol." Z.D. came back into their room, surveyed the zebra-stripped wallpaper and tiger print canopy bed, and opted for a yellow velvet armchair in the corner. "Maybe this is getting to be a problem for you."

"If we start talking about addiction, I would have to say that would make this the perfect birthday." Carol kicked her pumps off and sat on the edge of the bed. "Maybe I'll actually go get that psychic reading Tourmaline wants me to have."

"Psychic reading? Since when did you go woo-woo?"

"I'm not going woo-woo. She's giving it to me for a birthday present. The way my intuition is crapping out right now, I'm willing to give anything a try."

"Spoken like a woman committed to gambling."

"C'mon Z.D., let it drop."

"But I always let it drop. Think of it like a New Year's resolution."

"Jews don't make New Year's resolutions."

"You can't pull that on me anymore. If you don't do something, that doesn't make it a sacred cultural heritage."

"You know me too well. All right, then, so talk," Carol stood, took off the magenta vest her friends had somehow managed to get tailor-made to her measurements, and hung it up. She ran her hands down the soft silk, lost for a moment in the texture.

"I'm not sure what to say. Seven hundred's a lot of money. I know you've had some big wins before, but I don't want to see you pissing your mom's money away."

"Like the stock market crash? I lost more money in so-called socially responsible investments than I could ever imagine losing in the casino. I put almost all the money from the apartment building into Working Assets funds and they tanked. I don't like to even think about how much I lost." Carol rolled her shoulders.

"I expect you actually know to the dollar. But the stock market is going to go up again."

"So they say, Z.D. But, for instance, Molly left me Cisco stock that was over eighty bucks a share and now it's down to ten something. That's a long way back."

Z.D. drummed her fingers on the chair. "Are you worried about that?"

"I still have plenty, I guess. Probably it will come back and I've got time to wait. But I'm sticking with the tutoring for now." Carol arranged the pillows on the bed so she could use them for a backrest.

"All the more reason not to get any deeper into this gambling thing."

"One bad night is not a pattern. I agree it could be a problem if I was lying about something, hiding things, betting the rent. Something that would hurt someone else or myself. But I don't see that happening." Carol settled herself into the pillows.

"But how do we define hurt, especially in the early stages? Take your friend Sandra, for instance. She's always putting everything into her self-improvement schemes, which seem like the flip side of her alcoholism to me."

"I'm not sure I'm following you."

"You know, like going to the gym compulsively; or that time when she tried to convince everyone that water filters would change our lives." Z.D. gestured in the air.

"That was a hoot. But it didn't hurt anyone, and neither does going to the gym. And for all we know, water filters did change our lives."

"How can I put this?" Z.D. stared at the zebra pattern until she had to shut her eyes. "It's not any single activity—it's the loss of boundaries. She gets inside something and doesn't know when she's crossed a line, become completely convinced that a specific activity will save her, and us too, for that matter. It's a weird missionary zeal."

Carol nodded, considering. "But isn't that also, like, developmental? I mean, we've all had moments when we were true believers in something, and I gotta say, I miss that."

"Are we talking about the same thing still?"

"I have no idea. But twenty years ago I was certain I had the truth about not only the meaning of life, but how women became oppressed and what we had to do to change the world. I liked my mother's feminism and I'm sorry it went out of fashion. Maybe gambling distracts me from being disillusioned." Carol pulled at a loose thread on the bedspread.

"Maybe we should work on better illusions, then," Z.D. said.

"Aren't we always? But sometimes what I want is to get into that space where those—I don't know, what would you call them?—moral imperatives, I guess—where they don't exist, where I'm not worried—at least for an hour—about how I should send money to the Israeli women's peace movement or the Afghan women. Or that Bush is destroying the world. Everybody needs a break from being focused on current events."

"Don't tell me you're distracted by the news when you play craps. I've seen you. An earthquake couldn't break your concentration."

"That's what I'm saying. I don't have to think about the world when I gamble. It's a different kind of focus. I dare myself to up the ante, and it's exciting." She paused to consider what that excitement was about. "The thrill is you can know your fate in the course of a night, at least for that night, which is more than you can say about the fate of the rain forest."

"That's what scares me, honey." Z.D. shook her head.

"The fate of the rain forest? Okay, no joking. I understand what you're saying. Really. But it scares me not to. It scares me to spoon out my life in cautious, measured bets. I don't want to settle into being an old fart just yet. That doesn't mean I'm going to be stupid, but I want to take more risks, not less."

"I don't know, Carol. You could end up justifying taking risks that could destroy you. Or us."

"Damn, you're dramatic. And awfully puritanical for a dope dealer, you know? Talk about taking risks." Carol threw a small pillow at her.

Z.D. threw it back. "You know I gave that up—I just keep the

189

connections for my own stash and a couple friends. But dealing dope is a hell of a lot more respectable than having a liquor store in Oakland."

"Nobody we know owns a liquor store."

"Look, I'm worried, that's all. Sometimes it seems like you're just swinging around on the rope of the money itself." Z.D. slapped her left hand over her right fist, pleased with the image.

"I like that. The rope of money. It fits in with this jungle motif, don't you think? But I know the difference between swinging on a vine and a hangman's noose."

"For your sake, I hope so. So many folks get compulsive."

"Like your friend Nash and her computer games?"

"Well, maybe."

"Yeah, maybe." Carol bent over as best she could to examine the scarlet nail polish on her toes. Looking good. Only hippies do their nails and forget to check them. "See, when money's not involved, it's just time. You can watch your best friend blow days of her life, and as long as she goes to work and hangs out with you, what's the big deal about those lost hours? She's not doing anything that appears to have a physical effect—what difference do four hours of *Doom* at night make?"

"She says it helps inspire her set designs. Anyway, most of America watches television four hours a night. People gotta do something with their time."

"And we do lots of good, positive things, all of us. So what's the big deal about gambling? What is an addiction, anyway? I mean, what's the true definition?"

"I don't know. It's when you can't stop doing something."

"But why? I can't stop breathing—is that an addiction?" Carol put her hand on her chest with a flourish.

"Don't be flip."

"I'm not. I'm serious. I think we call too many things addictions. We've completely confused the difference between what's chemical and what's emotional."

"Aren't emotions all chemical, anyway?" Z.D. was getting both turned on and confused. She stood up and started to pace.

"Come on, you know what I mean. And I wish you wouldn't do that."

"Listen, Carol, just because you've got this all worked out in a neat package in your mind doesn't mean I have to agree."

"Agree with what?"

"With whatever you're trying to prove." Z.D. flopped back in her chair.

"I'm not trying to prove anything, for chrissake."

"You're trying to prove you're not an addict."

"I am no more a gambling addict than you're a dope addict. My mother would have said fiend. A dope fiend. How come we never use those good words any more?" Carol decided it was time to put on her nightgown.

"Because I'm not a dope fiend."

"And I am not a compulsive gambler. See—the difference is right there."

"What difference?" Z.D. got distracted, watching Carol take off her shirt and bra. She'd memorized the small arc of freckles over the fold of flesh that led into Carol's left breast and its appearance every night reassured her, the way, she imagined, that wild women centuries ago had been assured each night by the appearance of specific constellations in the night sky.

Carol was oblivious. "They say 'compulsive' about gambling, like having an obsessive compulsive disorder. It's not the same thing as addiction, that's all I'm trying to say. And I don't think I've been all that compulsive. Needing a break from reality, wanting to play a game, that's not necessarily compulsion." Z.D. started to say something, but Carol help up her hand. "Okay, I admit I've had some weird moments, but only a few. It's not that gambling can't be destructive—but it's a qualitatively different thing to have moments of compulsion than to be an addict, by which I understand you to mean being completely out of control. Out of your own control. Do I not seem to you like a woman in control?"

"Oh, very in control, I gotta admit. But I don't know why these semantics are so important to you." Z.D. leaned back, wishing she'd never started this discussion. How was she going to change the feeling?

"Because everything is semantics. How we construct our world view."

"Yeah, yeah—'Language is a virus.'"

"Very nice, Z.D. Who said that?" She pulled her nightgown over her head.

"Laurie Anderson, I think."

"No, she was quoting one of those old guys that hung around with Ginsburg—what was his name? You know, the one who wrote *Junkie*?"

"Oh, that was William Boroughs. I got something out of my college days after all."

"Yeah, that's him. See, Z.D., everything dovetails—dope and vocabulary." She pecked at Z.D.'s cheek before folding down the bedspread and getting under the sheet. At least the sheet was a solid color, even if it was black.

"You been smoking? Because you sound like you're stoned out of your mind."

"I'm not stoned," Carol said. "I'm thinking—it's just like you to confuse the two. That's what I meant about chemical reaction."

"Jesus."

"No really. You can be addicted to nicotine or hard drugs or caffeine—but if you like to start your day with a cup of chamomile tea, is that addiction?"

"Of course not. Up in the mountains of Peru—or somewhere in South America—they eat coco leaves, the stuff that cocaine's made of. The people say it gives them energy and helps them breathe at the high altitude. But Americans go in and say, hey, these people are all addicts. It's a cultural thing. We like to label some behaviors chemical and some emotional, but it doesn't make any difference. What counts is how you're judged for doing what you do, and what kind of power you give to the people judging."

Z.D. climbed into her own pajamas, which seemed somewhat silly to her, but what if one of the others walked in? Cordelia, for instance? None of the doors had locks.

"See, we agree." Carol patted the bed beside her.

"I'm not sure about that."

"But look Z.D.—Oprah gets on TV and says she's a food addict. How is that possible? Everyone has to eat. Is everyone a food addict? Is anyone who gains weight easily a food addict? So if someone eats twice as much as me, and rhapsodizes over the taste of spring flowers in the goat cheese, but is skinny, they're a gourmet, but if I get a craving for Cherry Garcia every couple months, I'm an addict?"

"You know I think that food addict stuff is crap. And I think you're gorgeous," Z.D. climbed in beside Carol and moved to bite her upper arm.

"Cut that out." Carol twisted away. "People can have eating problems, I believe that now, although it's complicated. That's what I mean. Eating is something we all have to do, but how we come to terms with what we eat is all social, it's call and response between us and our families and—"

"Yeah—and if I get a hunger to eat you?"

"Oh Zenobia." In Carol's mind, stacks of chips were falling, scritch scritch, a dull plastic wind chime. "I'm sorry honey. I know I should be, I *want* to be, but I'm just not in the mood."

193

17

"Take deep breaths," the psychic said.

"Okay." Carol watched Sophia close her eyes and roll her head—not like someone possessed in a horror movie, but as if she were stuck in traffic and stretching. After a few minutes, Sophia started to speak as if a robot had been programmed to talk in the throaty, growly voice of a 1940s movie star. "We are welcoming you, Carol."

"How do you know my name?"

"Sophia told us."

Well, of course. Carol almost laughed out loud.

"We are not Sophia," the voice said before Carol could respond out loud. Carol decided to try simply thinking her questions. Sophia kept her eyes closed, her hands on her knees. Silence spread like an oil slick across the room.

"Now we understand how you want us to proceed," the voice coming out of Sophia finally said. "Who are we? We are Javro. Let's say we are—how did you call it in your language?—on a crease many light years from your planet but enfolding it as well. We do not have a body in the sense you mean. We do have senses, though. It is not painful to speak through Sophia, but it can be tiring. We are not tired now.

"Why do we call ourselves 'we'? We do not think we are the Queen of England. Yes, we know who she is, but we are not involved with each other. We are many strands. Think of your DNA models. We are not like that, exactly, but it will help you understand. We are not what you call tricksters. We know what

194

you mean. We cannot tell you what to do. Although we do think you should use more yellow in your home. Because the color wants you. It is difficult to explain and not why you are seeking us.

"You are having trouble with inheritance. This is common in your species. We will discuss the physical presently. But we perceive you have something else unresolved. What you feel for the one who gave birth to you will settle. You have driven on dirt roads? The dust is kicked up by movement. It will settle. Yes, we do experience loss ourselves. We are not offended by your sarcasm. If you do not want us to talk about your father, we will not. Many women have anger they are ashamed of. But shame does not protect you from anger. It is possible you still enjoy this anger because it keeps your father alive. Yes, he is dead; he died in Asia. Your mother was correct. We do not know where they are now. We can only tell you what you have already learned from your science, energy is not lost in the universe. But we cannot always experience the place of balance. By 'we' here, we mean to include you.

"Now we will address your other question. Money is a complex human concept. We do not use currency, but we see that it is very important to you. You have a system of exchange in which many people cannot participate fully. We do not know why you organized it this way, although we do note your preference for—what is the word Sophia would use?—hierarchies. Pyramids. It is a misuse of the pyramid construct. They are meant for inside. To be inside them, where energy refracts and collects, where it could refresh you. To take the outer structure as a model seems to us like a joke for human bodies because if you sit on the top you must be very uncomfortable. We like points, but not culminations.

"Yes, we understand your problem. You have even such a pyramid on your American paper money. Is that correct? You yourself have a certain amount, which is finite. You might think of it like this. You could take all your resources and buy food. You would feed many hungry people. And yet you would still see before you as many hungry that you could not feed. And tomorrow you also would be hungry. Hunger is infinite. It is arrogance on your part

195

to think you can fix this. We do not advocate selfishness or what you would call hoarding.

"You are attracted to games of chance. We appreciate your impulse to take chances. Through chance, everything changes; you would call this evolution. But you must allow the change to change you. No, we are not trying to sound like your Delphic oracle. We only point out what you know. Repeating is molecular. But consciousness can apprehend pattern. When you apprehend it, you gain possibility. Mastery is the wrong word. The more skilled you become at recognition, the more you may choose among directions. You have the sport of riding on waves. You must know science, pattern, and your own ability in order to not be frustrated by your actions. The choices you make may still surprise you.

"We want you to think another way if you will. We want you to have pleasure. Even though we do not have a body in the sense you mean, we know from Sophia and from others about human pleasure. It is not what you might call duty, but sometimes it may come from responsibility. Responsibility is recognition of yourself in the other. So you see how it might be pleasurable for you to engage beyond your self. When you are having pleasure, you are not in pain. Pain is duty. We do not think you should be dutiful. We cannot tell you how to get this pleasure that is not duty although we—we appreciate your desire for instruction, for insight. We notice that you are in need of more cell salts. We recommend celery and blueberries. Now we are—tired. Sophia is tired."

Sophia's head jerked back slightly and she blinked her eyes. "That was weird," she said.

"Uh-huh. And what was weird about it for you?" Carol felt unexpectedly moved, but unsure about whether she'd been duped.

"Javro never tells people what to eat."

"She—he?—they? didn't tell me—just 'recommended.'"

"Well, Javro's always very polite."

196

A small laugh moved up from Carol's belly. "Yes, Javro's polite." Sophia gave Carol a tape of the session. She felt oddly light-hearted when she put it in her purse.

At home, Carol took out her brokerage statement, which showed a balance of $34,000 in the money market fund her investment advisor recommended. From a stack of old mail on her desk, she rooted out a donation envelope for Girls, Inc. Yvonne, the girl she'd been paired with—god, that was a long time ago already—had appeared sullen the entire semester they read together, Carol patiently waiting for her to spot the words Yvonne could recognize in children's books, the way Carol had been instructed. Even if it's only the "and"s and "but"s, the staff admonished, let her recognize them, let her take part. Slowly Yvonne began to sound out longer words, recognize more short ones. Carol did not want to parlay these small achievements into a premature success story; she saw the physical difference in the faces of girls whose parents picked them up, came to Girls, Inc. events. Those were open, generous children, who made jokes and put lots of sparkles on their art projects. The ones whose cousins or older siblings came because their single parent was working, fighting, sleeping off the night shift, had suspicion stamped on them already, and they were only seven, eight.

Seven. Eight. Breathing deeply into her stomach, Carol wrote a check for $500. She felt a tingle, or maybe it was more like a tickle, the sensation of a feather brushing her skin from the inside. Then she went into the kitchen and ate a bowl of yogurt and blueberries.

18

Her country was dropping bombs on Iraq. Again. Neither rage nor love stopped the patriarchs. Mass demonstrations appeared to have no effect, except on the marchers—Carol, Z.D., most of their friends had taken the BART into San Francisco in March for the huge rally. You had to show up for what was important. Carol looked at the children brought along to the demo, as if it were a picnic. She hoped none of those kids would ever find out first-hand how not-a-picnic war is. A small girl with elaborate braids stuck her tongue out at Carol, and Carol stuck her tongue out right back. Even though she'd worn sensible pumps, her legs ached while she strained to catch the speeches meant to whip them into action. What action now? They were marching already. E-mailing their senators did no good. Senator Feinstein had published an apologia in the paper, claiming she voted for war on the basis of her trust in the intelligence the White House gave the Senate.

"I'm a child of a flag-waving, working-class family, three thousand miles away from the fucking Senate, and I know they're lying. How can Diane Feinstein possibly believe this crap?" Z.D. threw the *Oakland Tribune* down on the breakfast table the day after the march. "It's like the whole country has amnesia."

"More like it's on a body-building kick," Carol said.

"Yeah, that's it. Nobody wants to be the ninety-pound weakling on the beach. We gotta flex our muscles and show the world."

"Your muscles are attractive, though," she said, coming up behind Z.D. and laying her head on her shoulder.

"But I don't use them to bully anybody. I just want to stay in shape."

"Maybe it's a fine line between being in shape and picking a fight." She felt a discomfort that started low in her abdomen. She straightened up.

"Picking a fight is always a choice. Those guys are assholes and they don't care about what we think or how many damn marches we go on." Z.D. took her dishes to the sink. "I'm going to work. You have students coming?"

"Not until the afternoon. I'm not feeling that well, Z.D. I'm going to get back in bed for a while. Seven a.m. is not exactly my time of day." Carol wrapped her bathrobe around her.

"You're sick?" Z.D. stared at her.

"Tired, probably. Don't worry, honey."

"I appreciate you keeping me company while I rant. Call me if you need anything."

Carol shuddered when the front door shut. Maybe it was menopause coming on, although her doctor said it would be unusual, since she'd started to bleed early. Maybe it was the war. Articles appeared announcing how we should not feel discouraged because it took a decade before the anti-war movement in the 1960s got a million people in the street. As if that war was gone. But everyday we still have Vietnam; Carol saw it in the grizzled men panhandling at the freeway exits and she read it in the news. She heard it on the radio, driving to buy groceries. Suddenly the men in charge had changed from World War II veterans to the men who dodged the Vietnam draft.

Not like my dad. What's the percentage of guys in the air force doomed to die? Maybe it's not that many more than get crushed in a 7.5 earthquake, statistically, which makes me a volunteer for someone's actuarial tables. But there's a difference between buying a ticket for a train and standing in front of it. He went and got himself blown up. Little Dad pieces falling onto the ground in a country I can only imagine. Is blood fertilizer, like bone meal? Are our cells fertile? Harold was in her bedroom, wiping blood off the buttons of his air force dress jacket. "Dad?"

It's all about three's, he mouthed, the three of us. He wasn't

199

speaking out loud—he was rubbing the buttons. But she could hear him. Don't drop the ball, stay close to home court. Something else about ashes. Dead people, why can't they just come out and say what they mean?

Rubbing his hands over his jacket, he looked up. "We're all naïve," he said. "For centuries generals dangle shock and awe. Was it a crime to want a medal for a reward, a medal to show you?" Puzzled, he patted his chest. His hand went through and came back dripping, coating the buttons with a fresh layer of blood. "Where's mine?"

This must be a pattern, she thought. War, numbers, courts, rewards. Sophia's Javro wanted her to surf the pattern. Know where you are, don't drop the ball. She was supposed to call Henry about the ball. About the women's basketball finals. Home. Home team? Chicago didn't even have a team, or Oakland. It was the Detroit Shock against the L.A. Sparks. Ashes come from sparks, but Detroit was certainly closer to home, and rising phoenix-like from the ashes of their terrible season last year. Homes were being destroyed across the globe. Shock and awe, her dad said. Something flared behind her eyes. Then Molly appeared, dressed in red—red shirt, red lounging pants, waving a red-tipped cigarette.

"Just like you to interpret things the way you want," her mother said.

"What way should I interpret them?"

Molly laughed. Cackled, actually. The dead do that. Was she still dead?

"C'mon, Mom, you said you were going to come back and bless me."

"I do bless," her mother said. "My blessing is a slam dunk."

"Thanks, Molly."

"Remember, you dream in your own language, kiddo, not necessarily mine."

Her father got on a bicycle. He turned to wave, and a shower of blood flew off the tips of his fingers, like a sprinkler. "Listen to your mother, honey. I wish I had."

When Carol got up an hour later, she called Henry. "Will you cover the women's basketball finals?"

"You know me. But let's talk personally."

"I can meet you in—an hour and a half?" Carol calculated the time it would take her to dress, go to the bank, get to Henry's shop, and be back in time for her first student.

"I can do that."

At the back of Henry's Steam Cleaning was a small alley, where a couple of vans with Henry's name on them straddled the sidewalk. Carol parked on the main street and walked halfway down the block to his back door.

Henry extended his hand to shake when she came in, but Carol stepped neatly sideways and sat in the chair next to his desk. "I'm not surprised you want some action on the WNBA finals, Rita. Even some of the guys are interested this year."

She played with the clasp on her handbag. "I want three thousand on the Detroit Shock—both in the first game and to win the series."

"Whoa, now that does surprise me. That's three times what you've ever bet before."

"I'm having a times-three inspiration."

Henry laughed. "It's sixty-six hundred with the vig. I can cover that if you can, but are you absolutely sure?"

"Are you my mother or my bookie?"

"Your associate, I believe." He rummaged through some papers on his desk, as if he hadn't looked this up before. "I can give you six points on Detroit for the first game. I'll tell you about the other two after."

"Sounds good," Carol said, looking at her watch.

"The game's not till Saturday. I'd like some security on that bet."

"I thought you might. Though I've always paid up, haven't I?"

"You're reliable as they come—and that's what we like, to keep everything nice and friendly. So I'm only asking for half, to cover that first game. What do they say in the movies? 'I ain't in this for my health.'"

"Oh, don't go gangster on me now, Henry."

He smiled and restacked his papers. "I'm just saying, it's another league when you start making these sizeable bets. I've got associates of my own."

Detroit lost the first game by 12.

Carol was at Henry's back door.

"I don't give refunds."

"I'm not asking for one. I want to double my bet on the Shock for tomorrow's game."

"Look, you just lost thirty-three hundred, and you're into me for another thirty-three. The Shock will have to win two in a row for that one to pay off. You want me to write another sixty-six? Rita, I got to question this."

"It's business, isn't it?"

"Yeah, but part of my business is making sure my customers stay healthy. I've known you for what, three years? You've never struck me as the out-of-control type."

"I'm not out of control, Henry."

"Losing what you can't cover can get nasty, and it wouldn't be me listening to your excuses. You understand that, right?"

"I figured," Carol said, looking him in the eyes.

"So you got that much cash?"

"If I lose, I can have it to you by Wednesday. Look." Carol pulled out her brokerage statement. Covering the account number with her finger, she put it in front of him.

"Nice," he said, "Very nice." Even deflated by the stock market crash, it was an impressive amount. He checked the statement's date, stroked the stubble on his chin, and chuckled. "And all this time I've been calling you Rita."

"Oops," Carol said, realizing she hadn't thought to cover her name.

"Oh, don't even think about it. My guys checked you out a long time ago."

"Really?" Carol felt a surge of bile make its way up her throat. All this time, some guys she didn't even know, not even Henry, had been scoping her out. That wasn't a position that good activists put themselves into willingly. Or any dykes. Maybe Z.D. was right—maybe it was time to quit. After this.

"Really. I'm not happy about this, though. I don't like taking away anyone's retirement."

"Happiness is vastly overrated," Carol said, pulling back the statement. "If I lose tonight, I can sell some stock when the market opens on Monday. You will absolutely get paid, and I won't have to resort to crime to pay you."

"This is going to be a big loss for you, ma'am."

"I would appreciate your not 'ma'am-ing' me, Henry."

"Thought you turned forty already. Isn't that when we get to call girls 'ma'am'?"

"You get to call women, women."

"Listen, Carol,"—he drew her real name out in a lengthy breath—"I'll write your damn bet if you lay off the feminist lectures. I can live quite nicely without them."

Carol folded up the statement and put it in her purse. He used to be so polite down at Diamond Lil's. "Then we have a deal?"

"Okay, but you only get two points on the Shock for this one."

"Two is fine with me."

"Deal, then, if you'll shake."

Carol extended her hand, and Henry sighed.

The Shock had a huge lead at half time in the second game, sixteen points. Then their offense stalled, and they were down four points with less than two minutes on the clock. Carol was alone, perched on the edge of the couch. She'd been relieved when Z.D. got a call an hour before about vandalism at the store. What kind of girlfriend does that make me when I don't want my lover to figure out how deep I am into the game? They were supposed to go over to Nash's, but Carol insisted she was okay at home—she had lessons to prepare for tomorrow anyway.

"Just some damn taggers, I think, but the cops thought someone might have tried to jimmy the lock. They think they're my pals now."

"Are they?"

"Cops are cops. Only yeah, there's a gay cop downtown, Gary, who works on the mentoring project with me. He says being a cop is a more honest way to give back to your community than being a politician. We argue, but he has a point."

"A hierarchic, state-supported point," Carol said, frowning.

"You notice I haven't invited him to dinner. Still, I have to check this out, honey. You sure you're okay?"

"I'm fine. A little guilty about not going with you."

"Hey, both of us don't have to have our Sunday afternoon ruined."

"I hope it's not ruined for you—why don't you go on to Nash's when you're done?"

"Yeah?" Z.D. wrinkled her brow, appearing pleased to have the evening open up. She hadn't hung out with Nash alone for a couple of months.

"Call me to let me know everything's alright—but sure, go over to Nash's, order a pizza, chill."

"Did I ever tell you you're a great honey?"

Carol grinned, straightening Z.D.'s collar. It didn't really need to be messed with, but she liked making the gesture. "Oh, go on, get out of here."

Now she was glad Z.D. couldn't see her agitation. She could feel Molly glaring at her from outer space. "You're not supposed to curse me, Mom. You promised."

"Did I know you were going to take such insane chances?"

"It's only money, Molly."

"The flesh of the living is fed with money, child."

Carol squeezed her eyes shut. Goddammit, goddammit. But then Holland-Corn got the ball. She heard the crowd shout, and felt the world lurch in a different direction. "Yes, Kedra, that's it, take the shot. Yes! Yes!" Kedra made a 3-point and the Shock were back. Nolan made her free throws and bam! The Shock by one. Carol jumped up.

"Yes, yes! Goddamit, I was right. I was fucking right. Oh, thank you, Molly."

"Hey!" Molly yelled into some September wind passing by, "you can't use me this way." But Carol wasn't listening.

Carol called Henry first thing Monday. "Let it ride, Henry."

"Are you nuts? You were lucky on that one. I'm willing to give you the twelve grand—"

"I get the vig back when I win, Henry. That would be twelve-six."

"Yes it would, if you're going to get technical on me. But if I wrote this bet, the vig would be twelve hundred. I'm not supposed to cover bets over ten grand."

"C'mon, Henry. You must be getting a lot of action on this."

"Bets are being made. And I'll grant you, mostly on L.A."

"So even if I win, you'll be fine, right?"

"I'm not in this to be fine."

"Henry. Let it ride."

"I expect you to show up with the ninety-nine you're going to owe me when the Shock lose Tuesday."

"I'll give it to you in quarter rolls."

"Very funny."

"I'm a funny kind of gal."

"So I notice." Henry let a stream of air out through his nose. "What are you chewing over there, Henry?"

"Antacids. You're giving me indigestion. Okay, this time you have to take two points on the Shock."

"You know you should be giving me two," she said.

"You want the Vegas point spread, go to Vegas. Take it or leave it."

"Taken."

The Detroit Shock won the WNBA finals on September 16th, a complete turn-around from their previous season, when they were worst in the league. NBA star Karl Malone watched his daughter Cheryl make four free throws in the final minute, sealing an 83–78 victory over L.A.

Nash, who had touched off Myra's jealousy again, was hiding out with Carol and Z.D., and even turned off her cell in order to concentrate on the game. Toward the end, she noticed Carol mashing potato chips up in her hand. "Something's wrong with your girl," Nash said to Z.D.

"She has been unusually agitated this evening," Z.D. nodded.

"Hush up. Look at Riley—and Nolan's going to connect for the trey! That's what I mean. Threes all the way." Carol was riveted to the TV.

"Yes!" Nash and Z.D. yelled simultaneously. "That's it, that's the game."

"I don't believe it," Carol whispered.

"Yeah, some come back," Z.D. said, getting up. "Man, you've done a number on those chips. You'd think you—" she stopped short. "Oh fuck, you had money on the game."

"Leave her alone, Z.D. She's always got money on the game," Nash said.

But Z.D. kneeled down in front of Carol. "On the Shock?"

"Yeah," Carol said, biting her lip.

"How much?"

"I—you're not going to believe me."

"Believe her," Nash yelled.

"Shut up, Nash. How much?"

"Counting what I lost on the first game?"

"Yeah, sure, counting what you lost on the first game."

"I won twenty-seven grand."

Nash stood up and started dancing around. "Twenty-seven grand? You the dyke! We are all im-pressed!"

Z.D. plopped on the floor. "Jesus fucking christ. I don't know whether to hug you or to leave you."

"Leave her? Why would you leave her?"

"Nash, think about it. She must have had something like fifteen grand riding on the last five minutes of that game. Five fucking points. She could have lost everything."

"I'm right here," she said quietly. "And I didn't lose. I won."

"How can you take a risk like that?"

Carol got up and shut off the TV, where Nancy Lieberman was

interviewing MVP Riley. She tapped her foot slowly. "Well, you know I checked the stats. But it's not all that logical."

"Try me."

"I think maybe I'll go order a pizza or something," Nash said.

"Stay here, Nash. I want you to hear this."

"It's not such a big deal. I had a dream."

"What!" Z.D. got off the floor and sat back on the couch.

"My father came to me in a dream."

"And told you to bet on the Detroit Shock? I'm not buying this."

"You don't have to. He didn't say 'Carol, I want you to bet the farm on Detroit.' It was how I interpreted it."

"You should write a dream book. Dream books are very big sellers where I come from. You could sell a million copies and stop gambling," Nash said.

"She could sell five million copies and not stop gambling. That's the problem, Nash."

"Este, Z.D., I know you are upset with Carol, and I agree that maybe she put too much on the line. But wouldn't the problem be if she lost? Shouldn't we be celebrating? Maybe, I don't know, buying a new car?"

Z.D. laughed. "You going to buy me a new Mustang, honey?"

Carol relaxed. It was going to be all right. She was not going to do this again, not bet like this. It was too much, Z.D. was right. She'd give the money away, half of it, anyway—LABIA had fallen apart, but she could give it to one of those Lesbian foundations she liked, Astraea or NCLR. Then the phone rang.

"Is this Rita—I mean, Carol?" A sneer materialized across the line into Carol's ear.

"Who's calling?"

"We're not going to pay you, dyke."

"Who is this?"

"Not your boyfriend Henry, that's for sure."

"Is Henry okay?"

"Henry's dandy. He wants you to know you're cut off. And don't go bothering him about this. He's a very busy man right now."

"He has to pay. He's always paid."

"Yeah? For what? You got a receipt?"

"He wrote my bet. We shook on it."

"He says you dykes fixed the game. We don't pay for that kind of shit."

"How could I fix the game? I don't even know anyone in Detroit."

"Do I sound like I care?" The man hung up.

"That didn't sound good. So much for honor among gamblers," Z.D. said.

"It's not funny, Z.D." Carol was poised to dial Henry's number.

"Let's think about this. Before it gets worse," Z.D. stayed her hand, but Carol shook it free in annoyance.

"How worse can it get? I'm calling Henry." She pressed "0" on her speed dial, and heard an unfamiliar voice.

"Jackson here."

"I'm calling for Henry."

"Henry's on vacation. How can I help you?"

"When will he be back?"

"Let's see—Carol, is it?"

"How did you know that?"

"Caller ID," Jackson said. "Not much of a mystery. But I don't think Henry will want to talk to you. You have a good day, now."

Carol and Z.D. stared at each other. Nash was putting away the chips and debris from their long afternoon in the living room watching TV. "I'm not bailing or anything, but I promised to go help out for Marga Gomez's performance over at La Peña."

"I'd like you to stay a little while if you can. We've seen those shows—how complicated can her stage be? It's a black set with lights." Z.D. asked.

"It's not how complicated the stage is. It's how complicated the woman's intent gets—how you arrange the room to receive it." Nash picked up her backpack and checked her cell for messages. "See?" she said, flashing the cell at them. "Seven messages, and only two of them from Myra. I gotta go."

208

"All right, Nash. Catch you later." Z.D. turned back to Carol. "How about I check this out? Make some inquiries."

"With whom?"

"The guys I know on the force—that cop I was telling you about last weekend, Gary. Remember?"

Carol sat down, feeling like the wind had been punched out of her. "I remember."

"And maybe that woman from PG&E who got me into those Chamber of Commerce meetings—"

"What would someone from PG&E know about bookies?"

"You'd be surprised what goes on downtown. What people with money know about." Z.D. rubbed her philtrum, which made Carol smile. "You know what she said to me?"

"I look forward to finding out."

"That the city movers and shakers are interested in tapping into what us 'alternative lifestyle' women are doing. She actually said that while 'gay men had more money, as a demographic, gay women were much more active in Oakland across the spectrum.' They want me because they think I'm a successful, traditional businesswoman who can report on the lesbians, because, get this, she said they found us 'opaque.'"

"Opaque?"

"Honest to god, fucking opaque. Anyway. I can ask around. How much did you actually lay out?"

"I gave Henry thirty-three hundred on the first game, which I lost. He had me down for another thirty-three for the series. I doubled my bet on the second game and he gave me credit because I showed him my Schwab statement—and I never backed out of a bet. Then after I won that one, I let it ride on the third, that's how it got so big. But I only actually gave him the thirty-three." Carol sighed. "I could write it off as continuing education."

"You are something else. No wonder the bookies are scared of you."

"I'm a little scared of them tonight myself."

"Don't worry. Z.D.'s here to protect you."

209

"Yeah, but Z.D., don't you think it might be risky to go to the cops about this? Like we could set something in motion that could be much more dangerous than losing three grand?"

"Didn't you say you won twenty-seven thousand dollars?"

"I learned from the stock market crash that it's just paper until you've got it in your hand." Carol bent over and rebuckled her sandals. And then rebuckled them again.

"So you think we should fold? Give up as soon as some assholes growl at us?"

"We? You're taking this on now?"

"You bet I am." Z.D.'s started to pace.

"And you know how I like to bet, Z.D. But how come—for the money, or to protect my honor?" Carol admired Z.D. when she got like this—riled up, intent on figuring out how to fix something. It almost made her smile.

"Well, almost anything for your honor. But really because I don't like to see women pushed around. And I don't like it that there's some—what?—some gang of guys out there who think we're such pushovers."

"I don't like it either, you know. But they don't play fair."

"Not right now. But think about it—they're in business too. They don't want it going around that they weaseled out on a bet, right? Or that they roughed somebody up for winning."

"Probably not, probably not even if she was a dyke," Carol agreed, considering.

"Then let me try to take care of it. Okay, babe?"

19

The red strobe startled Carol. How long had the cops been following her?

"Okay, ma'am. Do you know why I stopped you?" The policeman shone a flashlight directly in her eyes.

"Um—" Fuck. What are you supposed to say? She hadn't been speeding, had she? Run a stop sign? "Sorry, officer, no clue." Polite honesty, that should work. She smiled at him, pulling her head away from the bright light.

"You were all over the road. Been partying, huh? Let's see your license."

Partying? She'd been over at Tourmaline's with Kaneesha and Tina, talking about why LABIA had run out of steam. Mostly, they agreed, because no one wanted to deal with giving the money away—too fraught, too time-consuming, too subject to recriminations. They'd gone back to holding once a year community "educationals"— discussions about how and why to share resources, how to deal with class. If twenty dykes showed up for one of those, they considered it a success. "We should write a pamphlet and give it up," Tina had said, in-between mouthfuls of the vegan lentil stew Tourmaline made. Not bad for vegan, Carol thought. Even the wine was vegan—organic, no sulfites, lowers cholesterol. She'd had one glass. Right? Not more. That had to have been a good hour ago.

"Step out of the car, ma'am."

In restaurants, when wait-people called them "ma'am," her friend Ginny always said, "We're not ma'ams—we're dykes!" Clearly this would not be a good strategy now.

"Recite the alphabet backward, ma'am."

"Excuse me?" Carol shook her head. What was going on here? It was after ten, and San Pablo Avenue was very quiet. The few cars going by didn't even slow down to look. She wouldn't have either.

"You heard me." The cop's tone turned nasty. Up close, she could see a day's beard growth, and smelled garlic and beer on his breath. She should be paying more attention, she realized. He was a good foot taller than Carol, probably ten years younger, white. He had a small scar under his left eye.

"Okay. Z Y X uh W V U—" Carol squinted, picturing the alphabet in her mind. It would have been easier to count backward from a hundred by sevens, but you can't choose your sobriety test.

"That's enough. Now turn around—" he thunked his flashlight hard on her shoulder.

"Ow! What—"

"Motor response. Go on, turn around, walk a straight line to that lamppost and back."

Carol pulled herself in, together. She walked what she thought was a very nice straight line.

"Yeah," the cop said. "You been partying all right. Big night out with the dykes, huh? You know what DUI means? You'll have to come down to the station."

"I'm not drunk!"

"You arguing with me?"

"Aren't you supposed to give me a breathalyzer test?"

"You arguing with me?" he said again, more loudly, in her face, holding the big, metal flashlight up.

"No."

"I'm taking you in. You can lock your car before I cuff you."

"Cuff me?"

"This isn't twenty questions, you cunt."

With the handcuffs biting into her skin, Carol got into the squad car. Not giving her the breath test meant she could get this thrown out, she knew. But how do you throw out this powerless-

212

ness, this rip in your life, this way a man can invade you, force you into his trip? And when Z.D. came to bail her out, how would she get treated? The best she could hope for was unapologetic snickering. Snickering into our faces, our relationship. Suddenly familiar, safe Oakland turned and snarled, a tiger jumping out of the night, tearing, tearing at her flesh.

20

Take care of it. Protect her. Who do I think I am, Bruce Springsteen? Z.D. squinted at the vein in her left eyelid. Now that she was forty-five, it made her look distinguished, she decided, and took the focus off that softening happening around her neck. She was staring in the crizzled mirror of the tiny bathroom next to her office, with its view over the floor of her discount paper empire. She'd been promoted to regional director a year ago, which, among its many benefits, gave her the opportunity to see her parents every couple months—short visits, an afternoon, the perfect length.

Getting old. She slapped her cheek as if all her skin needed was a stern reminder to move back into place. In some seniors' lecture her ma had dragged Dad to, they'd been told that reading prevented Alzheimer's, and her dad, who had never bothered with anything besides instruction manuals, suddenly became a reader. He read everything on the bestseller lists, whatever got nominated for a prize. Z.D. would come to visit and he'd be sitting in his recliner with a beer, reading *Angela's Ashes*. She was relieved—not that she cared that much about his mind, but now when he talked he actually had things to say, and most of the time he was too engrossed to say anything besides hi, which took a big burden off her ma. And besides, if her dad could change, it meant anyone could.

People can change, she said out loud. Carol could change. Would she want to? Do I want her changed? A while back, co-dependency was the psychological catch phrase of the day, co-dependent and enabler. But what was that about, anyway? We are actually desperate to enable each other, to make an impact on someone else. Maybe we got more sophisticated about the human condition. Or maybe the fad got supplanted by something else, because you could say all those guys willing to enlist for Iraq were co-dependents, enablers of the war machine. And guys don't like to get that sticky women's psych stuff all over them. What is it we do now? Perform ourselves—nah, that can't have trickled down to Indiana yet. Z.D. cocked her head, checking out her own performance. "Change your own damn self," she said out loud.

Back in her office, she fiddled with her mechanical pencil, adding more lead, sticking in a new eraser, while she stared at the snapshot of Carol standing in front of Latourell Falls on that trip to the Gorge they'd finally taken the year before Carol's mom died. Carol looked happy. She'd been fucking happy. I used to make Carol happy, and I bet she'd insist I still make her happy, but I'm not so sure.

When Carol came up to me that day in the theater, it was like—what does Nash say it is in Greek drama?—deus ex machina, a goddess dropping down in a basket to change my plot. As if Madonna, Bette Midler, and Nell Carter all morphed into one big femme and fell in my lap. A fucking fairytale. Maybe I'm the real addict here. Every time I come home, I'm amazed she's still there, still wants me. No, she put her fingers up to her lips, no, that's not right. She wants me. What am I afraid of, then? That she wants something else more than me? And I've become too tame to her, too predictable.

She cracked her knuckles. Her store manager, Patrice, a tall, stocky African-American woman, knocked on the glass door, startling Z.D.

"That last shipment of paper from Cascade was two cartons short of what the invoice claims," Patrice said.

"Can you take care of that?"

"No problem. I wanted you to know, in case it shows up in other stores."

"I appreciate that. Patrice—"

"Anything wrong, Z.D.?"

"No. Thanks for not calling me Miz Dallas anymore. You're doing a good job down there."

Patrice flipped the beads at the end of her braids. "Told you you wouldn't be sorry about promoting me."

"Never crossed my mind." She had been sorry to fight with upper management about it, though. They'd acted like she'd double-crossed them by hiring too many women. Too many Black women. Not that they'd actually said it that way, here in the new millennium. "We want qualified people. We want to make sure we have an appropriate applicant pool," was their mantra. You have to treat that shit carefully, with documentation as thick as diapers. She snorted at the image and took a swallow of cold coffee. Kind of amazing they'd ever let her get this far. Maybe they'd known her so long they'd forgotten she was a woman.

Do men ever forget dykes are women? If Dad, Billy, Jake, Amos, and Jed were a representative sample, then no. They all had their different ways of reminding her, polite or violent, it didn't make that much difference—some kind of invisible door got shut. She knew plenty of guys who were nice enough in business, because they had a stake. And Gary and even his straight cop partner, whom she'd talked to yesterday about Carol, were OK. Turned out that catching bookies was lower on their priority list than marijuana busts—white-collar crime, kind of. They'd hinted that the cop who tried to pin that drunk-driving charge on Carol two nights ago might be on the take. That confused Z.D. "You mean he didn't stop her because of how she was driving?" she'd asked them.

"Maybe not," Gary said, hooking his fingers in his belt, trying to look as not-gay as he could for his partner, Z.D. figured. "Personally, I think somebody told him to harass her." His partner frowned. "Off the record. You didn't hear it from us."

"Hear what?"

The partner let out his breath. Right answer, Z.D. thought.

Then he said, "Maybe your friend should go on a trip, leave town for awhile. That mentoring program you started, that's okay. I got a couple kids you could try to find spots for, you think?"

"Sure, ok—" Z.D.'s confusion slipped into her voice.

"Quid pro quo," Gary said, smiling.

"College boy," the partner said, and Z.D. saw that he explained away Gary's queerness by chalking it up to class.

"We could try to smooth things over, negotiate," Gary said.

"Okay, yeah," Z.D. agreed. They must have gone to diversity training in order to handle both their own rogue guys and queers with such calm. Oakland's a big, integrated city and she'd seen its gay police contingent marching in the San Francisco Pride Parade on TV. Things have changed.

But underneath—not always—but enough—or when you touch some nerve, question the wrong thing—this power struggle stuff squirts up in your face, gets all over you. Carol was so humiliated the other night she couldn't even look at Z.D. Put up your dukes and fight like a man. Oh, you're not a man? Ha ha, our mistake, little lady, have a nice day. It must be something to pass, like the drag kings and trannies do. But then you have to always worry that somebody like Jake would find out—he'd stomp the piss out of a passing woman or a trannie without batting one of his beautiful long eyelashes. Suppose she told Michaels, the guy who owned this outfit, she was transitioning? He'd laugh in her face. Probably. She leaned back in her desk chair.

Never felt like a woman, whatever the hell that is, and don't want to be a man. Why wasn't it enough to be a dyke? She didn't want to transition, no matter how often her workout-buddy Willy said, "Don't knock it if you haven't tried it." Willy said T made you feel like a horse, and it would help that sag on her jawline too. Z.D.'s hand went up to her chin. How would that be different than some straight woman getting a face-lift? Why is this always such a big fucking deal? Fucking gender identity.

Not that she hadn't thought about it—how could you not? Everyone was on about butches getting in touch with their masculinity.

217

She didn't like it. Sure, maybe some people are born miserable in their skins and nothing can help them except changing sex. She had to allow for its possibility, although it didn't strike her as right. It's messed up that some boy needs to cut his prick off in order to wear a dress, and a woman needs to cut her tits off to do construction. On the other hand, one of her dad's great aunts used to tell her that if god had meant men to fly, he'd have given them wings. You don't hear that much anymore. Technology morphs the world, our expectations of the world, so why not let it change our cellular structure too? Maybe she was stuck in the past, some outdated twentieth-century conception of a fixed body.

Maybe. And maybe butch is really about getting past masculinity. Opposites attract, blah de blah—sure she liked it when Carol did her "real woman" thing—the lace panties, the nail polish, the bustier. It was fun. But it was on the surface. You can't help being molded by your place in time—you could see it in the ducktails and rolled up sleeves in photos of '50s butches with femmes in flouncey poodle skirts on their arms. All the butches wanted to be James Dean. But underneath all that, what you did, what she and Carol did when they were in tune, jumped over that. Leaped clear through. That was what was so great about being a dyke—inside you could be free, not have to get stuck in being boy or girl.

Did those dykes mainlining testosterone ever stop to think that maybe they were responding to all the militarism going down now? It seemed to Z.D. that the world had taken a giant step backward into woman-hating. Hate us if we wear a tie, hate us if we take the veil, hate us if we show up naked, hate us in disguise. She scribbled her "hate us" litany in a small spiral notebook she pulled out of her desk drawer.

She glanced at the page before, where she'd written, more than a month ago, "I am not a boi not a man I am not strapping it on I am not worshipping cock I am not glad we're at war I am not envious oh yes, oh yes I am. I got big time envy. I am jealous of lieutenant control. Give me the damn remote, you're going to destroy the world. And damn if they don't." Kind of a theme

218

emerging there, Z.D. said to herself. Nash knew Z.D. was a closet poet. Nash was on her case about hiding it. "You think it's weak? That why you hide this stuff in your desk?" Nash had a nasty habit of opening drawers. Maybe it came from being the kid of doctors, hanging out in offices with cabinets full of shiny, mysterious equipment.

"Hell, no. You got to be tough to be a poet—Audre Lorde, June Jordan, Chrystos, Anzaldúa, Alix Olson—I'm just not any good. And it's a sign of strength to admit your failings." Nash dragged her to poetry slams sometimes, when she wasn't dragging her to some play. Once she'd heard a trannie read a poem about how, now that he was full of testosterone, he fantasized about raping women when they got in the elevator with him. He was cool, he was a real man. The audience actually clapped. Nash had turned to her, grimacing, whispering, "What the hell is going on here?"

If that's what transitioning did for you, no thanks. Besides, messing with her hormones made her nervous. She'd studied enough biology and gone to enough of those holocaust movies to figure out that queers were a dispensable population, and doctors loved to experiment with people nobody gave a shit about. Everybody's so desperate for a little power—maybe it's because the world is so overcrowded.

It's good to have power, though, she murmured. I want power. Hell, Carol wants power, that's what all that gambling is about. Some of it, anyway. I want the power to make those dicks give her the money, and stop harassing her. Not like she can't take care of herself. But I've got contacts she doesn't. Is that what power is, who you know? Who you know, who you are, what you've got. Both her desk line and cell phone rang at the same moment. She took the business call. Back to reality, buckaroos.

When she'd finished yelling at the supplier, she called Nash back. "Hey, buddy, what's up?"

"Can't remember your place in phone tag? You called me."

"Oh yeah. Listen, Nash, I want to ask you a favor."

"What else is new?"

219

"Hey, I don't ask for much."

"Actually, you never ask for enough in my humble opinion."

"Well, then. You busy this week?"

"Not very. I finished the sets for *Mother Courage*, and my next gig with Theater Rhino doesn't start for three weeks. The Rep wants me to submit sketches for their next production but that's not a big deal. Why you interested in my schedule?"

"I was thinking maybe you'd be willing to take a trip with Carol."

"Me? What's wrong with you?"

Z.D. could hear the skritching Nash's old-fashioned steel pen made. Better than playing video games while we're talking, she thought. "I'm jammed here, and besides, I want to stay in town and follow my leads."

"I don't know, Z.D. What's Carol say about this?"

"We talked it over last night. She was really knocked for a loop by that drunk driving ticket."

"Yeah, that's fucked up. It's not Carol."

"No, they don't have a breathalyzer on her or anything. I'm pretty sure we can get it thrown out. Anyway, at first she didn't want to go."

"See, she never liked me, my friend."

"Dammit, Nash, it's not about you."

"Hey, compadre, dial it back. I'm joking."

"Sorry. I'm a little uptight. And I've never seen Carol so unsure of herself, shaky. I appealed to her sense of intrigue, and she finally agreed it might be a good idea." Z.D. got an image of them all dressed in '40s film noir clothes—Carol in a dress with one of those long, scalloped hems and her and Nash in fedoras, with watch chains hanging out of their pockets. Maybe we've all seen too many movies. Me and the bookies.

"That's some favor you're asking," Nash said, stalling.

"You said I never asked for enough."

"But when you do, you sure know how to ask big."

"You don't like my girlfriend?"

"You're not going to trap me with that, amiga. I am very fond of your girlfriend. She's an interesting lady and quite a handful, in more than one way."

Z.D. frowned. "Be careful there, Nash."

"You know you agree. We have different tastes in handfuls, that's all."

"And that's why I feel comfortable asking you. Unless you think Myra would be upset."

"Myra and me—" Nash sighed. "I think I've got to give that up for good this time."

"That bad, really?"

"She's too insecure."

"You have stepped out on her more than once, Nash."

"Okay, I'm too immature. I've given her reason. I'm commitment phobic. I have ambivalence about going with white girls. I am polymorphously perverse."

"I'll pick perverse for five hundred dollars. But that does free you up to leave town for a week."

"A week with Carol?" Nash still sounded dubious, but the skritching had stopped. Maybe she was giving in.

"She doesn't fucking bite. I'd like it if you could keep her away from casinos."

"Pick a place without them. I'm not going to be her police."

"Sorry." Z.D. closed her eyes, apologizing to Carol too. Wanting to fix things has a way of spilling over into trying to control things. Even your lover, whose wildness you profess to admire. "But you'll do it?"

"I walked right into that one." Nash laughed into her handset before she snapped it shut.

21

"Those damn waves," Carol said, fanning herself with the hotel bill, "can't they do something about them?"

"It's not a sound machine they can turn off. People travel hundreds of miles for this rural peacefulness," Nash said as she folded her boxers neatly in the second bureau drawer, which was cedar-lined. Nice touch, she thought.

"It's not peaceful, Nash. Rural peace is a damn myth. First the flies, then the waves, and the racket all those seagulls and crows are going to make in the morning!"

"Some people are up in the morning."

"Some people! Next you'll tell me some people have binoculars and they're out at dawn identifying the damn species." Carol banged the wooden hangers around in the closet. She didn't like herself like this—grumpy, tight.

"Well some people do. Even your enamorada, Z.D., has been known to gaze at a bird or two. It's not like being convicted of DUI."

"I was not convicted of anything. The charges have been reduced to running a stop sign—which I did not."

"You were lucky."

"Luck has nothing to do with it, and I should know. One glass of wine was all I had—it was a potluck postmortem for LABIA. You've been in enough meetings with me to know I don't get drunk when we're talking about community."

"I'm not doubting you, Carol."

But Carol's exasperation made her feel like she wasn't being heard. "You've been known to drink considerably more than that some afternoons while you hammer away on stage. You know I was set up. That's why that cop didn't want to give me the breathalyzer—it would have showed I was sober. Z.D.'s friend on the force says if the cop who wrote the ticket doesn't show in court next month, the whole thing will be dropped, and they've persuaded him not to show." Carol shook her head. "Who knew we'd end up so cozy with our sworn enemies?"

This was going to be a hell of a long week, Nash realized for the fifteenth time. How did she end up here? Friend of a friend who knew a writer who went to a retreat near this hotel, recommending it for a hideaway holiday. A night in Minneapolis, a rental car, a sunny drive, and here they were. She'd only had to dodge one casino on the way up.

"We're in the middle of nowhere. Wouldn't it be fun to see Minnesotans in their natural habitat?" Carol had said when she spotted the billboard.

"Didn't you say you were going to cut back on the gambling?" Fuck it, Nash had thought, sparring already.

"C'mon, Nash. Think of it as sociology."

"I'm sure we'll have enough of that sociology around the lake. And anyway, isn't the point keeping a low profile?" She'd found it momentarily funny, helping Z.D.'s wide girlfriend cast no shadow.

Now Nash hung a Guyabera shirt she was particularly fond of next to Carol's blouses. 'Rican fashion could be a wrong choice up here in white-land, she thought, grimacing.

"Stop smirking, Nash, it doesn't become you." Carol picked up the pamphlets on the night table and plopped on the bed. "I don't know how much lower profile you can get than Lutsen, Minnesota. Did you look at this tourist brochure? They are actually touting a haying. I mean, a haying? Isn't that when men on tractors mow their overgrown lawns and ball it up for the cows to eat? What is to tout about that?"

"Give me that." Nash pulled the pamphlet out of Carol's hand. "They don't hay here, we're on the fucking shore. See, this is inland." Sitting down, she stuck the picture of a boy admiring a haystack under Carol's nose.

"It indicates their mindset, doesn't it? That the tourist bureau would pick a picture of a haystack over these stupid tiny waves. People—all those people you invoke as the normal standard—like pictures of waves. I know."

Bright, clear blue water surging against the ancient walls of Old San Juan flashed in Nash's memory. She'd never seen a blue like that anywhere in the States. She sucked her lips in and ran her tongue along their surface inside her mouth, which made a puckering noise when she released her lips to speak. "Normal standard. You've got me there. It's been a long time since we've been normal, hasn't it?"

Carol reached across the bed to ruffle Nash's hair. "Remember 'fluffing your aura'? Huh? I bet I could fluff you up good out here in the boonies."

"Cut that out," Nash said, standing up and straightening her polo shirt. "I'm not interested. They've got a bar downstairs. And a pool table."

"Oh that would be low profile—two city dykes playing pool among the Swedish and Canadian white folks."

"And you are what, silver?—and don't give me any crap about the construction of the races—they'll look right through us. As long as you don't start hustling someone or pick a fight with me, they'll tell their daughters not to stare and try to pretend we don't exist. You're not famous—not even infamous except to your friends and bookies."

"Who's trying to pick a fight now?"

"Carol, you want a drink or not?"

"Since when did you get to be such a barfly?"

"Isn't that what people come here to do, drink? Neither of us are driving anywhere tonight and we're under no obligation to start the seven steps."

"It's twelve steps. Seven stations of the cross. Or is that seven deadly sins?" A wisp of confusion crossed Carol's face.

Nash laughed. "Nice to see you Jewish girls keeping track."

"That's what we're supposed to do, keep track. I can't believe I agreed to come to this goyish place the day before Rosh Hashona."

"You had plans for Rosh Hashona?"

"I like to make a chicken and light a candle."

"No doubt they have chicken on the menu, and we can find a candle. It's one of those portable holidays, true?"

"All Jewish holidays are portable, Nash—we're a wandering people. At least we were." Carol fanned herself again, this time with the tourist brochure.

"Apparently, you still are." Nash was getting restless. "You'd think a fancy lodge like this would have air conditioning. It's not supposed to be this hot at the end of September." She struggled to get the window up the last two inches of the frame. Although she succeeded, some of the paint flaked off on her hands. She washed them in the sink.

"The better to hear the waves, don't you think?" Carol fidgeted with her cuticles.

"Stay here if you want. I don't care. I'm going to the bar. Maybe I'll find you that candle." Nash checked her reflection in the bathroom mirror, caressing her hair flat, and headed for the door.

"I'm coming, I'm coming," Carol said. "What's that smell in the hall?"

"Chlorine's my guess—the pool's at the end of the corridor."

"At least I can swim," Carol said with a faint smile.

Nash had a Becks on tap. Carol had a Bloody Mary, "How I like my vegetables," she said.

"That's original."

"Play nice, Nash."

"I'm bored already," Nash shredded her napkin into three neat, separate piles.

"There were those signs—"

"We're not going."

"C'mon, Nash, it's just an hour north of here."

"There's a casino an hour from everywhere in the damn country now. We're not going."

"It's dinky. Just a couple blackjack tables and slot machines."

"How do you know? Oh, never mind. You must know the layout of every casino west of Biloxi."

"I looked it up on the internet before we came out here. I was in Biloxi once, though, the second or third summer I drove to college. I thought it would be romantic to take a southern detour, see the crabbers walk out into the Gulf of Mexico with lanterns at low tide. But it was before they had casinos there. I really liked that one south of Albuquerque." She bit into her celery. "South? Yes, the one on the north side only had blackjack. But they had a good crap game to the south—it was my first big win." She had a quick flash of Kylie's Cat in the Hat boxers, but she wasn't about to share that with Nash.

"Jesus Christ. I thought you were full of remorse for your bad habits."

"I'm waiting for Yom Kippur, the day we're supposed to repent. And remorse isn't what I feel about gambling—about much of anything. I learned a lot from gambling; now seems like a good time to maybe learn something else." Carol swished her celery stick in the Bloody Mary, then crunched it as delicately as she could. "But really, Nash, you're being so serious. I'm just messing around. I'm sorry you find my interests so tedious. Tedious, or disgusting?"

"That's ridiculous, Carol. Don't you remember how excited I was when I thought you were actually going to collect on that bet? But Z.D. asked me to babysit you for a week—"

"Babysit! That's cute. You don't think I would have been just fine alone?"

"Este, I apologize. Really. But it's going to be a miserable week if we start playing mind games. I like you, your gambling femme self is fine with me. I'm not saying it again."

Carol leaned back and cracked her spine. "Babysit. I like that. Z.D.'s got a nerve."

"Isn't that what you admire her for? Anyway, she didn't say that. It was the wrong word, and it was my fault."

"Get me another drink, please."

"Get your own."

"I don't have any money. Z.D. did somehow manage to convince me not to bring any. I must have been more rattled than I realized to agree."

"I'd be rattled too," Nash said, trying for sympathy.

"Then? A drink?"

"Now who's the barfly?"

"This is very unpleasant, Nash. I could sign the room number you know."

"Sign it then. That's fine with me. And I wasn't making any judgments."

"Look, I agreed to this trip as an experiment, but last time I checked—and I know there are many signs to the contrary now—this was a free country. At least, free enough that you couldn't stop me from leaving."

"Who's stopping you?"

"You have the car keys and the cash."

"You have feet, a thumb, and wits, or so I've heard. But if you want the car keys and money, I'm not going to keep them away from you."

"Fuck you, Fred."

"Nash," Nash said. Carol's emotions were up and down tonight, quick, like those small waves breaking on the grit they called shore outside.

"Natividad. What does that mean, again?"

"Birth. Like the Nativity. That's me, the second coming."

"Is that why so many girls find you irresistible?" Carol tried to muss Nash's hair again, but Nash batted her away.

"No scenes. Pool?" Nash asked, finishing her beer.

"I'm not going to swim this week unless you let me go to the casino."

"Sink or swim," Nash laughed. "But I didn't mean that pool."

227

"I know. I'm not very good."

"I don't care—just something to do."

On the way to the pool room, they were startled by a stuffed giant polar bear in a glass case, its paws out, as if it had been paralyzed in the act of reaching for its prey. "Jeez, Louise!" Carol whistled.

Nash put her face up against the glass. "Looks real. But why do they have a polar bear in the Minnesota woods?" She had a moment of disorientation, her sense of set control, of appropriate props, undermined.

"Nice place you've taken me to. Z.D. and Kaneesha are always on about how male casinos are. So they send me up here to stare at some poor bear that got slaughtered for a guy's pride. She couldn't find a nice women's b&b?"

"You don't have to look at the bear."

"But now I know it's here. Rrrrrr," she coaxed a growl out of her throat. "I am the spirit of the polar bear and I'm goinnnng to eat you!" Carol whispered, bringing her magenta nails up into claws, as two teenage boys passed them on their way to the Mortal Kombat video machine.

"In your dreams," Nash said, following the boys into the game room. "You wanna flip for the break?"

"I want to flip you," Carol said.

Nash grimaced in the direction of the boys, who were already deeply involved in shooting electrons at imaginary targets. "Call it."

"Heads."

"Tails. I break," Nash said, flicking the quarter at Carol.

"Oh great, now I can make a phone call."

"They're fifty cents. You're stuck in the last century."

"I liked the last century," Carol said, pocketing the quarter anyway.

"You can't mean that." Nash broke, getting two solids in the pockets.

"Good," Carol said, "I like the stripes better. And I do mean it.

228

About the last century. Barbarism met technology and shook hands, but at least—"

"At least what?"

"I was going to say something witty, but you know, thinking about it, the only good thing about the last century is that it's over. I just don't have a good feeling about this new one."

"Who does? But it ain't in your hands—unlike the cue. Pick your shot."

"Four in the side pocket." She missed, and so did Nash after her.

When it wasn't Nash's turn, she squatted, holding the stick straight in front of her, as if she were sighting some distant point.

"Back bothering you?" Carol asked, missing her third shot in a row.

"It's been a long day."

"Look, I concede, you've already won. A swim before dinner?"

"Changed your mind already?" Nash straightened up, unfurling her spine. She tried to imagine it like a fern in the rainforest, slowly curling toward the damp light. Slow and focused, that's the cure.

"It's a woman's prerogative, is it not?"

"I'm not in the mood. Let's play it out."

Nash won in the next two turns.

"What next? Air hockey?" Carol gestured sarcastically to an old table across the room.

"I like air hockey, don't knock it."

"I think I will sign for that drink now."

Nash's sleep prickled; the cedar scent pinched along the route the gin had taken through her gut. She was lying on her side, and her ribs ached. In her dreams a shark tried to speak, but her mouth was full of sand. She had been young—how old, ten?—when her teacher had the class troop down to the rock jetty near her school in Isla Verde. A fisherman had caught a pregnant shark. They all lined up to look at the babies in a neat row inside the shark's sliced-open gut. One of the boys retched. Not Nash. She'd seen pictures of a lot worse in her parents' medical books.

She reached for the mug of water she'd left on the bedside table, arching so as not to dribble on the sheets. The electric clock glowed: 5:07 a.m. She lifted the muscles in her forehead, trying to focus on the mass in the other single bed. Carol. She twisted her neck. Not Carol. Pillows, not even convincingly shaped. What? She sat up. "Carol?" she called toward the bathroom. No response. She got up. No Carol in the bathroom, so she peed and pushed her fingertips into the sides of her temples. Temple, she thought. Whose idea was that for the place that throbs? Where the hell is Carol? She flushed, since there was no one in the room to wake up, and checked her jean pockets for the car keys. Still there. That rules out the casino, Nash figured. Maybe she found the Minneapolis business guys who run the all night poker game. Nah. Maybe. Nah. Maybe. She checked her wallet—nothing missing. Still, Carol could have a stash of money Nash didn't know about, at least a credit card she'd secreted in her bra, and probably did.

She bit the loose flesh on her wrist, trying to come to consciousness. She didn't like to dress before showering, but she could shower later—clean underwear, yesterday's pants and shirt. She sniffed her socks. No, clean socks, she had plenty. Bending to tie her shoelaces, she stretched and frowned. Damn her stupid games. Hide and seek in the Lutsen Lodge. She walked quietly through the halls of the smoking rooms, since she couldn't imagine a poker game without smoke. She doubted that Carol had hooked up with a secret Wicca of vegan scent-free card sharks who played by their altar to Isis. But aside from an occasional cough, the few rooms with light sliding under their doorsills seemed too quiet.

What's open at 5:30 a.m.? Would they be serving breakfast already? Swedes or Norwegians or whatever, they get up early, go fishing—cold winters make them want to suck up the end of summer through straws. Straws. Where the hell is she?

Downstairs she heard the rattle of staff getting ready, but they didn't start serving breakfast until 6, though the coffee service was out. Nash poured a cup of coffee into styrofoam. First light was coming up over the water and she stood at the lobby window watching the day smear itself ingratiatingly over the far rim of the inland sea they called a lake. Sunrise was something she rarely saw. Amusing palette, she said to herself, but a redundant form, don't you agree? A seagull on the shore turned toward her as if to answer. Something's wrong, she thought. The coffee hit her empty stomach and it gurgled and spit acid. Carol wouldn't get up to walk on the beach for the damn sunrise; it's too out of character, even for someone who likes to swim.

Although Nash had grown up by the sea, she didn't learn to swim well until she went to college. Puerto Ricans don't learn how to swim, she said: we experience a chill in winter no matter what you norteamericanos say; in summer the ocean is full of tourists, and the pools are all in hotels or private clubs. Her parents did belong to a country club somewhere, and the boys swam. She had a dim vision of a pool carved into the volcanic rock at El Yunque, the rain forest, the water cool and murky, her brothers daring her to dive. She shook her head. The water was a thing, a separator of continents, a gathering of monsters—barracuda, sailfish, giant squid. Would you leap into the mouth of a dragon? She squinted at the lake and a fish broke the surface, flipped out of the pinkened blue, and was gone. The pool, she thought.

She put the styrofoam cup next to the felt checkerboard in the lobby and pulled herself up the stairs, back past their room. The main door to the pool was locked. She went back through the women's bathroom entrance—where Carol's flowered nightgown hung from a peg. Shit. The floor past the shower was slick, and Nash started to slip but righted herself with a hand against the wall. Then she was running over the non-skid mats past the sauna to the pool. The surface was completely still. What? She squinted. Close to the deep end, she made out the shadow of a form on the bottom. The form squiggled in the refractions, or perhaps it moved. The sun had started to glare on the east windows of the pool structure, filling it with a chapel-like light.

Nash kicked off her shoes and jumped. The cold slapped her awake

231

more than the coffee. Scandinavians. Then she was paddling above the woman's shape, whose ass was up, face down. She dove, getting halfway to Carol underwater when her lungs threatened to burn a hole in her chest and she had to surface. This time she pulled in as much air as she could hold and went back under water. She hooked her arm around one of Carol's. Desperate, she clawed at the water, trying to carve a handhold that would pull them up. Up up up, she screamed at herself. The surface of the water was too far. I won't drop you, you asshole, we're not drowning. She fixed on the surface, which looked hard as ribbon candy, and then with the last strength she owned screeching its way through her muscles, broke through. Gasping, she fought her impulse to let Carol drop back. If I can carry a bucket of tar up a theater scaffold, I can drag you. Nash pulled her up on her thigh and side-stroked with her free arm toward the shallow end. As soon as she could stand, she stopped and took a breath. Carol floated behind her, puffy in a bright teal bathing suit, her blond hair framing a halo around her head, like some medieval annunciation painting.

Gently now, trembling, Nash struggled to get her over the tiled, wide stairs, her arms under Carol's armpits, stumbling up backward. As she was pulling, the morning guy unlocked the main door and stared at her, startled. "Ambulance," she yelled, "help!" The guy disappeared. Nash bumped Carol's limp ass and legs. Damn you, damn you, her nerves bawled, bunching and releasing, you can't die on me on a Thursday morning in Lutsen, Minnesota. You can't. You can't. She knelt over Carol and positioned her palms over her chest the way she'd seen people do it in the movies, trying to get the water out. Get the water out? Do CPR? Breathe, dammit. Live, push, live, push, live you idiota, live, push. Carol moaned. A gurgling started in her throat and Nash pushed her face to the side. Vomit poured out, a slick of chlorinated vodka and tomato juice. Carol groaned.

"That's it, asshole. Vivas," Nash said, turning Carol's face up to meet her lips. The paramedics found her blowing into Carol's reeking mouth, shivering in her wet clothes.

"We're here now," one of them, a teenage girl chewing gum, said to her, while the older, a stubble-faced guy, felt for Carol's pulse. He pulled her eyelids up and shined a light into her eyes. Then he ran the thin battery end of the flashlight along her instep. Nash saw Carol's toes wiggle—maybe not as much movement as a full wiggle, but at least they responded. Hotel people were in the doorways with their "what's going on?" and "how can we help?"

"I need a volunteer for the stretcher," the paramedic said, and one of the young hotel guys stepped forward.

"Is she—" Nash started to shake uncontrollably. The girl put a blanket over Carol's body, and another over Nash's shoulders.

"I think your friend's gonna make it," the paramedic mumbled.

"What?"

"She's okay to move. We're taking her to Grand Marais—you better come along. Can you stand up?"

Nash pushed against the cement with her palms. The room rubberized, light bending along the soft pillars of wood. The girl held out a hand. "Take a deep breath. Good. Now hold on to me." She pulled Nash up and deposited her in a deck chair while the hotel guy helped the paramedic get Carol on a stretcher.

"Big girl," the paramedic said.

"Hey," Nash said.

"No offense. You OK to follow us?"

"I think so." The girl took Nash's arm. When Nash looked at her she realized that she was probably in her late 20s. Fit, blond, serious, chewing. Woman, Nash thought, she deserves to be called a woman. She started to laugh, but it hurt and she coughed.

"We just have this one flight to get down," the woman said. "Are you cold?"

"Cold?" A wind picked up along the back of Nash's neck and she started to shiver again. Wasn't it hot yesterday? Where'd this chill come from? The woman put her arm around her. An unknown pain started in her right knee, as if an old rusty pull tab was caught in the joint.

233

"It's warm in the ambulance—just a couple more steps."

A crowd was gathered around the van. "Why are so many people up?" Nash asked the woman.

The woman looked confused. "It's 6:30," she said.

"Oh, of course." Nash and the woman turned to appraise each other's sanity.

"You're from the city," the woman said.

"Oakland, California. I'm Nash. That's Carol."

"Hildy," the woman said, satisfied. In front of them, the crowd parted to let the men lift the stretcher into the ambulance.

"Is she going to be all right?"

"Mike said so. He usually calls them right."

"Usually?"

"The rest is up to—"

"Shh," Nash raised a finger to her mouth, and Hildy seemed to take it as part of her physical state. But when Nash lifted her leg to get up on the ambulance, it wouldn't go.

"Take it slow," Hildy said.

Nash's knee buckled. Eight arms seemed to materialize before she hit the ground.

"What's wrong?" a male voice asked.

"My knee—"

"Get her up here, we'll take care of that later," Mike yelled from inside. He had an oxygen mask over Carol's face.

Nash closed her eyes and leaned on her left leg as someone pushed and someone lifted and someone else pulled her onto the bench next to Carol. Mike was staring at her.

"You're not going to throw up, are you?"

"No."

"Good. Your friend—she have epilepsy?"

"Epilepsy? No. Why?"

"She had a short seizure when I got her in here—it's over now. Maybe mild hypothermia, maybe pulmonary edema is all."

"That sounds serious."

"Don't worry. It's regular with near drowning."

Carol's lips were blue, but she seemed to be breathing all right. The woman waited until they were out of the hotel's driveway to start the siren. Nash's memory shoved up pictures of ambulances parked in front of her neighbors' houses and downtown hotels, days when she felt impervious, though she understood it was only time, a trick of time, before she'd be the one it came for, or for someone she loved. It was different from inside, different when it was you, a Nordic stranger driving you to an unknown hospital, the middle of nowhere. Not nowhere for them, she thought. Nowhere for us. She had an image of the set she'd built for a college production of *A Streetcar Named Desire*—one of her first sets. She hated this, having to depend on, having to trust, some strange guy.

"Regular." Nash pushed Mike's word against her teeth, trying to nail this reality into place, or turn it into a stage set. If this was the script, she was ready for a rewrite. "Is she going to die?"

"Eventually," Mike said.

"That's not funny."

"Sorry. I don't think so. You know how long she was under water?"

"No. She was underneath when I got there. I—I thought I saw her move a little."

"Might of." Mike considered. "If you did, that would be a good sign."

Carol shuddered and opened her eyes. It seemed to Nash as if Carol was staring inside of Nash's skull, and it made her scalp itch.

"Not going to die," Mike said.

"How do you know?"

"Her pupils are responding to light. See?" He shone his little flashlight in her face again, and she blinked, tried to raise her arm, gurgled, and then her eyelids fluttered shut.

"Turn that off," Nash said.

"You wanted to know. It means probably no lasting brain damage."

"Is there such a thing as temporary brain damage?"

Mike fidgeted with some straps. "Look, the doctor will explain it to you. Oxygen deprivation. Looks like you got to her in time, though. Good job. How's your knee?"

Nash tried to bend it and grimaced. Mike leaned over and pulled it hard. Something popped. "Try again."

This time it bent. "Hurts. But thanks. What did you do?"

"You probably tore something when you were kneeling. If it pops out again, you should see an orthopedist."

"Great. Some vacation. She almost drowns and I lose my knee."

"Not lost yet," Mike said, adjusting a dial on the oxygen tank. Hildy took a curve in the road hard. "You sisters?"

Nash was about to echo him, sisters?, when she realized it would be best to say yes. But who would really think so? Carol was shortish, dirty blonde, fair, fat; Nash was tall—well, taller, brown, her face marked from the bad time she had with chicken pox, different build entirely. 'Rican and Jew looked different, didn't they? Maybe in Oakland. Ethnic, that's what they'd see here. We're ethnics, and we're gonna be on the evening news. "Sisters-in-law," Nash said, quickly enough to appease him. That should take care of it, give her access enough. She hoped. That would make her Z.D.'s sibling, Z.D.'s brother, compadre. Okay, that was almost right. But was sister-in-law close enough for the emergency room? No one else was going to be able to get to Grand Marais today, clearly. They'd have to make do with her. At least her cell phone would work in Grand Marais. But her cell was on the nightstand. Dammit.

22

Carol wasn't sure she was dreaming. She was too wet to be dreaming. She'd been sitting on the side of the pool, dangling her legs, singing a song to her toes, rosy toes, she sang, rosy toes, who knows what trouble you can make, I've had all the trouble I can take, maybe the new year will be a piece of cake—and then she cracked herself up. Laughing, laughing. When she was little, maybe nine (it was—yes, after Dad was gone, goodbye Dad, you were had) she'd been on a swim team. They used to hold their breath and swim the width of the pool underwater. She could do that. She took several fast breaths. Dolphin, orca, manatee, they ain't got nothing on me. She spit the breath out laughing again. Huffed up, to fill her lungs with oxygen. Wouldn't Z.D. be pleased to see her taking such good care of herself, getting exercise at first light, inspired by the healthy folks of this northern place. Laughed again. C'mon, don't be such a damn drunk sissy, she thought. Anyone can be brave without going to war. Every day, dykes face the guns of the patriarchy, all that malarkey, and manage not to kill anyone, not even each other. Isn't that what we should applaud? Take a bow, take a good long breath, take the plunge. Giggling, she sliced into the calm surface of the pool, made it easily to the other side, and turned around under water. A half of a half of a half of a half of a breath is infinite. That's one of the thousand paradoxes—you can slice something into forever, halving, no matter how thin or thick. Thick water, thicker than usual. Butterscotch pool, she thought. She could breath butterscotch. It didn't taste so bad.

Then what? Nash was doing something that hurt her, and she

was telling Nash to stop, but Nash didn't seem to hear; she was sure she was pushing Nash away, but Nash was still on top of her. Z.D. wasn't going to like this. She didn't like this. A crack zigzagged up her spine and shook her out like a flag in the rain. What did that man want? Then noise. Was she still swimming? She felt her body curving, something snapped her into a curve, but she wasn't in the water anymore. If she wasn't in the water, why was she wet? What was happening? A light popped in her face and she struggled against it. Something else was on her face—she opened her eyes and Nash was sitting next to her, looking like a brown dog thrown against its will into a lake—matted, disconsolate. Why aren't we kinder to animals? Suddenly everything stopped, the noise, the rocking, and people were yelling at each other, jerking her around. She should sit up and make them be quiet. She needed to sleep, to get back to the thing she was dreaming about, to make sure no one slipped on the cutting board where time was being sliced, oh give me a slice of that sweet rye bread, infinity needs to come out even, wasn't that her responsibility? Infinity, infantry, air force, no one can force me now. I'm a steady hand, halving the halves.

Carol woke alone in the night, her head slanting to take in the limited view, shapes of trees heaped on a trading blanket of darkness, so close to the border of Canada, the inland waterways where canoes bumped into the muskets of ghost fur traders and missionaries. After the pudding water, breathing air didn't taste good. In America, she mumbled quietly to herself, although she was aware that the bed next to hers was empty, the water is filled with sewage and the air is filled with blood. Who will ever taste the wild earth again?

Maybe in Antarctica. She knew a scientist once—met her at a party, that is, met a scientist at a party who studied penguins in Antarctica. Everything was made of ice. Ice dorms for the biologists. Was that right? Pipes in the ice humping heat into ancient accretions. But there, maybe there on the frozen shelf, when they

238

open their mouths and the cold plays their teeth like a xylophone, the almost numb tongue can reach into the clear centuries before smoke lacquered sense. I'll never get to Antarctica, Carol realized, not me, not now.

Damn. 4:15 a.m. She could make out the numbers on a wall clock like the ones they used to have in classrooms. No true darkness inside a hospital room, but outside the world was black. She thought summer light came early up here in the north woods. Was it still summer? Maybe she had it backward. She used to be so good at logical propositions and facts. Outline of branch, body of branch, leaf detail, and eventually dawn. What happened to Nash? Nash, gnashing. It's odd to feel so rubbery. It's odd to feel. Who needs it? Feeling. Everyone says femmes are good at feeling and detail. As if a heart could be read in the act of sewing sequins on a skirt, as if what people need would be revealed by looking ever more closely—oh auntie femme, read us them tea leaves again!

Carol turned to the light in the hall. Tea would be nice right about now. Hot English breakfast tea and a blueberry scone. That would be an advance for civility in hospitals—when they come in to draw your blood, and oops, 4:39, they'll be here soon if Myra was right, wasn't it Myra who complained about mornings on the recovery ward?—they should bring you tea and scones, and maybe a flower. Or a bullet. Bulletin: I'm sick of this, the stink of myself, the smell of hospital soap, which they must make out of ground-up cockroaches boiled in lye, what else could smell like that, medicinal and insect secretion all in one? Maybe it's black flies or mosquitoes or moths. What is that called, the study of bugs? Icthy-something. No, that was fish. Fish out of water, devoured by bugs. Here in the country, different bugs. But so what? You still have to fence yourself off from them, put up the plate glass, the screen, rub on deet, cover your extremities, be extreme. Oh wilderness, you can't get me sentimental, I've seen you naked and covered in deer shit, your hawks going straight for some rodent's eyes. Who decided we had to all be environmentalists

239

anyway? Maybe the Republicans have it right: swallow the earth up, hack it to bits, extract what you can, leave the mess for some woman to clean up, and if it can't be cleaned, tough. It was only a little planet in a small corner with jungles that ate men alive, men like my dad who fell out of the sky and—. Oh god. She heard footsteps in the hall. First sound, then a shadow. She turned back to the window, feigning sleep. She wanted them to think they'd woken her.

"Good morning, dear."

The voice was loud and cheerful. She didn't budge. A hand reached for her wrist, and she became aware of the IV line in the back of her hand. It ached when the nurse touched her. How could she see leaves outside the window in Lake Superior light and not notice the tubes that bound her to the bed? She swallowed, guiding a ball of sludge down her esophagus.

"Can you sit up?" The nurse checked her paperwork. "Miss Schwartz? We just have to get a few samples for the lab, now."

Carol turned toward her and the nurse pressed the button that jerked Carol into sitting position. "There we go. Turn your arm over."

Carol complied. She decided compliance was this morning's word. Word for the day. She was turning it over in her mind. Comp lye hence. Hench. Henchmen—women—of the king. Who's king here? Someone in white, somewhere else. Molly was right to want to die at home. But I'm not dying. Am I? The nurse tied a band around her and thumped at the vein, frowning. "You must have been very dehydrated," she said.

How could that be? She was in water. She suspected that this was all the result of nearly being drowned. How can you dehydrate by drowning? And isn't the body made of water? She knew her physics. The body is a trick of light, a sleight of hand, the thick bucket of flesh we think we know is open space with a few particles whizzing around. Why doesn't water slosh in from the fat cells, for instance, to feed the blood? Is blood a constant volume?

"Ow."

240

"I'm sorry. I'll try the other arm." Tie, thump, cluck again. Ow again. "I think we have it this time."

Carol watched her blood trickle into a tube, slow at first, then a gush. The nurse filled three tubes with different colored stoppers, pulled the needle out, put a bandage on.

"Not so bad, was it?"

"Not so bad," Carol said, thinking it was wise to stay on the nurses' good sides, to make them believe they were doing good. Maybe they were doing good. Maybe once you decided to comply it was a slippery slope to surrender. Slippery slope is among the twenty-odd logical fallacies. Gay marriage does not lead to dog marriage, although she was not sure now what the big deal would be about allowing folks to marry their dogs. Marriage is all about licensing, isn't it? A dog license is clearly a property contract, as is marriage, so not allowing queers the same rights as dog owners doesn't make sense. Everything depends on the angle of light. One exception does not make a hundred necessary. Some people hold their balance on the edge, others fall. Maybe chaos theory has a formula that will tell us who. Who slips on the muddy slope. Who is pulled back at the last minute. That's not chaos theory, that's a prayer.

Molly wasn't big on religion, but the memory of being dragged by her bubbe to High Holy Day services at the conservative synagogue made Carol draw a deep breath. That awful perfume smell again, perfume on old ladies who haven't bathed, on patients who only get sponged off. On Rosh Hashona it's written, on Yom Kippur it's sealed, who shall live and who shall die. Who shall drown and who shall be resuscitated. Up there, in the big book of god, moving finger, finger in flame, burning words into the stratosphere, not even comets can erase them. That's what Jews said. They went to temple for days and meditated on their sins. Our sins. But sin isn't causation. That's where so many folks make their mistake. Babies get written in for death, your mom's cells turn against her, but mass murderers—presidents, dictators— thrive. Isn't the point of all that praying the idea that we can

241

change it by our deeds, by the purity of our hearts, in the ten days between Rosh Hashona and Yom Kippur?

That can't be right. It doesn't make sense that 355 days god is a jealous god, a vengeful guide, shutting the gates of the garden of Eden, but hey, here are the ten days god will soften, or at least look the other way, and let people be in charge of their own fate. That cannot be Old Testament. Carol rubbed her head. Her hair felt sticky, unpleasant. Was it Rosh Hashona yet? How long had she been asleep? She wondered if there were Jews in Grand Marais, a congregation. When Nash came, maybe she could get her to find them, to loan her a prayer book. Maybe the guy they have who comes around to hospital patients to find out if they want to pray has a stock of prayer books for everyone. A High Holy Day prayer book. A Koran. A Bhagavad-Gita. Because the lakeshore is full of tourists all summer long.

Probably lots of them almost drown. Maybe it's a conversion experience, a baptism. By the time Z.D. makes it to here, I'll have turned into a Christian. Carol laughed out loud. A nurse stuck her head in the door. Hospital so well-staffed its walls listen. "You need anything, hon?"

"For instance?"

The nurse came in and checked the IV. "We're not giving you much for pain—the doctor wants to monitor your vitals. But if you're in pain, you tell me and I'll give him a call."

"Thanks." Now go away. The doctor is trying to decide if I have brain damage, and my brain must be whizzing along fine if I've figured that out. Whizzer of a mind. I'll lie here and repeat the times tables, that'll be fun. Odds payoffs. No, no, you promised. What did I promise? No more big bets. No more sexy money. Money rubs up against your body, flicks its serpent tongue in your ear, oh my dear, what we could do together. But it's only a paper moon, paper mandala, a symbol. Marx said money is a symbol of something else we value. Hhmm hmmm hmm. There's your clue, kiddo, Molly would say. Where is Molly? Cashed in her chips—which implies you get to take what you have left with you, even

242

though we know it's not true. The chips are stacked against you. Or was that the cards? If the cards are stacked, that must be divination, an ancient reference to the tarot embedded in idiom. The three of swords pierces a heart, my heart is pierced, and bleeding idioms. Damn tarot cards, somebody else's symbols, insinuating themselves into your subconscious. Who wants to dream of towers falling in ancient Egypt? Carol looked back out the window, half expecting an apparition of her mother's face shimmering in the morning light. Molly must have saved me from drowning.

Someone cleared her throat. Carol lifted her head slowly off the pillow and made out Nash.

"It's me you better be giving credit to," Nash said.

"Was I talking out loud?"

"Whispering and grunting. But I speak Carolish." Nash threw a box down on the other bed.

"You saved me from drowning." It came out flat, a fact, a kick in the head. "It couldn't have been easy."

Nash puckered her lips. "You have a gift for understatement. I brought you some donuts from a place that says it's the world's best donut store. They have this world map stuck with hundreds of pins showing where their customers come from. Este, even Puerto Rico. Very international up here."

"You brought me donuts?" So simple, better than being saved from death by water, a gift of food to the fat girl, taking for granted not deformed appetite but common hunger, universal hatred of hospital food. A civilized, humane gesture. Carol started to cry.

"Hey! No big deal." Nash was embarrassed, went to the box, ate a donut. "Pretty good. And a thousand donuts consumed while knocking out sets makes me an expert. Maybe not the world's best, but close enough. We can share, okay?"

"Sharing is good." Carol watched Nash eating and realized she felt nauseated. "I hate to tell you this, but I'm going to throw up."

"Ay—I'll get the nurse." And the nurse was there with the basin in the nick.

243

In the nick. She was quick. Carol twisted her neck and felt her brains slosh. They'd never sloshed before. Maybe she got wet inside. Was that possible? To take in the pool through your ears?

"Thanks, Nash."

"For getting the nurse?"

"For sticking by me. For being such a good friend. To Z.D."

"You think I wouldn't do it for you?"

"Maybe you would, but I never asked you to."

"You don't think lying face down in a swimming pool is a call for help?"

Carol considered. A call for help—Myra would have said that. Had Myra rubbed off on Nash? Rubbing off, pollen on the hairy legs of bees, if we cross-fertilize that would imply we interpenetrate, become each other. Then why are we in so much pain? SOS, I got the soul sickness, the Ancient Mariner's grief, the wandering Jew orphan blues. Call for help. Could be. Ich. Giving into deep sorrow was more sentimentality than she could bear. Maybe she'd throw up again. No, she checked her stomach—it had calmed. "Well."

"Well, what?" Nash had started playing solitaire on her cell phone.

"Well, could be. But please don't let them sic the local therapist on me. I don't think I could bear it. Speaking of therapists, what's going on between you and—"

"C'mon on, Carol, I told you I don't want to talk about that." Nash sucked her teeth but kept her fingers moving on the tiny buttons.

"If not to me, who? If not now, when?" Carol got a shiver full of the shades of the dead—not just Harold and Molly, but all the Jews she came from—disapproving of how she shaped Rabbi Hillel's ancient exhortation to engage social justice into a clever bon mot that Nash wouldn't even get.

But Nash looked up and pointed a finger at her. "You know, I saw that on a billboard once. Something like it. When Reagan was running for re-election. The woman I was driving with had a fit,

244

because he was stealing a famous saying of one of your rabbis, true?"

"That must have been almost twenty years ago, Nash." Carol scrunched her eyes to calculate. Bush, Clinton, Bush, Reagan—how come our years are numbered by those guys? "How do you remember that?"

"It was a big fit she threw. Cultural appropriation, robbing her ancestors' graves. Plus I have good visual memory." Nash shrugged. "See, that's the thing. Me and Myra—we're so different. We want to trust each other, but even when we say 'trust,' the word has a different color, a different shape in our mouths."

"You didn't cheat on her again?"

"No, actually, I did not. But I was, well, thinking about it. It's spooky when someone can hear you think."

"Sounds like the problem isn't that you have different—what? languages? definitions?—but that she gets too close."

"That's what Myra would say." Nash looked down longingly at her cell phone, wishing she could stop talking and get back to her game. "I don't know. I've been thinking about it. You, you could have been dead—"

"I'm grateful, Nash."

"No, that's not what I meant, for you to thank me again." She held up her palm in the signal for stop. "I meant, sometimes I'm guilty, you know, of acting my life, like it was theater, and if the script is a little tragedy, so what? Next week, new plot. But maybe not. Maybe you only get two or three plots, if you're lucky, and it's up to you to make a happy ending. 'Happy endings, nice and tidy, that's a rule I learned in school—'" Nash sang.

"*Threepenny Opera*, right?"

"Yeah. Hard to go for happy endings anymore without getting snarky."

"It's because the world looks so doomed now that personal happiness seems like copping out." Was that it? Was that right?

"But we still live personal lives. I'm only thinking I could maybe live mine a little better. When I get home, I'm going to try to talk to Myra." Nash took a deep breath. "Not just talk. Fix myself with her. If I can."

"That's good, Nash. I hope so." Out in the corridor, in the nurses' station probably, a deep man's voice penetrated the lull. Dan Rather, maybe, was talking on the radio about how it might be the wrong war, now, in Iraq, but the men and women who go to fight, go for the right reason—the best reason, to serve their country. My country, right or wrong, I'll be its cannon fodder, its mass of bodies, its blanket of slogans, I'll go, I'll swear by the lines on the map and the parchment under glass, that war is good, nutritious, builds character eight ways. No one will ever shove sand in our faces, not the sand of the ancient deserts, not the soft mud of the Delta. Carol suddenly felt two hundred years old, worn out in every cell. "Isn't Z.D. coming?"

"Tonight, I think."

"Doesn't she love me anymore?"

Nash cleared her throat. "You'll have to ask her that. But you know it's not easy to get here. Her plane gets into Minneapolis in the afternoon, then she has to rent a car and it's a long drive. I got her a room at the Harbor Inn, no view—turns out it's peak season, even after Labor Day, because of fishing and foliage."

"Fishing and foliage," Carol repeated. "What time is it now?"

"One seventeen."

"Are there still donuts?"

Nash handed her the box. Carol pulled one out and sniffed it. "Cinnamon. Cinnamon smells good."

"Yeah," Nash agreed, glad to finally get back to her cell phone game.

Carol's hand dropped to the sheet. She closed her eyes and felt the texture of sugar, of dough crumbling under her thumb. When she opened them again, Z.D. was standing over her, wearing an A's t-shirt.

"You're not blending in, you know. They root for the Twins out here," Carol said.

"Hello yourself." Z.D. put her hand on Carol's cheek and ran it slowly up through her hair, gently untangling the knots she encountered.

Then Carol began to cry. She didn't know how or why or what about, at least not at first. She was crying because her hand lay in a puddle of donut crumbs, because her lungs felt like crumpled dollar bills and her mind as if it had turned to silt and was slowly draining out her tear ducts. She was crying because her mother was dead, her father had gone to war, because she was sure Rosh Hashona had started without her participation, because she had money and women in Iraq, India, West Oakland did not, because she thought about the world before she thought about her home, because what kind of home did they have, anyway, because how could Z.D. have convinced her to go away, how could she have agreed, banished for gambling, was that such a sin, to get a little thrill from scrying—was that what it was called?—divining the future through the intersection of statistics and dreams, all she wanted to do was . . . was—what was it she meant to do? "What are we doing with our lives, Z.D.?"

Z.D. sat on the end of the bed, and Carol felt the bounce move through the mattress into her cells. Was she more alive because she was half-dead? How can anyone be half-dead? Isn't it a simple duality—life, death, life, death, the heart of cosmic dust beating, some serpent twinned around the galaxies flicking her tongue?

"I'm so glad you're still alive enough to wonder," Z.D. put her forefinger under Carol's eyes, wetting it with her tears. Then she licked her finger, and squinted. "Nice salt aftertaste, but I'd say your electrolytes were out of balance."

"Oh, Zenobia, thank you for coming. My mind feels like it's dripping out of me." Carol smiled and squeezed Z.D.'s hand.

"Nah, it's just tears, see?" Z.D. put her finger in Carol's mouth, and Carol sucked it. Behind her eyes the serpent glided away, into green brush, and the brush circled a clear, turquoise pool.

Z.D. heard the nurse coming first, and pulled her finger out quickly, to Carol's sigh.

"Excuse me. I have to check vitals now. You can wait outside, sir."

Carol started to cough and laugh at the same time. "She's a woman and she can stay."

"Hospital policy—"

"We're registered domestic partners in California," Z.D. said, standing and pulling the folded-up certificate from the secretary of state out of her back pocket, the last thing she'd grabbed on the way out of the house.

"Oh, well. Oh. Well. I don't know if we—in Minnesota, if we—well, I'm only taking blood pressure and temperature, so I guess it doesn't matter." The nurse looked at the wall while she fumbled with the cuff and thermometer.

"Is that the right size cuff?" Z.D. tried to engage the nurse, who busied herself with the gauge.

"They've got plenty of fat folks in Minnesota and I've been here for days—"

"Please don't talk with the thermometer in your mouth," the nurse said, marking her readings in the chart.

"Only since yesterday morning. You have to believe I got here as soon as I could."

"Mmmmhmm," Carol said, and the nurse pulled the thermometer out. "Isn't there a newer technology for this?"

"Disposable temperature strips," the nurse nodded, "but we're—" she stared at Z.D. and back at Carol "—old-fashioned out here."

"I didn't mean to offend you, nurse—" Z.D. looked at her nametag "—Jensen, really. I appreciate everything you're doing."

"Thank you," Jensen said. "I have to get going."

"Maybe you should bring the nurses some donuts or something. They make the best donuts in the world here—see?" Carol held up a pile of donut crumbs she'd been shielding under her left arm after the nurse was clearly out of earshot.

"You must be sick if the best you can do with a donut is pulverize it. I'll call Nash to bring something over. She's leaving in the morning, and you're not getting rid of me tonight."

"She was so good to me."

"Yup, Nash is good."

248

"When we get home, let's throw her a party."

"I'm not sure she'd be comfortable with that."

"We can call it the not-dead-yet party, and everyone can tell everyone what's important in their lives." What is important in my life, Carol repeated to herself, and the thought got stuck, as if it were a needle skipping in a scratched groove on an old vinyl record.

Z.D. suppressed a laugh. "Wouldn't it be easier to buy her, like, a toaster oven? And anyway, let's concentrate on the getting home part first. Looks like you don't have a roommate. Maybe I'll camp out here."

"I don't know if they'll let you stay the night in old-fashioned country, cookie."

"Your mother used to say that."

"What?"

"Cookie. On the phone, she always said, 'Cookie, let me talk to my child.'"

"I miss Molly."

"I bet you do. But she's not ready for you to join her."

"Z.D., do you think I was trying to drown myself?"

"Well, weren't you?"

Carol turned her head away. "I don't think so. Why would I?"

Z.D. sat down, close, and tipped Carol's face back. "Because you're freaked out. Because the cops and robbers scared you. Because you don't know what you're going to do with your life. Because taking risks makes you high."

"Is that what you think?" Carol began to cry again. Maybe Z.D. was right and what she longed for was danger, the cold tip of the dagger against her breast. A dagger pressed to the heart, that would be hot, wouldn't it, not cold? Women who slice their skin, the cutters, say they do it in order to feel. To bloodlet—there's an old idea, medieval, the blood has humors, humor me, and let it bleed. Is that what I want, to tear myself open, in order to see the horrible pulsing vein, in order to smell the rot, maybe the strength, of my own organs, kidney, bowels, pancreas, exposed below everything that cushions me, am I ashamed?

"Well then, what, Carol? What were you doing on the bottom of that pool?"

"Can I get back to you on that?"

"No." Z.D. stroked Carol's cheek with the back of her hand, knuckles ruffling the slight blond down.

Carol pursed her lips. She shifted her eyes away from her, and then back, experiencing Z.D.'s patience as if it were a flannel jacket that Z.D. had gallantly draped over her shoulders, cozy, butch, comforting. "I was lonely."

Z.D. gave a grunt and cocked her head, waiting.

Carol scrunched her eyes shut. "I want to say I was lonely for you, and in some ways I was. But I was more mad at you than anything. Goddammit, Z.D." Her eyes flew open and she pushed Z.D.'s hand down. "I was so pissed at you. Don't just sit there nodding like some Buddhist confessor. What made you think it was such a good idea for me to get out of town?"

"It seemed like a good idea at the time." She tapped the soles of her shoes against the linoleum, too embarrassed to admit it was because the cops told her so. "How could I foresee you'd take a drunk dawn plunge?"

"Even if I hadn't—"

"No, you're right." Z.D. frowned. "I guess I started to feel like every day you made things more complicated and I had to clean it up. And I couldn't if you were, you know, coming up right behind where I was sweeping, and throwing more dirt."

"Throwing dirt? And who asked you to clean up after me?" Carol struggled to sit more upright.

"You've lived with me long enough to not have to ask."

"Oh, I see. We have some kind of secret bargain in which I mess up and you come to my rescue, prince and damsel in distress."

"Something like that." Z.D. smiled and relaxed.

"It's not funny, Zenobia. Maybe it's how you've coped with me lately. I know I haven't been easy—don't give me that look, I'm apologizing. But I didn't need you to bail me out."

"I did, though."

250

"What are you talking about?" Carol squinted against the bedside light, which seemed to be making a halo around Z.D.

"Well, first I dealt with the insurance company and the hospital for hours. Some hoops they got."

Carol had an image of Z.D. in the middle of a three-ring circus, jumping through a ring of fire. Wasn't there a song about that? "Thanks, honey. The insurance companies can run you in circles, I know."

"You're welcome. And compared to dealing with the underworld you got involved in, it was a breeze. But finally the bookies agreed to return your original bet, with a little extra for the misunderstanding, and leave us alone. Gary—that gay cop I told you about?—helped me negotiate. They gave me five grand, and they insisted it was a payoff for your never betting with Henry again, or talking to anyone about this."

"Some deal."

"Well, they insisted we had inside information. They knew that we knew that they knew that it was bullshit. But they'd thought it would be simple to push dykes around, and they had to save face when we pushed back."

"If you say so," Carol grumbled.

"Listen. I love you. I love you more than my Mustang, more than the damn waterfalls out in the Gorge. But if you can't find a way to—"

"Oh, nice, here I am recovering from a near death experience, and you're threatening me."

Z.D. got up. She raised the blind on the window, revealing a clump of trees outlined against the growing dark, last light lingering on red and yellow leaves. Nice to see a little autumn. "Not threatening." She turned back to look at Carol stretched out on the bed. Everything was so neat in this room, so like a nun's room, really, if you ignored the IV. "I'm not threatening you. I want you. I want you back." She pulled the folded paper out of her pocket again. "Domestic partner."

Carol bit her lip. "I've never been all that good at domesticity."

"But you have been a hell of a partner."

"Not lately."

"No. Not so much lately. That's what I'm talking about."

"But you—"

"I know, I know. We didn't talk enough, I took advantage of your confusion, packed your bag, and pushed you out the door. I was wrong. I wanted to fix everything and I thought it would be better if I did it alone." Z.D. held up both her hands, palms open.

"Only butches think they can fix a relationship by themselves."

"Well you haven't been giving me a lot of help lately. Every time I tried to get close, you shoved me away. I'm a dyke of action."

"Come here, dyke of action." Carol patted the mattress, and Z.D. sat down again. Out in the hallway, they could hear machines being rolled to distant rooms. "I want to tell you something."

"What's that?"

"I'm tired of casinos and bookies. It's—not really all that much fun anymore. You know, I got scared when I got all that money after Molly died. What if I blew it? It was like some kind of bizarre test. How do you feed every mouth in the universe that's hungry, how do you provide for your own old age, for the people close to you that you love? Then the stock market crashed and I thought, hell, I can take this into my own hands. And I was good at it."

"I have to agree, you were good at it." Z.D. noticed that lines had formed around Carol's mouth. When was that? When Nash was trying to resuscitate her? When she was learning the math of bookies?

"I can be good at something else."

"Yeah?"

"Why not? We're still young."

"I'm not so sure about that." Z.D. put her fingers to the lines around Carol's lips, tracing them.

"Young enough. Old enough. I mean, we can still—have ideas. Take chances with them."

"Haven't you taken enough chances yet?"

"Not by a long shot." Carol started to laugh, and it came out as

252

choking. Z.D. held a cup of water up. "Mmm. Thanks. No, really. I want to take chances that matter, that make a difference."

"Oh, those kind of chances. What the hell are you talking about?" Z.D. put the cup back on the tray table.

"Start a housing cooperative. Buy up a city block. Find some architects, investors." Carol pressed the buttons to adjust the bed until she was sitting upright. "Make something. Not just hold dances and ration out rent money." She felt a wave of righteousness suffuse her, warm and encouraging. Maybe she could stand up soon, maybe they could leave the hospital and start changing the world again. Tomorrow.

"Nothing wrong with rent money."

"That's not what I mean."

"No, I think I get what you mean. You want to start building Lesbian Nation." Z.D. put her fist over her mouth. It seemed funny to go back to the granola visions of the '70s feminists, but maybe that wasn't fair. Actually, acting on those visions suddenly seemed overdue.

"Don't laugh at me."

"I'm not laughing. Okay, I am laughing. But you're right—land is power."

"Power," Carol said, noticing how her tongue lay flat when she said it, how the word was in her lips, her face. "You know what? I'm hungry."

"Imagination and appetite—those are prime signs of life. I don't think they have to be worried about your brain anymore." Z.D. patted her on the head. "Oh yeah, I smell that too. They must be bringing around dinner."

A nurse's aide appeared, fumbling with a tray. "Schwartz? You can start having solid food tonight." She fiddled with putting it down and getting the table over Carol's lap, while Z.D. moved herself to the chair by the window.

"So what is it?" Z.D. asked, once the aide had left.

"Some kind of overcooked white fish, white potatoes, mushy green beans. Culinary masterwork."

"This is a long way from the Bay. Sorry."

"I don't think our local hospitals would do much better." Carol ate some fish, arranged the green beans in lines around the plate. "Want some?"

"Uh, maybe I'll see what Nash can find."

"Wise child." Carol put her fork down. "Molly would say that."

"Say what?"

"Wise child. I miss my mother."

"I know you do. I miss her too. She was great."

"And you know what? I miss my father too."

"You always have."

"Really? You think so?" That rubbery sensation returned momentarily. Which wave is this? Can I not find my power until I dive through the undertow, excising my father's corpse? Corpses left unburied drown memory.

"Every since I've known you, sweetheart, you've missed your dad and refused to own up to it."

Carol looked down at her lap, and then at the neat lines of gray green beans on her tray. "Something's gone wrong with this world."

"A disturbance in the force again, Luke?"

Carol threw a hard roll at Z.D., who ducked and laughed. "It's Friday night, isn't it?"

"Yup. Takes more than a little water to fry your brain."

"Shut up, Z.D. It's Rosh Hashona now."

"Oh. I forgot."

"Why should you remember?"

"Because we've been together for fifteen years. You know when Christmas is."

"Everyone knows when Christmas is. Jews are more subtle."

"I'll grant you that. How about if we do something big for Rosh Hashona."

"Oh god, Z.D., you're such a Catholic girl at heart. The Jewish idea of doing something big is saying you're sorry to the people you've wronged. Some year, the Israelis might even say it to the Palestinians. If we're lucky."

"Wouldn't that be something big?"

"Absolutely, but I'm not holding my breath. Personally, I think I've atoned already for this year. But I do apologize. Are we right with each other yet?"

"Yes," Z.D. said, stroking the side of Carol's face. "Yes, we're right with each other." She was quiet for a minute, listening to Carol breathe, her own breath echoing.

"You know what, I got an idea. Let's do something anyway—take a trip, you and me. We haven't gone anywhere together for a while."

"What about the store?"

"I left Patrice in charge. She's turned out to be great. She can handle it another week or two. I've got weeks of vacation stored up, and the Northwest region can survive without me for a little while, anyway."

"Where should we go? Paris? Rome? I didn't bring my passport."

"How about D.C.?" Z.D. fiddled with Carol's blankets.

"D.C.?"

"You usually do better than echoing me," Z.D. said. "It just occurred to me we should find your dad's name on the wall."

"Maya Lin's wall?"

"The very one. What do you think?"

"The Vietnam memorial," Carol said softly, looking down at Z.D.'s hand picking among the folds of her bedclothes. "I never went there."

"I know."

"I'd like to. Maybe that would help me make things right." She saw the black slabs glinting in grainy fall light as if in documentary footage. Maybe Maya Lin had been inspired by the monolith in Kubrick's *2001*, hurtling through space, surprising the apes who invented murder, using bones as the first weapons. Bones were the first dice and the first instruments of insurrection. Take a chance on violence. Beat some sense into them, the soldiers said. Our bones know the truth of war, but our fingers itch. Pull the trigger, drop the bomb. Wanna bet we hit our target? Wanna

255

place a small wager on that? "Or maybe we should go to Vietnam."

"You don't have your passport, remember? But I bet you have your driver's license. We can leave for D.C. tomorrow if they'll let you out of this place."

"Can we drive?"

"Tempting thought. Maybe I can find some farmer selling his pickup—it should only be—" Z.D. looked at the ceiling and squinted "—oh, two or three days from here."

"Really?"

"Where's that roll you threw at me when I need it?" She made a mock survey of the floor. "Of course not. I gotta return the car I rented in Minneapolis—we'll fly from there, and then home. Patrice is good, but I can't leave the whole region for the time it would take to tool back and forth across America."

"But tooling around America sounds good to me."

"Mmm. Gotta agree with you there, honey. But when we get to D.C., we'll drive around the coast, get us some soft shell crabs, watch the sun rise over the Chesapeake Bay before we have to go home."

"Okay. So spring me."

23

Why have people gotten used to flying in airplanes? Carol looked around at the mid-westerners getting themselves to the Capitol. Well, they look used to it anyway—maybe they were all congressional aides who had to make the trip weekly. A well-dressed crowd, oblivious to the fact that we're scraping the belly of god up here during the new year, the Days of Awe. In the old days, folks knew how to be awed. Awesome, we say now, for an iPod or a pair of jeans. The capacity to know when awe is called for— when did we lose that? Why aren't we all jumping up and down and screaming, "We're flying! We're flying!" like the Darling children in *Peter Pan?*

Now we're all too darling to care. Even Z.D. is calm, flipping the pages of the in-flight magazine, scoping out the diagram for the Reagan airport. Was my father that calm, did he get so used to zooming up in the sky that he forgot where the danger hid? Memory runs like veins of ore, deep below the surface. The mind doesn't care what's important, it simply lets the elements seep into tissue and collect. Maybe memory space is fragmented like a hard disk—50k of lying at the bottom of that pool buried in the limbic system, then a long stretch embedded in the frontal lobe where Dad preens in front of a mirror in his uniform, followed by a snapshot of Nash in the ambulance stashed away in the cerebellum.

Carol saw her mother's hand, the middle and index fingers nicotine-stained, on top of hers. How old could she have been— thirteen? "Stop," Molly had said, "you cannot solve the riddle of consciousness here, by tracing the brain. No one knows how we are able to think that we think." Is that what Molly said? Maybe she offered me a drink—that would be more like her. The doctor said not to drink for a couple more weeks, at least, so if any residual problems cropped up from oxygen deprivation, they'd be clear. Residuals have something to do with the stock market as well as the body. Residual currency floating in the veins. Currency of what?

"Are you okay, honey?" Z.D. looked up.

"Fine, I guess. Why?"

"You keep sighing. Are you worried?"

"How can I be worried when you've arranged everything?"

Z.D. smiled, stuck the magazine in the seat back pocket. "Yup. Best arranger west of the Rockies."

"But we're east of them now."

"Somewhere out there my East Coast doppelganger's trigger finger is itching for an arranger duel."

"What would that look like? Two dykes on computers in a library with a list of things to accomplish?"

"Good idea, actually. Twenty-first century gladiatrixes." Z.D. grinned at the idea.

"Gladiatrixes? You've been hanging around Nash's theater crowd too long. Anyway."

"Anyway, what?"

"I was remembering something about Molly."

Z.D. put her hand on Carol's.

Carol savored the weight of Z.D.'s palm. They were on the two-seat side of the plane, and she figured middle-aged women holding hands were discreet enough. If butches and femmes traveling together could ever be considered discreet. In Saudi Arabia, they beheaded gay men last year—beheaded? Crushed them under a falling wall? Maybe that was saved for a woman accused of adultery. Capitalism requires more freedom. If we're going to be able to choose between sixteen brands of chunky and smooth peanut butter, we have to be left alone in the bedroom, however grudgingly.

258

Z.D. shook her head. "You know, I think it's pretty normal to miss the dead."

"How would you know?"

"That's not fair. Janet, Larisa, Bobby—" Z.D. held up her hand and folded down the fingers for their friends who'd died of cancer and the one who'd had a heart attack last year. "Not to mention, I miss Molly too. So I'm not as close to my mom, so what? I can imagine that when she dies I'll feel like—I don't know—like—"

"Someone amputated your left arm?"

"Is that how you feel?"

"Sometimes. Something I needed that I didn't know I needed is missing. It will always be missing now."

"Are you talking about Molly or your dad?"

Carol looked out the window. Clouds crowded out the fields below. "My dad, I guess. Molly—" she turned and looked into Z.D.'s open face. Z.D. trusted her again, trusted her to try to tell the truth. It's hard to tell the truth about death, to know it, to hold it—it slips out of your hands, as if you were a bear on a riverbank trying to grab a salmon. Only the bears are probably more successful. "Molly comes and goes, she doesn't feel gone, exactly. Maybe I'm in one of those stages of grief, still, bargaining or denial, but sometimes I can hear her voice. Do you think that's crazy?"

"No," Z.D. whispered.

"No, me either. Maybe it's cellular—you know our cells interpenetrate, migrate from skin to skin. We really do rub off on each other."

"She was your mom." Z.D. smiled.

"Yeah, she was a good mom. A good woman." Carol fished in her purse for a tissue. "I read that at the Vietnam memorial, they have a statue for the women soldiers—and the women are cradling some wounded guy."

"Typical. No bravery for women unless they're saving a man's ass."

"Shhh—you want us to get thrown off the plane?"

"I don't think they can throw you off a plane."

"Yeah, but they can make an emergency landing and lock you up in Des Moines."

"Okay," Z.D. lowered her voice to a growl, "is this better?"

Carol gave a small giggle. "Better. So why are we going to this patriarchal war memorial again?"

"So you can bury your missing limb."

"That's a little over the top."

"Hey, I'm not the one who brought up amputation. We'll go take a look, okay. His name will be there, on the list, carved in. Your whole life has been shaped by that damn war."

"I like to think I have more free will than that."

"Not just you. All of us. The way I see it, the whole world has post-traumatic stress from war after war after war, and keeps dealing with it by creating more trauma. We have to acknowledge what's going on and stop it," Z.D. said.

"If it could be stopped by looking at war memorials, it would have ended by now. Unless you think the women still have a chance to fix it. The Cubs will win the World Series first."

"You didn't bet on that, did you?"

"They actually have a shot this year, but I'm not a fool, even for the home team. Besides, I promised."

"See, that's what I mean. People can change. We can still change how things turn out."

"What'd you do with my Z.D., the cynic?"

"I changed her," Z.D. laughed, "like water into wine."

"Then I'll have to drink you up."

"Anytime." Z.D. turned to the window as they felt the descent begin, a variation in pressure, squeezing them out of the sky.

The plane banked to land. Under its wings, the polished black granite of the memorial reflected end-of-September light, with reverberating yellows beginning to tinge the deciduous trees lining the mall. Visitors saw their own faces echoing back from the surface between the rows of names. Carol meant to be clear—about men, her father, war. About gambling with nations and nature.

About women—her mother, the women she loved, herself, the ordinary lives that take the greatest risks to create. But how can you be clear in a ruined world? Not ruined yet, she had to hope, not entirely.

We can still claim our lives. The risk to feel, to create, to take a chance, to trust—those all are good risks. How does it change to violence, to an endless self-absorbed loop of adrenaline justification? We take so much for granted, and never ask the questions at the root, the place where the equations that end up killing us start. My father took the risk that war would make him whole; my mother took risks for me, took risks I never saw. Nash jumped in the pool without hesitation. And every day my friends risk contempt and their livelihoods in order to survive with integrity. Integrity. She took a deep breath.

I want new risks, Carol decided, squeezing Z.D.'s hand. Z.D. turned to meet her gaze. We can still make something together, join our grief and joy, our amazing luck to be women who have slipped out of time, slipped through to our own juice. We can not let our stories end with war.

Elana Dykewomon is an activist, an author, and a teacher. One of the finest thinkers—and writers— the women's movement has produced, she has worked for the last fifteen years as an editor and teacher of composition and creative writing, both independently and for San Francisco State University. She is the author of *Beyond the Pale, Riverfinger Women, Moon Creek Road, They Will Know Me By My Teeth, Fragments from Lesbos,* and *Nothing Will Be As Sweet As The Taste: Selected Poems 1974-1994.*

www.dykewomon.org

Bywater Books

RED AUDREY AND THE ROPING

Jill Malone

Fight or flight? Jane Elliott has tried both. Surfing, letting the waves take her. Teaching Latin, clutching at its rules to feel safe. Safe from a lover, safe from her friends, safe from her mother's death—and her guilt. A guilt that has her flinching from love and embracing pain. And now she lies in a hospital bed, alone.

Set against the landscapes and seascapes of Hawaii, this is a story of one woman's courage and her struggle to find a balance between what she desires and what she deserves. Gripping and emotional, *Red Audrey and the Roping* is also a remarkable literary achievement. The breathtaking prose evokes setting, characters, and relationships with equal grace. Splintered fragments of narrative come together to form a seamless suspenseful story that flows effortlessly to its dramatic conclusion. This is a journey that will transform its readers as well as Jane.

Red Audrey and the Roping *is the winner of the third annual Bywater Prize for Fiction.*

Paperback Original ◆ ISBN 978-1-932859-54-6 ◆ $14.95

Available at your local bookstore
or call toll-free 866-390-7426
or order online at www.bywaterbooks.com

Bywater Books

VERGE

Z Egloff

"Verge is powerful, quirky, and fresh."
—Alison Bechdel, author of *Fun Home,*
Time Magazine's Best Book of 2006

Claire has three goals: to stay sober, to stay away from sex, and to get into film school. So far she's blown two of the three and her drunken affair with her professor's wife means she might just have blown the third. Stuck without the camera she needs to complete her course work, she turns to Sister Hilary at the community center for help. Sister Hilary has a camera to lend, but the price is recruiting Claire as a reluctant volunteer. The only trouble is, Claire's more attracted to Sister Hilary than to helping out.

Claire ought to know there's no future with a nun, but can't this two-timing, twelve-stepping, twenty-something film freak get a chance at happiness?

Verge *is the winner of the fourth annual Bywater Prize for Fiction.*

Paperback Original ♦ ISBN 978-1-932859-68-3 ♦ $14.95

Available at your local bookstore
or call toll-free 866-390-7426
or order online at www.bywaterbooks.com

Bywater Books represents the coming of age of lesbian fiction. We're committed to bringing the best of contemporary lesbian writing to a discerning readership. Our editorial team is dedicated to finding and developing outstanding voices who deliver stories you won't want to put down. That's why we sponsor the annual Bywater Prize. We love good books, just like you do.

For more information about Bywater Books and the annual Bywater Prize for Fiction, please visit our website.

www.bywaterbooks.com

Bywater Books

BABIES, BIKES & BROADS
The Third Cat Rising Novel

Cynn Chadwick

Cat Hood doesn't want to go home. She has a new life and a new love in Scotland. But her brother, Will, has been widowed and left with two small children. So there's no choice for Cat now. She must return to Galway, North Carolina, the place she left when love got lost.

But it looks like love wants to get found all over again. When Cat gets back, she comes face-to-face with Janey, the lover who betrayed her all those years ago. And with only the slender thread of a phone line to bridge the gulf between America and Scotland, Cat can't help fearing a new betrayal.

As Cat helps her brother to rebuild his life, she starts to see that her own needs attention. That maybe it's time to acknowledge this is her home. That maybe it's time to leave behind the pain of the past.

And maybe it's time to get over Janey. If she can ...

Babies, Bikes & Broads *is a runner-up for the fourth annual Bywater Prize for Fiction.*

Paperback Original ◆ ISBN 978-1-932859-62-1 ◆ $14.95

Available at your local bookstore
or call toll-free 866-390-7426
or order online at www.bywaterbooks.com